DEATH AT DARRINGTON MANOR

NANCY WARREN

Storm
PUBLISHING

Ebook ISBN: 978-1-80508-112-8
Paperback ISBN: 978-1-80508-114-2

Cover design: Emily Courdelle
Cover images: iStock, Shutterstock

Published by Storm Publishing.
For further information, visit:
www.stormpublishing.co

ALSO BY NANCY WARREN

An Abigail Dixon Mystery

Murder at the Paris Fashion House

Vampire Knitting Club

Tangles and Treason

The Vampire Knitting Club

Stitches and Witches

Crochet and Cauldrons

Stockings and Spells

Purls and Potions

Fair Isle and Fortunes

Lace and Lies

Bobbles and Broomsticks

Popcorn and Poltergeists

Garters and Gargoyles

Diamonds and Daggers

Herringbones and Hexes

Ribbing and Runes

Mosaics and Magic

Cat's Paws and Curses

Vampire Knitting Club: Cornwall

The Vampire Knitting Club: Cornwall

The Great Witches Baking Show

The Great Witches Baking Show

Baker's Coven

A Rolling Scone

A Bundt Instrument

Blood, Sweat and Tiers

Crumbs and Misdemeanors

A Cream of Passion

Cakes and Pains

Whisk and Reward

Gingerdead House

Village Flower Shop

Peony Dreadful

Karma Camellia

Highway to Hellebore

Luck of the Iris

Vampire Book Club

Crossing the Lines

The Vampire Book Club

Chapter and Curse

A Spelling Mistake

A Poisonous Review

In Want of a Knife

Toni Diamond Mysteries

Frosted Shadow

Ultimate Concealer

Midnight Shimmer

A Diamond Choker For Christmas

The Almost Wives Club

The Almost Wives Club: Kate

Secondhand Bride

Bridesmaid for Hire

The Wedding Flight

If the Dress Fits

Take a Chance

Chance Encounter

Kiss a Girl in the Rain

Iris in Bloom

Blueprint for a Kiss

Every Rose

Love to Go

The Sheriff's Sweet Surrender

The Daisy Game

For Lizzie, who was there from the beginning. With love.

"The fascination of shooting as a sport depends almost wholly on whether you are at the right or the wrong end of the gun."

P. G. Wodehouse

ONE

Tuesday, April 14, 1925

Abigail Dixon strode into the editorial offices of the *Chicago International Post* in Paris. She didn't mean to stride but she was tall and athletic and always in a hurry, so that was her usual mode of walking. As she entered the busy newsroom she was assailed as usual by the clack of typewriters, the mix of American-accented voices all speaking English, which was a relief since her French wasn't coming on that well. The coal fire in the grate and the number of bodies made the room pleasantly warm. April wrapped around Paris like a fashionable coat. The leaves were bright green interspersed with pink blossoms and the sun lightened everything from the grimy buildings to madam's poodle.

Inside the newsroom, however, spring had not penetrated. The men wore the same gray suits and sweat-stained shirts every day of the year. She felt like a spring flower bravely blooming in her pale blue coat from Paul Joubert's spring collection, the matching drop-waist dress and low black-heeled shoes.

She blinked against a miasma of cigarette smoke, most of it coming from the desk of her editor Walter Strutt.

As she headed toward Strutt's desk he glanced up and didn't look delighted to see her. However, she was used to this. She put on a determined smile and sat down across from his desk which was laden as usual with piles of paper, an overflowing ashtray, and a notebook filled with the incomprehensible scribbles that only he could read. He was a gaunt-looking man as gray as the cigarette smoke that drifted around him.

"Abby," he said wearily.

She had practiced all the way up Avenue de l'Opera what she would say when she got here and she took a deep breath and plunged in. "Good morning, Walter. I wanted to talk to you about some story ideas. I've been working for the paper now for several months and I've proven I can report hard news."

She'd chosen a Tuesday morning to approach him, since Mondays were often busy with stories from the weekend. He made a sound that could have been him clearing his throat, or it could have been a sound of derision. She chose to assume the former.

He reached for his cigarettes and lit one, his eyes narrowing against the smoke.

"I want to write an article about the anarchist who was arrested trying to blow up the Eiffel Tower."

Before she could say another word, he cut her off. "Already got Robinson on that one."

It was so unfair. Robinson had only been at the paper for a few weeks. Okay, he had a Pulitzer, but maybe she'd win a Pulitzer too if anybody ever gave her a chance. She was twenty-five years old, had a college degree in journalism, and she'd helped solve a notorious crime. Didn't that count for anything?

In case he'd forgotten, she reminded him. "Walter, my byline graced the front pages of this very newspaper reporting on one of the most notorious murder cases Paris has ever seen."

He blew out a stream of smoke. Not exactly in her face, but in her general direction. "You were also on the front cover of *Vogue* magazine. Think that qualifies you for hard news stories?"

Once again the bitter sense of unfairness felt like it was choking her and tightening its hold. "I didn't write the article, I was interviewed."

"You looked real good too. In your couture clothes and your fancy new haircut."

She couldn't help it, she put a hand to her bobbed hair. She still wasn't used to the shorter style but she'd learned to love the ease with which she could get ready in the morning and the lack of restriction both from the hair pinned high on her head and the clothes she'd once worn.

"I'm not sending a *Vogue* model into a men's prison," he replied with an air of finality. "They'd chew you up and spit you out."

Perhaps the pale blue designer dress had been a mistake. "Obviously, I wouldn't wear this outfit to interview an imprisoned anarchist."

"Doesn't matter what you wear. You're not doing it. I've already got you an assignment."

The way he spoke, she suspected it wasn't any one of a million hard news stories she would love to cover.

He said, "It's a society wedding."

Her worst fears were realized. "A society wedding? Since when did I become a wedding reporter?" And she thought about it for a second. "I didn't even know we had one."

"We have a wedding reporter when I say we do. And today I say we do." He inhaled smoke and blew it out so his next words emerged like curly ribbons of smoke. "And you're it."

She supposed she could get through one society wedding if she had to. Maybe she could bargain with him. Maybe she'd agree to do one society wedding if he let her do one news story.

If she'd learned one thing about Walter Strutt in the months she'd worked in the Paris office of the *Chicago Post* it was that he could be pushed. She'd tried not to do it unless absolutely necessary, but she was also a very determined young woman and she hadn't come to Paris to write about hem lengths. The *Chicago International Post* was the biggest English language newspaper in Paris, beloved of expats who longed for news of home as well as local stories that interested them. Unfortunately, a lot of that was society gossip.

He pushed an envelope toward her. To her surprise, her name was typewritten on the front of it.

She was mildly shocked that he'd gone ahead and opened it before she'd even seen it. Usually when people wrote to her at the newspaper the envelopes were left unmolested. Most of her mail was from people, mainly women, telling her how much they admired her. Abby had been quite famous not so long ago when she was implicated in the murder of her stepmother, a crime that took place in one of the up-and-coming couture houses in Paris. The tentacles of the story had reached back into the Great War and the coverage had been sensational.

She'd briefly been the most famous woman in Paris, and readers back home in the States as well as here in Paris had eagerly awaited the next installment in her first-person account of her ordeal. Who didn't love a story about a young woman unfairly accused of murder? Certainly the readers of the *Chicago Post* had lapped up her first-person accounts and begged for more.

There was talk of a book deal.

Reporting on high society weddings was not the way to fulfill her destiny, Abby was positive.

Still, she opened the envelope and discovered she was looking at the personal stationery of Lady Victoria Wimborne with an address of Darrington Manor, Somerset, England.

She glanced sharply up at Walter Strutt but decided to keep

reading to the end of the missive before saying a word. The Wimborne wedding must be taking place in Paris.

Abby would be bored to tears, but she could manage a few hours at the Ritz or Le Meurice. She'd write something lovely about the bride and groom and what she wore and who'd styled her hair and who'd cried at the wedding and what important dignitaries were present. And then she'd make Walter Strutt give her something better.

However, as she read down the letter she discovered this was not only an invitation to attend the wedding of The Viscount and Viscountess Wimborne's daughter The Honorable Cressida Wimborne to Reginald Mitchell Esquire, but it turned out her presence was requested not just for one day but a full week of festivities taking place at Darrington Manor. In Somerset. In England.

Lady Wimborne had not gushed but stated quite plainly that she would be honored if Abby would attend on behalf of the newspaper, and she enclosed a list of events so she might prepare her wardrobe accordingly. The activities ranged from a masked ball to a fishing expedition.

When Abby had read to the end, she didn't know what to say. She looked down at the crisp paper, the elegant signature of Lady Victoria Wimborne, and then glanced up to find an expression in Walter Strutt's eyes that was somewhere between sardonic amusement and evil glee.

"You didn't even assign this story," she said, confused. "She's invited me as a guest. But I don't know the family. I've never heard of the Wimbornes."

He said, "But I bet you've heard of Charles A. Mitchell."

That got her attention. "You mean Charles A. Mitchell the car king?"

"You got it. Charles A. Mitchell not only revolutionized the automobile industry, but the Reginald Mitchell who's marrying whatshername Wimborne is heir to the Mitchell company and fortune. And it seems Charles A. Mitchell is one of your fans. He read all about your harrowing adventures being accused of murder, the poor little American girl in trouble and all alone in Paris. And he thinks you're quite the plucky young dame."

She shuddered. If there was a word in the English language she had come to loathe it was plucky. She didn't think there was a single article that had been written about her that didn't use the word *plucky*, usually along with *heroine*. She couldn't entirely blame Walter Strutt for being sardonic. She'd cry out that it wasn't her fault she'd been implicated in the murder of her own stepmother, but she knew she'd be wasting her breath.

"Well, I'm going to turn it down," she decided. "It's lovely of Lady Wimborne to invite me to her daughter's wedding, but I'd feel awkward at a private house party, among people I don't know."

Walter Strutt leaned forward and stabbed his cigarette in her direction. "Think again, missy. Lady Wimborne may have sent you the letter, but it's Charles A. Mitchell who wants you there. And what Charles A. Mitchell wants, Charles A. Mitchell gets."

"But I'm not an automobile customer or anybody he wants to impress."

"That's as may be, but he thinks you're a plucky heroine and he phoned Charles Abernathy personally and said how much he wanted you to be the on-site reporter at his son's wedding to a British Lady. With the amount of money that Charles A. Mitchell spends in advertising in our newspapers, you can imagine that Abernathy was quick to say yes."

She was outraged. Seriously outraged. "But that's editorial interference! He can't do that. If it's not against the law, it should be."

The sardonic gleam—no, it was definitely edging toward evil glee now—became more pronounced.

"He's not interfering in an editorial about his cars, not keeping road accident statistics out of the paper or trying to influence the news. All he wants is for his fancy son and the son's fancy fiancée and their fancy wedding to get reported in our papers. And it's exactly the kind of thing the *Chicago International Post* does. Our readership is composed of expats who read about who's coming in on what ship and what they ate for lunch. Yes, we present news as well, but it's about social connections more than anything. You've been here long enough to know that."

She had, but still her journalistic feathers were seriously ruffled. She could tell from the quiver in his lower lashes that Strutt loathed the interference of an advertiser in editorial affairs as much as any newspaperman, but he'd had his orders and she had hers.

"What if I say no? I've never been to a house party in a manor house. I have no idea what's required. Besides, I have duties here. I can't take a week off work."

"You won't be taking a week off work. This is your work. It's a take-it-or-leave-it proposition, Abigail. You want to keep working here or don't you? Frankly, my life would be a whole lot easier if you flounced out of here in your designer clothes and didn't come back."

And the awful thing was, he was telling the truth. Walter Strutt would never fire her. He wouldn't dare. She was here because of a family connection with Charles Abernathy, who ran the *Chicago Post* and had been a close friend of her father's; he was no relation but she did call him uncle. Walter Strutt had been wanting to get rid of her since the minute she arrived. So, he couldn't fire her but if she refused to take an assignment or chose to quit he'd be in the clear.

As annoyed as she was, she wouldn't give him the satisfaction. She liked her job. Well, she liked her job when she got to do the kind of stories that interested her. And she had proven herself. But this was not the time to cut off her nose to spite her face, as her father would have said.

She picked up her invitation and rose. "Fine." And then, because these things mattered, she said, "I assume there will be some kind of expense account to get me to and from this house party? There will be train fares and I'll have to tip the servants." She really had no idea. If only her mother were alive, she could consult her. But sadly, she was an orphan, alone in the world.

She'd ask Paul Joubert, the owner and designer of a top couture house who'd become her good friend. It was the kind of thing he knew.

Walter Strutt didn't look particularly excited at the idea of having to finance her journey, but even he could see that she wouldn't be going if it wasn't for the newspaper.

He gave a short nod. "I'll see to it. Now clear your desk, get all your assignments in to Ru for editing. You leave for England a week today." Ruth was in her mid-forties and her main job was to keep up with who was coming into Paris on what ship. She was the only other female in the newsroom and often edited Abby's work.

A week. So little time.

With what dignity she could muster she said, "Thank you." And then she went to collect her mail. She didn't have a permanent seat in the newsroom, which was another bone of contention. She had to sit in whoever's desk was vacant. She saw Robinson head off, patting his pocket to make sure he had his notebook and grabbing his hat off the hat stand, and she subsided into his desk.

Her mail was the usual. Letters of support after her ordeal, questions on how she did her hair, and there was always one earnest letter asking how the young woman in question could also become a world-famous journalist.

Well, Walter Strutt might not take her seriously but there

were plenty of young women in America who believed in Abby. And she was determined not to let them down.

Abby worked for a couple of hours at the desk. In spite of her desire to write hard news, her assignments were always for the women's page. When she'd become a sensation, she'd received a generous bonus of one thousand dollars from the publisher of her newspaper, who was determined not to lose the plucky young heroine to a rival publication. He'd also doubled Abby's salary to one hundred dollars a month. She kept quiet about the windfall, knowing her fellow reporters didn't make that much, but despite her value to R. J. Hunnicutt, the publisher, she was still under Walter Strutt's rule and he assigned the stories. She had an article to finish on the latest trends in hats. And then she headed home feeling quite dispirited.

TWO

It was only a few blocks from the newspaper office on Avenue de l'Opera to the apartment she shared on Rue Saint-Hyacinthe. She took the elevator up to the fifth-floor apartment to find her roommate, Vivian O'Connell, had just returned home from her job as a sales clerk in a *parfumerie*. And as usual, Vivian smelled of flowers. Part of her job was to liberally spray herself with perfume and then suggest to the men who came into the shop that they should buy the scent for their wives or sweethearts. Vivian was blond and pretty and curvaceous and the men who came into the shop bought a lot of perfume.

However, Vivian also had a susceptible heart. She unashamedly told Abby that she'd come to Paris looking for love. Unfortunately, she wasn't the only young woman who'd come to Paris for romance, but too many young men had been killed in the Great War. There were a lot of lovely single women hoping for a husband and family and not enough healthy single men to go around.

Abby could see from Vivian's red nose and weepy eyes that her latest love affair had ended in disaster. As they tended to do.

"Do you want to talk about it?" she asked her gently.

Vivian dabbed a damp hanky to her eyes and said, "I'm such a fool. I really thought he loved me."

Abby had heard these words before, but to Vivian every fresh heartbreak was like the first time. She patted her friend's shoulder and said, "I know." And then listened while Vivian poured out the story of the latest betrayal. It was always a variation on the same theme. He'd met someone else. Or there'd always been someone else. Or he was married.

At the end of Vi's tearful recitation, Abby said, "Shall we go to the bistro? A little red wine and steak frites will set you right up. It's on me."

Vivian perked up at that. The little bistro round the corner had seen them through plenty of heart-to-heart talks. Vivian's usually about her love life, and Abby's usually about her work battles or her legal troubles.

"That's enough about me. Tell me about your day," Viviane said, dabbing her eyes one last time.

And then she was able to tell her the latest: that she had to go to England and cover a society wedding. Abby's tone might have been sepulchral, but Vivian opened her eyes wide.

"You're going to England to cover a society wedding?" She sounded both excited and envious. She leaned forward. "Gosh, I'd give anything to go to a society wedding. I've never been to England."

Abby was going to say you could go in my place, but stopped herself because obviously they couldn't swap places.

"Golly, you'd better get right over to Paul Joubert. You can't go to a week-long wedding with British aristocrats without a full wardrobe." Then very seriously she said, "Abby, you'll be representing the United States of America. You have to look your best."

"Don't worry. I'm going to see Paul Joubert tomorrow. One

of these days he's going to cut me off, and I can't blame him. But until then, I am so lucky that he designs for me. Can you imagine if he suddenly refused to create beautiful clothes and not even charge me? Then what would I do for clothes?"

Vivian shook her head. Working in the perfume industry, even if she was in the retail end of it, she had a pretty shrewd notion about the importance of being aligned with the right personalities to sell a brand of perfume or a clothing designer or a milliner or a maker of shoes.

"So long as you remain an important figure in Paris, Paul Joubert will continue to design for you. Besides, he loves you."

With Vivian's words still in her mind, Abby felt a little more confident when she approached the atelier of Paul Joubert the next morning. There had been a shake-up in his atelier in the months since she'd known him. The woman who'd always opened the door, who'd reminded Abby of a black crow, had been replaced by a very pretty young woman, much like Vivian only French.

"Bonjour, madam." And she asked how she might help Abby. Abby replied in her slightly awkward French that she had an appointment with Paul Joubert, and the young woman immediately slid into English and said, "But of course. I am delighted to meet you. Monsieur Joubert is expecting you."

And in she went, into the hallowed halls of Paris couture. She'd yet to get over the thrill of walking up the steps to the inner sanctum where the designer himself created gowns that were the envy of the world, worn by society hostesses, film stars, royalty.

When Paul Joubert saw her he jumped up from his desk, broke into a beaming smile and spread his arms wide. "Abigail, my muse." He kissed her on both cheeks and then stood back. She'd dressed with care in one of the outfits he'd given her, and he kissed his fingertips in appreciation. "You give my life purpose!" Then he said, "And how may I serve you?"

She simply handed the invitation to him and let him read it for himself. At the end of it he looked up with sparkling eyes and said, "But this is marvelous. You attend this wedding?"

She didn't feel as delighted as he sounded. "I have to. I've been assigned."

"*Bien sûr*, and it's a great honor. But you will need a full wardrobe."

"I know. I came immediately. Paul, I have some money now. I can pay you."

But he shook his head impatiently. "One does not ask one's muse for money. Abigail, you changed my life. A man does not forget those things. Besides, you wearing my clothes brings me prestige and, not to be vulgar, riches."

She felt a little better. "Thank you. Then I put myself in your hands."

"Extremely wise." Then he perused the sheet again. "A masquerade ball, *très bien*. Dinners and breakfasts. Evening attire. Croquet. What is this passion the English have for croquet? And fishing?" He glanced up as though she might understand the peculiar tastes of the English.

"It is an English country house. Fishing's no doubt part of their entertainment."

"*Beh*, England in this weather. It could be so variable." He twisted his mouth as though he smelled something bad. "Damp tweed. I will think on this carefully. But the dress ball. *Merveilleux*. I will make you a glorious costume."

"But nothing too flashy," she warned him.

"Abigail, nothing I do is flashy." He sounded so offended she apologized.

"I just meant I don't want to draw too much attention to myself at a ball. I'm meant to be there as a reporter."

He looked at her and his eyes were very wise. "You and I both know, *ma mignonne*, that that is not so. You are there to be associated with these bright, young things. In the same way that you bring a certain something to my atelier, so you will lend a certain *je ne sais quoi* to this society wedding."

"Does it seem wrong to you that it's only through being implicated in a murder that I've become so famous?"

He tutted. "One does not argue with the god of fortune. One smiles sweetly and puts out one's arms."

Since he was currently holding a measuring tape, she had to smile even as she obediently spread her arms like wings. Even though he must know her measurements better than she did herself, he always measured anew. She sometimes felt that each errant croissant or extra glass of vin rouge was noted and recorded.

When he had finished, he said, "Leave it to me."

"That's it?"

He looked at her down his nose.

Realizing any further input from her into the garments' design would not be welcome, she meekly replied, "No. Thank you."

Before she left, he tilted up her chin. "Make sure you get your hair trimmed before you leave."

She remembered to ask him about tipping the servants. He said she would definitely be expected to tip the servants without appearing to do so. Then he said, "And, naturally, you will require your own lady's maid."

She was shocked. "What? I don't have a lady's maid."

"Well, unless you want these English people to despise you, you had best hire one."

She couldn't imagine Walter Strutt approving that addition to her stingy expense account. Surely she could manage for one week without a maid.

As though he'd read her thoughts, Paul said, "Abigail, you must find someone. It is imperative."

"But—"

He held up a hand. "Also, I do not want you scrambling into

my beautiful clothes and twisting around yourself to fasten buttons. No, and no, and no. I can suggest an agency who will hire you a maid."

"Thank you," she said, wondering how she'd become someone who traveled with a maid. No doubt the woman would speak only French and look down her nose at American Abby. There had to be another solution.

When she left Maison de Joubert, she walked along the Rue du Faubourg Saint-Honoré which was as fashionable as the women who shopped there. She nearly shuddered when she recalled her first time walking down the elegant street with its white ornate townhouses trimmed with lacy black wrought-iron balconies. How old-fashioned she'd been; her hair, clothing style and even her shoes were from a different era. At that time Abby would have said fashion was a frivolous pursuit and she was more interested in her career. Occasionally, she still felt this way, but she'd learned to appreciate the artistry behind couture and, having become a fashionable young woman, from her bobbed hair to the tip of her silk-stockinged toes, she had no desire to return to her previously dull appearance. Vain that might be, but she'd discovered the exquisite satisfaction of knowing she was one of the best-dressed people in the room and it was a heady experience.

It was all thanks to the master of Maison de Joubert, the great Paul Joubert himself. He'd been buzzing with ideas and Abby knew Paul would work miracles in creating her a wardrobe that would allow her to fit in, sartorially at least, with posh English people.

In the meantime, she had assignments to finish. She was banging away on her Underwood typewriter when Vivian arrived home with a fresh bouquet of flowers and some samples of perfume. Obviously, her heartbreak was easing a little.

Viv asked, "How was your day today?"

When Abby recounted her meeting with Paul Joubert, and

his insistence that she hire a lady's maid, her friend was as stunned as she was. "You have to have your own lady's maid?"

"I know. It's only going to be a one-week assignment, and the wedding's not even in London; it's to be held in some old manor house in the middle of the English countryside. Who knows if they even have indoor plumbing or electricity?"

"Oh, Abby, it won't be that bad."

"It will. And I'm sure the maid will despise me for dragging her all that way, and it's going to feel so odd having a stranger dress and undress me. Can you imagine?"

"Silly, you and I help each other all the time with buttons and zips, and I've seen you in your undergarments countless times."

"But that's different. We're practically family." Abby pulled a sheet of paper out of the typewriter with a ripping sound. "Where am I going to find a maid who will travel to England for one week? Oh, and she has to speak English."

Then Vivian's blue eyes went wide and a delighted smile spread across her pretty face. "You're looking at her."

It took Abby a second to realize what her friend was saying. "I beg your pardon?"

"I am hereby applying for the position of lady's maid. Getting away from Paris would be the best thing to help me recover from a broken heart." Vivian stood up straight and said, "My qualifications are: I keep up with all the current fashions, I'm very good with hair, you know I do your makeup better than you can do it yourself. And besides, I've never been to England. And we'll have each other, so when you get fed up with those stuffy English people, we can hide in your bedroom and eat candy."

An answering smile slowly dawned on Abby's face. "Are you serious? But what about your job? What about your boss? Won't he miss you?"

"Truly, we're not very busy at the moment. I think he'd be

perfectly happy to do without me for a week or so." She snapped her fingers and uncapped one of the samples, waving it toward Abby. "Especially if I tell him that you'll be wearing his perfumes." Then she gazed at her friend blissfully. "Think of it, Abby—England. Maybe we'll meet lords!"

Abby had to laugh. "Maybe we will."

THREE

When he saw Abby in the flame-colored silk gown he'd designed for the masquerade ball, Paul Joubert's eyes filled with tears. "Abby, my heart is at your feet."

He turned to Maison de Joubert's new premiere and issued a string of quick instructions in French, then in English said, "She has the height, the long limbs of an athlete, but slender as a lily. Large dark eyes that smolder, the long neck, the shoulders. Perfection."

"Mademoiselle looks very well," the woman agreed in heavily accented English.

Vivian, who'd watched the exchange wide-eyed, never lost a moment after that in imitating Paul Joubert as she described Abby's "eyes that smolder, but slender as a lily," until the two of them were doubled over laughing.

Paul had insisted that Vivian accompany Abby to the atelier for the final fittings so that he could instruct the newly appointed "maid" on how a beaded shawl was to be arranged, which shoes, hats and bags accompanied which gowns. What jewelry to wear. Vivian had borrowed one of Abby's reporter's notebooks so she could scribble down all the instructions. Clearly gratified to have someone who understood the importance of each detail, Paul Joubert had then sent her upstairs to the atelier to be instructed on how to press the delicate garments.

The clothes duly arrived and Viv insisted on packing Abby's trunk. "Because I know what you're like. You'll scramble everything together and I'll spend my week ironing."

"Are you certain you don't object to being my maid?" Abby asked more than once. It seemed horribly elitist to take her friend along as a servant. "We won't even be allowed to eat our meals together."

"It's an adventure, silly. Serving you is no different than serving the customers who come to buy perfume, and at least you won't pinch my bottom when no one's looking." She sighed. "Besides, I'm twenty-five and I've never been to London."

"Well, I'm twenty-five and I've never been to London either. We'd better go before it's too late and we're twenty-six!"

The two young women took the train from Paris to Calais and then the ferry to Dover and then another train to London, where they stayed overnight and spent a few hours exploring. Next morning they boarded yet another train to a small town Abby had never even heard of called Frome. The trip was a lot more fun when she had Vivian traveling with her. They'd laughed at the eccentricities of some of the other travelers and had already begun the pretense that they were mistress and servant, to the great amusement of them both.

The train wasn't crowded, so Vivian and Abby sat across from each other and beside the window watching the English countryside roll by. It was as if they were looking at paintings rather than scenery: green fields dotted with placid sheep, picturesque villages and ancient churches passed by. A large man read a newspaper and puffed a pipe, grunting from time to time as he turned the pages. Vivian flicked through the latest copy of *Vogue* while Abby wrote in her notebook, trying to come up with questions for a series of articles about the upcoming nuptials of the Honorable Cressida Wimborne and Reginald Mitchell Esq. She was just wondering if one could die of boredom in a week, when the train pulled into a station and the pipe-smoking man disembarked leaving his newspaper behind. Abby reached for it.

She'd read the London papers that morning, but this was a local newspaper. What were the burning issues in southwest England, Abby wondered. Could there be a story for her outside the world of rose petals and wedding vows?

"Just look at this bathing costume," Vivian said, when they were alone in the coach. "Why, I'd blush to wear it." She showed Abby, who had to agree that bathing attire was becoming more about fashion than athleticism. "According to this article, Greta Garbo was spotted someplace called The Riviera, wearing one."

She folded open the newspaper the man had left behind. The front page had her muttering, "Golly."

"What is it?" Vivian asked, looking up.

"A young woman's been strangled."

Vivian put her small hands to her throat. "On the train?"

"No. In London. I read about it this morning in the London papers, but it seems the young woman was from Darrington. That's the village connected to Darrington Manor."

While Vivian looked appalled, Abby began to perk up. Her wish for a hard news story in the depths of the English countryside seemed to have been granted.

All thoughts of bathing attire forgotten, Vivian leaned forward. "What does it say?"

Abby read aloud: "*Local girl found strangled to death in London...*"

She skimmed the paragraphs, recognizing in the prose the excitement of a bored reporter with a genuine news story. Unlike the account in the London paper, which stated that the young woman was from the countryside, this story emphasized her ties to Darrington. "*Gladys Trotter, nineteen, was described by all who knew her as a bright young woman who dreamed of being an actress,*" she read aloud.

"Well, who doesn't?" Viv asked. "I was certain I was going to be the next It girl when I was nineteen." Then, after a pause, "But what was she doing in London?"

Abby shook her head. "No one seems to know. She told her mother she'd be working at Darrington Manor. Seems she worked there on a casual basis and, with the wedding coming up, they must need the extra staff. When she didn't return home last night her mother didn't worry as she'd often stay for days at a time when she was needed." She glanced up. "So, our budding actress was a part-time servant at Darrington Manor."

She read on. "Her body was found in a room at the Standard Hotel, a modest establishment in a less salubrious area near Paddington station."

"Paddington station? But we got the train from Paddington station," Viv cried out. "We could have passed the murderer."

"Vivian, there are millions of people in London. The chances of us coming across a killer are quite slim." She read on. "The young woman was strangled with her own silk stocking. There was no sign of the murderer but the hotel receptionist remembered her with a young man who wore a muffler and a hat."

She paused, picturing the scene. "That would make him difficult to recognize. It suggests the killer had planned his crime."

"Oh, that's simply too horrible. And how could a barely employed servant have afforded silk stockings?"

"That's a good point, Viv." She read on: "*The man signed them in on the hotel register as Mr. and Mrs. Smith. Police are investigating the crime but so far have made no arrests.*" She put down the paper. "You know what this means?"

"No. But I don't trust that expression on your face."

"It means that the police have no clue as to who killed this poor young woman. Viv, there's a story here, a real human interest story. So while I'm writing about a society wedding, I can also find out more about Miss Gladys Trotter. And you will be my eyes and ears below stairs. Who was she? Why did she go to London? Did she have a beau? Could the motive for her murder be found in Darrington Manor? Or perhaps there's a strangler operating in London and she was the first victim. We must keep our eyes open, Viv. This is a genuine mystery."

Viv was much less excited than Abby. "The last time you got involved in a murder investigation you were nearly killed."

Before Abby could reply to her poor-spirited assistant, the whistle blew and their stop was announced.

They both got up at the same time and Viv ushered her to go first. "After you, miss."

Abby realized that it was a good thing they'd been practicing because otherwise they would have given the game away by giggling every time Viv had to say "Yes, miss" to her roommate. When they alighted at the platform in Frome they both accepted that the charade had now become real. As she watched the train lumbering off down the track, the steam wreathed around the carriages lending the scene a dreamlike quality, Abby had a sudden urge to jump back on, as though continuing on to Darrington Manor would be a mistake.

It was a momentary sensation, probably brought on by reading about that poor girl's untimely death.

Emerging from the cloud of steam, a young man who'd

stepped out of the second-class carriage approached them with a jaunty stride. He was tall and wore what looked to be his best suit, as though he had been to a wedding, or a funeral perhaps. He was young and nice-looking. When he passed, his eyes met Abby's and he touched his hat with one finger in a slightly cheeky manner. She definitely got the feeling he had noticed she was young, and also female. Then he strode toward the exit so quickly that Viv, who'd been organizing their suitcases, never even noticed him.

"I think it's colder here than in Paris," Viv remarked, shivering.

"It's certainly damper."

As Abby reached for her suitcase, Vivian scolded: "Don't touch that case. That's for your maid to do. I'm sure there must be a porter here somewhere." She glanced around but the only porter seemed to be helping an older gentleman with a great deal of luggage.

"I can't get used to the idea of you picking up my bags and ironing my clothes," Abby admitted.

"Well, you must get used to it. Besides, I've let you pay for my journey. It wouldn't feel right if I didn't work for you in return." She grinned, her blue eyes lighting up. "Besides, I'm enjoying myself. I feel like an actress preparing for a role. And so should you. You've managed to fit in with grand people in Paris. You must do the same thing here."

"You're right, of course. I suppose I can't even link arms with you as I'm dying to do."

"Certainly not. You will act like a grand lady, and I'll scamper behind you like the dutiful servant."

They both laughed. Not that Abby imagined anything too terrible would happen if she admitted that she didn't have her own maid. How many reporters did? But it was important to Paul Joubert that she treat his couture garments like the priceless treasures they were. She was so grateful to him for all the clothing he had provided, she was willing to live the fantasy that she was the kind of woman who traveled with a couture wardrobe and her own dresser. It was a pleasant fantasy in any case. And Vivian had taken on the role of keeper of the wardrobe as if it were a sacred duty.

They'd been told someone would meet them at the train station and sure enough as they stood on the platform looking up and down a young man came toward them with a welcoming smile.

Abby's heart began to sink because he was exactly the kind of romantic young hero type that Vivian always went for. He had sandy blond hair that flopped down over one eyebrow, big, dreamy eyes, and a sensitive mouth. He was tall, broad-shouldered, wearing a suit and tie and a cap. But there was nothing servile about his manner as he approached and said, "Do I have the pleasure of addressing Miss Abigail Dixon?"

She said, "You do. And thank you so much for meeting us."

"It's my pleasure." And then he turned to Vivian, who gushed, "And I'm Vivian. Miss Dixon's maid."

"I'm Ned Corcoran. The car's just through here," and with that he picked up the two heavy cases, leaving Vivian with nothing but a dressing case to carry. They followed him to what Abby was fairly certain was a Rolls-Royce and he opened the back door for her before stowing the cases in the back.

As Vivian got in beside her she whispered, "Isn't he dreamy?"

And her suspicions were confirmed. Of course Vivian had fallen for him. Abby was half in love with him herself.

"We're only here for a week," she reminded her susceptible friend. "Besides, he could be married."

Vivian sighed. "I know," she replied, pausing briefly, "but he doesn't look married."

"But then they never do."

They fell into silence as he got into the front and they

headed away from the train station. "You're American, I understand?" Corcoran asked.

"Yes," Abby replied. "And it's the first time either of us have been in England. Well, apart from changing ship at Southampton when I travelled from America to Paris."

"I hope you'll enjoy your trip very much. Darrington Manor takes a little getting used to." He twinkled at them in the rearview mirror. "It's not as modern and convenient as you're accustomed to, but it's a lovely old place."

He spoke with such affection that Abby had to ask, "Have you lived there long?"

He chuckled at that. "All my life. My father was the gamekeeper and I grew up in one of the cottages on the property. I was lucky enough to get a scholarship to a decent school, but I'm back again. I work as the estate manager. But our staff is so small that I often act as chauffeur. Mum says I ought to go make my fortune in America. Or at least go as far as London. But I haven't the heart to leave."

She could hear the affection in his voice and thought he must be very close to his mother. It was sweet. She could almost feel Vi melting beside her. She'd have to keep an eye on that girl or there'd be trouble before the week was out and yet another broken heart.

They bumped and rattled over narrow country lanes and she looked about with interest. It was mostly rural and agricultural with fields of sheep, including playful lambs, and cows, green fields being planted with various crops. She glimpsed limestone houses and thatched cottages and had to shut her eyes when another vehicle came toward them on what felt to her like the wrong side of the road.

"That's the village of Darrington," he informed his passengers as they passed a pretty village that looked to Abby like a picture postcard of rural England. Darrington was where the murdered young woman hailed from, she recalled with a shiver.

Then he turned into a long, steep drive that was rather bumpy and lined with beech trees. "Here we are," he said, as Darrington Manor came into view.

It was a large rectangular-shaped home built in golden stone that glowed in the early afternoon light. Green lawns spread out like a luxurious carpet and a stone chapel came into view with an attached graveyard. The lawns were ringed with woods but behind the manor house she glimpsed fertile fields stretching as far as she could see. "Oh, how lovely," Abby cried.

Ned spoke with pride. "The Georgian manor house stands in a hundred acres. It's almost two hundred years old."

Their wheels crunched over a circular gravel drive and pulled up in front of Darrington Manor's imposing front entrance. Ned got out and opened the door for Abby. "I'll get Vivian settled and make sure your cases are taken to your room."

She thanked him and headed up the steps to the main entrance to the manor house. Viv would be taken to the servants' entrance, leaving her feeling suddenly very much alone. As she approached the carved wooden double doors, they opened and a butler appeared. Conscious of his scrutiny, she tilted her chin up, refusing to be intimidated.

Once again she was grateful to Paul Joubert for providing her with a complete wardrobe for the week. Her travel clothes were a little creased, but she knew she looked as though she belonged.

"Good afternoon, miss," he said.

"Good afternoon. My name is Abigail Dixon."

He stood aside to let her enter. "Her Ladyship has been expecting you."

Abby stepped into the flagstoned hall. An enormous chandelier hung from the center of the high ceiling, illuminating a polished mahogany table on which stood a crystal vase with an arrangement of spring flowers. A fireplace took up most of one wall and a hallway led to the back of the house.

From this hallway, a woman came toward Abby with her hands held out in welcome.

"Miss Dixon. Thank you so much for coming. I'm Victoria Wimborne."

Abby shook her hand. She'd been reading a copy of *Debrett's* on the way over so she knew how to address Lady Wimborne. "It's so kind of Your Ladyship to invite me."

"Not at all. And you must call me Victoria. I'll take you up to your room myself."

Lady Wimborne was a beautiful woman with soft blond hair that she wore pinned up and a sweet-tempered face with china doll blue eyes. She was dressed in expensive clothes but they weren't the height of fashion. Abby had spent long enough covering fashion for the women's page and associating with Paul Joubert to know that Her Ladyship's clothes were several years out of date.

Being shown to her room by the lady of the manor was presumably a great honor, but Lady Wimborne put her at ease, chatting to Abby as she led her up a flight of stairs and down a corridor lined with bedroom doors. "You must be terribly fatigued after your long journey," she said.

"No, I love traveling. And it was very exciting, spending a night in London."

"That's nice. I always find traveling rather tiring. You've got your own maid with you, I understand."

Abby was certain she heard approval in the tone. Or maybe it was relief. Perhaps there weren't enough staff here to spare a maid to look after Abby. In any case, she was thoroughly glad that she'd brought Vivian.

Lady Wimborne opened a door and said, "This is one of my favorite guest rooms. We call it the pink room, for obvious reasons. I hope you'll enjoy your stay with us. And please do let me know if there's anything you require."

Abby took a quick glance around the room and was delighted. The curtains and bedspread were clearly quite new in a pretty pink chintz, and her window overlooked a walled garden. There was even an en suite bathroom. "It's beautiful. Thank you."

Lady Wimborne nodded. "I'll leave you to get settled. Your cases will be up shortly. I hope you'll join us for tea at three o'clock."

"Of course. Thank you."

"Tea will be served in the library."

And then her hostess left her. Abby went to the window and looked out. Apart from a walled garden where an apple tree was coming into blossom. Beyond the garden she could see a large pond fed by a stream, and beyond that a wooded area and then fields. The view was tranquil and timeless. While she stood contemplating the scenery, there was a soft knock on the door and then Vivian opened it and came inside. Behind her was a strong young man carrying Abby's suitcases.

Vivian announced, with a twinkle in her eye, "Here are your cases, miss."

But Abby was looking at the person carrying them. It was the young man from the station. "I believe you were on our train," she said to him.

He looked at her and nodded. "I was visiting my family for a few days, miss. My mother's been ill."

"I hope she's better?" Abby asked politely.

"Aye, she is. Thank you, miss."

In front of the young manservant they kept up the appearance of mistress and maid, but the minute he shut the door behind him, Vivian broke into a peal of laughter. "You should have seen your face. You'd completely forgotten I'm here as your servant, I could tell. You were going to say something that you'd say to a girlfriend."

"You're right. I'm not used to having a servant. I'm far too democratic."

"Good. Don't get used to it. When we get back to Paris, you'd better not expect me to dress you."

They both found this exquisitely funny and then each set to work on one of the suitcases, unpacking Abby's stylish clothes into the wardrobe and chest of drawers in the guest room.

While they were doing that she asked, "What's it like downstairs? Did you meet any of the other staff?"

"It's all hustle and bustle down there. I don't think they're used to entertaining on this scale. The woman who rules the kitchen seemed very efficient, but also run off her feet. She kept muttering about being understaffed. But isn't Jerry nice?"

Abby was confused. "Jerry? Who's Jerry?"

"Silly, he's the one who brought up your cases. How funny that you saw him at the station and I never did."

"You were busy acting like a good maid."

Vivian said, "He was very impressed to hear that I live in Paris. He wants me to tell him all about it. He's asked me to go to the pub when we get our time off."

Abby shook her head. "You do work fast. What about the young man who drove us here? I thought you liked him."

"Ned Corcoran. It turns out he's not really a downstairs man, nor does he fit in with the family. He's somewhere in between, in a sort of British hierarchy no man's land. And he's much too busy to gossip with the likes of me. He very properly introduced me to the housekeeper, declined the cook's offer of a cup of tea, and left. But Jerry has lots of time, especially when the butler's not watching over him. He's a laugh."

"So, you've already discounted Ned and moved on to Jerry?"

Vivian glanced up with a grin. "I'm only here for a week. I have to move fast."

"I don't suppose you found out anything about that murdered young woman?" Abby asked.

"I've barely had a chance to start asking questions. Besides, I'm already scared to death of the housekeeper and the cook, and the other maids were running around like crazy. I get my own room, by the way. It's not as grand as this one, but it's clean and I can see the chapel from my window. Anyway, Hazel—she's Miss Wimborne's maid—showed me my room and I said we'd read about that poor girl. She glanced behind her as though the housekeeper might be eavesdropping, but there was no one around, so she said, 'Poor Gladys. She was so young and pretty, but had her head full of ideas. She said she was destined for bigger things and was going to be an actress.'"

Which was pretty much what had been reported in the newspaper.

"Hazel said the cook had been relying on Gladys to help over the coming week, and when she didn't turn up she threatened to murder her with her bare hands. That's what Hazel said. So you can imagine how dreadful she must have felt when she found out the poor girl was dead."

"Golly. So they were expecting her here, then."

"Hazel said—wait, let me get this right." She paused and, in a fair imitation of the local accent, continued: "'You should have seen that Gladys swanning around in a red dress that was too tight—unseemly, it was, but she didn't care. Dropped hints that one day we'd be waiting on her.'"

Viv dropped the accent and in her own voice went on: "Even Jerry said she used to be a real laugh, but recently she's been too full of herself. He said she had ideas above her station."

Abby digested this. From what Vivian had told her of Jerry, she suspected every girl was fair game. Abby suspected Gladys

Trotter had rejected him and that was why he'd said she had ideas above her station. Still, she filed the gossip away.

Then Abby checked the time. It was just after two o'clock. "I'm having tea downstairs in the library at three. Do you think the turquoise day dress? Or the dove gray two-piece?"

Vivian took a moment before replying. "Well, if it's a library, it's going to be full of books. Perhaps the gray?"

"Fine then. The gray."

She took her toiletry case into the bathroom and freshened up, emerging to find that Vivian had laid out her outfit on the bed including the pearls, hosiery and even the shoes and handbag. As she stepped into the outfit and Vivian did up the buttons at the back of her blouse, Abby asked her, "How did I ever manage without a dresser?"

"I think being a lady's maid is great fun. I'm not sure I could do it forever, but I'm definitely a somebody among the servants. They all want to know what you're like. I think everybody read about your ordeal in Paris and thinks you're wonderful."

Abby was pleased that Vivian was getting on well with the house staff, but somewhat horrified to discover they'd all read her articles. But then, what had she expected? She was the one who'd written most of them and the case had been sensational. However, one day she'd really prefer to be known as something other than the innocent girl caught up in a scandalous murder in Paris.

When she was dressed and Vivian was satisfied that Abby's appearance was perfect, she was allowed to go downstairs.

"Will you be all right?" she asked Vivian. It seemed wrong that she should be having tea while her friend wasn't invited, but Viv seemed to have embraced her temporary role.

"I'm going to press your dress for dinner. It became shockingly creased from being packed for travel," Vivian said with a look of deep concentration.

"I feel that I should do my own ironing. You're my friend, not my servant."

But Viv looked shocked at the very suggestion. "Paul Joubert would have my head if I let you take an iron to his gorgeous fabrics. You're a wonderful writer, Abigail, but no one who's seen you with an iron would ever let you near their creased garments. Now, go on down and enjoy your tea. It's up to me to make sure you're the best-dressed woman at dinner."

Abby thanked her, swore to herself that she'd make it up to Vivian somehow, and then with a last swift glance at her appearance, headed down for tea. What would aristocratic ladies talk about during tea? With luck, they'd have read the newspapers too and maybe she'd find out more about the murdered local girl.

FOUR

The library at Darrington Manor was a somber room, heavy with oak paneling that had darkened with age and smoke. Abigail glanced out of the tall windows onto an emerald lawn where gardeners were at work trimming the grass.

Inside the room a fire crackled in the fireplace notable for the carved oak frieze above it, patterned with trees and the Wimborne family arms. The Wimbornes had been as steady in holding on to Darrington Manor as the house itself had remained barely touched year after year while wars raged, monarchs died and were replaced, and other families of the landed gentry lost their stately homes.

That the Wimbornes were hanging on to Darrington by a thread was evident in the faded fabric on curtains and furniture and Lady Wimborne's less than fashionable outfit. Still, it was clear every effort was being made for Lord and Lady Wimborne to give a lavish entertainment to send their only daughter into married life.

Inside the room were three women. Lady Wimborne was the only one she'd met. Her hostess rose and welcomed her with a smile. "Miss Dixon. What a lovely suit. I do envy you living in Paris and having access to such clothes."

"Thank you," Abby said, feeling like a terrible fraud as she couldn't afford Paul Joubert's creations any more than Lady Wimborne herself.

Her hostess indicated an older woman of at least seventy who had an impressive hook of a nose, deep-set brown eyes, and hair and clothes that proclaimed her preference for the fashions of the last century. "Lady Constance Harroby is a cousin of my husband's and Cressida's godmother."

At Abby's "pleased to meet you," the woman gave a slight nod as though it was naturally an honor for Abby to be in her presence. "Beside Constance is Beatrice Ashby."

Beatrice said, "How do you do?" in a soft voice. She was rather colorless, nervous-looking and about forty years old.

Maybe her hopes to be a hard news reporter had temporarily been dashed by her Paris editor, Walter Strutt, but Abby was an optimist and determined, if she had to cover the wedding of a British aristocrat to an American industrialist's heir, she'd do her very best.

She couldn't, wouldn't, give up hope. Yet, here she was on another tedious assignment. She couldn't help but notice that the two people she was meant to be writing about weren't present. Lady Wimborne waved her to a two-seater couch and brought her a cup of tea and a plate of lemon cake.

While she sipped tea in the faded library and kept up a light flow of conversation with Lady Wimborne, her thoughts drifted to the Paris newsroom. Had Robinson managed to interview the imprisoned anarchist? The murdered local girl was a news story, but how could she make it relevant to her Paris readership? She pondered this while she and Lady Wimborne chatted about hem lengths.

"Does she have money?" the piercing voice of Lady Constance came to her ears. "Tall gel. Dresses well. American.

They all seem to be rich, these American gels. Would she do for Peter, do you think? He'll have to marry money, you know."

This embarrassing outburst was clearly about Abigail and directed at the colorless woman named Beatrice.

"I really couldn't say, Your Ladyship," Beatrice replied in a hushed tone.

"You must find out. It will take more than one fortune to put this family back on its feet. And a gel's inheritance is so much more useful as it comes to Darrington. It's all very well Cressida marrying an American fortune, but the money will stay in America, won't it?"

As Abby glanced out the window trying to pretend she couldn't hear the old woman asking in a very loud voice if she might do for the young man of the house, she saw a beautiful young woman with a blond bob strolling across the lawn. As she rounded the house a man's hand appeared to reach out and grab hers. She couldn't see anything of the man, only his hand, which seemed to be trying to pull the woman toward him. With a shake of the head and look of pain, she prized herself away and hurried on.

There was a pause in the conversation in the library. Abby decided that any subject would be better than Lady Harroby's loud questions about her marriage prospects. "I read on the train coming down here about a young woman who was murdered in London. It seems she came from Darrington?"

She felt the shift in the atmosphere. Lady Wimborne looked at her as though she'd come to the library via the fields and tromped cow manure onto the fine rug. "Yes," she said, clearing her throat. "I heard about that. Poor Gladys. She was a very sweet girl who worked here at Darrington occasionally."

"What's that?" Lady Constance bellowed. "You talking about that dead gel? Lightskirt," she said ominously. "I had her work for me last Christmas, do you remember, Victoria? Pretty but brainless. Instead of polishing the furniture, which I'd instructed her to do, I found her kissing one of the farmworkers. That fellow whose wife left him during the war. What was his name?" She seemed to be dredging up memories then nodded sharply. "Smith, that's it."

Abby felt something like an electric shock run through her. The killer had signed the hotel register as Mr. and Mrs. Smith. Could he have been using, not an alias, as everyone suspected, but his actual name?

"The Trotter family have been part of Darrington for generations," Lady Wimborne said as though determined to move to more socially acceptable conversation. "Her mother is terribly upset, as are her brothers and sisters. There are six of them. I believe she was the youngest. I shall make a visit of condolence to her mother, naturally."

Feeling that to pry any more would be social suicide, Abby just nodded and let Lady Wimborne lead the conversation back to a concert she'd attended recently.

Five minutes later the door to the library opened and the ethereal young blond woman she'd glimpsed earlier stood there, looked about her and blinked. Lady Wimborne put on her most gracious smile.

"Cressie, darling. You're just in time for tea."

Was there a slight note of reproach? Presumably she'd expected the bride to show up on time for tea with her guests. Cressida obviously felt the reproach for she colored slightly and said, "I'm terribly sorry to be late, Mummy. I was seeing to Colonel. He's strained a forelock."

Abby could only assume that the Colonel in question was a horse and Cressida a keen rider.

Abby wasn't in the habit of calling a woman she'd never even met before a liar, but she was fairly certain the stables weren't in the direction that the young woman had come walking from. Ah well, what young woman didn't keep the odd secret from her mother?

Lady Wimborne said, "Let me present you to Miss Abigail Dixon. She's come all the way from Paris."

Cressida Wimborne was very like her mother only in stronger colors, as though a painter had begun with watercolor when creating the mother and moved to bolder oils to paint the daughter. Her hair was more gold than flax, her skin pinker and her eyes a much deeper shade of blue. Unlike her mother, Cressida was dressed in the height of fashion.

The deep-blue eyes studied Abby with what she felt was disdain. "How lovely of you," she said in a cool, cultured voice. "I'd never have thought I was important enough to have a reporter at my wedding."

Lady Wimborne gave a trill of laughter, reminding Abby once more of her own late mother, who'd had a knack for smoothing over awkward social moments, especially if Abby had made a social gaffe. However, she didn't think Cressida Wimborne had uttered an accidental gaffe. There was deliberate hostility there. She felt like telling Cressida that she didn't want to be there any more than Cressida wanted her there. It seemed they were both stuck due to the machinations of Charles A. Mitchell, the car king.

Sure enough, her mother said, "Don't forget, Cressida my love, that your future father-in-law particularly wished Miss Dixon to be present."

With a glittering smile Cressida said, "And my father-in-law-to-be is very good at getting exactly what he wants." Then she stepped forward and held out her hand. "It's lovely to meet you, Miss Dixon."

Since Abby perfectly understood how it felt to be forced into a situation one didn't wish to be in, she responded with great friendliness. "It's a pleasure to meet you too. Congratulations on your upcoming wedding. And please call me Abby."

After a small hesitation the woman said, "My friends call me Cressie."

Now that any awkwardness had been smoothed over, Lady Wimborne brought a cup of tea over to her daughter, who had sunk gracefully onto the settee beside Abby. Perhaps she felt bad for her slight rudeness.

She said, "I understand there's to be a photographer."

"Yes. I heard that too. I don't take photographs myself. I'll merely be reporting on your gown and the guests and that sort of thing. The details that our readers love."

"One has to wonder why they would be so interested in the nuptials of a person so unknown to them," Cressida said pointedly.

Abby didn't think Cressida Wimborne was that naïve. She didn't rise to the bait, she just said, "I'll do my best to get the details right and spell everyone's name correctly. That always seems to be the most important thing. You can say the most dreadful things about someone and if their name ends up in the paper they will not mind. However, say the most glowing thing possible and spell their name wrong and they'll complain loudly."

"Heavens."

"Will you be making your home in America or here?" Abby asked Cressida. She felt, since they were seated together, that she might as well begin interviewing her in an informal way.

Cressida dropped her gaze and rubbed at the enormous diamond engagement ring gracing her finger. "I believe I shall spend quite a bit of time in New York," she said softly, sounding the very opposite of excited by the prospect.

Before Abby could think of anything to say in response, Lady Constance piped up again in her loud voice.

"It's terrible the estate taxes now. Perfectly wicked. Death duties have beggared many a fine family and it was a tragedy that the Wimbornes had to sell both the Van Dyck and the Lely. It's a shame Peter doesn't spend less time on his sporting pursuits and more time finding himself a rich wife. You must find out, Beatrice, whether this gel has money. Shame she's American, but beggars, you know, can't be choosers."

In a low voice Cressida said to Abby, "My godmother is quite deaf. She has no idea that everyone can hear her plainly. We just ignore her. It's the easiest thing to do. My apologies if she's embarrassed you in any way."

Abby said, in an equally soft voice, "No. It's fine. And I don't have any money, by the way."

Cressida gave a soft laugh. "Even if you did, I wouldn't recommend my brother Peter as a bridegroom. He's a good enough man in his way, and one day he will inherit what's left of this estate, yet he's completely obsessed with sport. He has no other interests. I expect he'll end up marrying the gamekeeper's daughter. That's who'd make him happiest. But, I suppose he'll be forced to marry for money." She didn't say the word "too," but it seemed to be implied.

Very soon the door opened again and the butler announced Mrs. Mildred Mitchell. Abby was quite curious to see the wife of the famous Charles A. Mitchell, car king. The woman who entered wore a fur-trimmed suit, and a great deal of jewelry, all of which was large and sparkling. She wasn't a tall woman but she had enormous presence, twinkly brown eyes and a ready smile.

"I'm so sorry to be late for tea," she said in a booming American accent. "My husband telephoned."

Lady Wimborne rose and said, "That's quite all right, Mildred. Do sit down and let me get you some tea." And she gestured to Abby and said, "I don't believe you've met Miss Abigail Dixon?"

Mildred Mitchell said a quick hello to the ladies she knew and then walked straight over to Abby and shook her hand. "I can't tell you how delighted we are to have you here, my dear. Especially my husband. He's a man who knows what he wants and goes for it, and he felt quite strongly that you were the person to report on our only son's nuptials." And then she beamed at Cressida. "And we could not be more happy with his choice. Cressida is a lovely young woman, of a good family, and exactly the sort of person I believe will make my son very happy."

It took Abby a second to realize that Mildred was doing her best to write Abby's copy for her. Naturally, they wanted everything about the wedding to appear in a good light in the newspaper, but Abby could have told her she didn't need to worry. Walter Strutt had made it very clear that Abby was to turn in a glowing report of the affair. If the groom fell headfirst into the wedding cake drunk, she'd mention how much he had enjoyed his first slice of cake. And if one of the bridesmaids fainted or fell down in a fit she'd simply witter on about how moving the wedding party found the vows.

So she listened politely and said, "I'm very much looking forward to meeting your son. And your husband."

"Well you're in luck, my dear. They're on their way and should be here in time for dinner. They're driving down from London. And Reggie's dearest friend Oliver Platt will be coming with them. Oliver's the best man, you know. I'll make sure you get all the proper names and spellings, my dear."

There was a stifled giggle from Cressie and Abby's voice wobbled a little as she said, "Thank you very much, Mrs. Mitchell."

"I do love afternoon tea, don't you? It's so *English*," she gushed, squeezing in beside Abby. "Did Cressie tell you the good news?"

Having no idea what that could be, Abby said, "I don't think so."

Mrs. Mitchell's smile was wide and rather smug. "Why, the great Coco Chanel has agreed to design Cressida's wedding gown," she said in breathless tones. "And she's coming to

Darrington Manor for the week. It's a great honor—although I'm sure I don't need to tell you that, you living in Paris."

"Coco Chanel is coming here?" Abby asked curiously.

Mildred Mitchell nodded, full of satisfaction. "We expect her for dinner. Cressie was going to have some local seamstress make her gown."

Cressida made as if to speak but Mrs. Mitchell kept going: "And it would have been just darling, I'm certain, but my husband said, 'Millie'—he always calls me Millie—'you get on the telephone to Miss Coco Chanel and tell her who you are and what you want. She's a smart business woman, I wager she'll agree to design Cressida's gown if you tell her...'" Mildred Mitchell petered out. Abby was fairly certain the words she stopped herself from parroting were, "If you tell her who we are." The implication was clear. Coco Chanel might not deign to produce one of her famous gowns for a nearly penniless aristocrat, but for the daughter-in-law of Charles Mitchell the car king, she'd drop everything, not only to design the wedding gown but to be a guest at the wedding.

And so, it seemed, she had.

Abby had met Coco Chanel in Paris and admired her both as a clothing designer and as a woman who'd made a success of herself in business. However, she wasn't certain that spending a week with the diva of Paris fashion was going to be as joyous as Mildred Mitchell seemed to think it would.

FIVE

Tea finished and then the ladies were invited to retire to their rooms to rest before dressing for dinner. Abby wasn't used to being cooped up for as long as she had been between taking the train down from London and then being confined to the library for afternoon tea. She simply had to get out and get some air, and if it meant scrambling into her dinner clothes at the last minute she was certain Viv would forgive her. Besides, dressing was so quick when a woman had her own maid.

She needed to get outside and stretch her legs, breathe in some fresh country air after the stale, smoke-filled atmosphere of the train and the small talk of the library interpolated with loud and embarrassing comments from Lady Constance.

As they left the library she turned to Cressida. "Is there somewhere I could go and have a walk outside? I feel the need to stride out some of my fidgets. I've been sitting still too long."

"I completely understand what you mean," the young woman said. "I'd come with you, but I've promised Mother I'll help with a few wedding-related tasks." Then she said, "It might rain, so make sure you borrow my anorak, which is hanging by the back door, and you'll find some Wellington boots there. I'm sure there will be a pair that will fit."

Abby thanked her and scurried off. Sure enough, when she followed the directions Cressida had given her, down a corridor past the dining room, a ballroom and a small sitting room, she found an entrance at the back of the house that was obviously used by the family much more than the front door. There was an array of rubber boots, most of which showed signs of mud and wear, and several waterproof coats. She happily swapped her designer footwear for a pair of muddy boots, slipped into a raincoat, and stepped outside. She strode out following a path that led toward the pond and woods. It wasn't raining but there was moistness in the fresh air and she breathed in deeply. She thought of Paul Joubert's comment about damp tweed and immediately understood what he meant. If you spent much time in this kind of atmosphere your tweed and pretty much everything else would be damp. Still, she found it pleasant and rather invigorating. She strode out, letting her arms swing by her sides.

The pond was quite large and ringed by bulrushes and wildflowers where butterflies danced. A tangle of budding lily pads floated on the surface along with a family of ducks who appeared inured to the weather. When she turned back to look at the manor house it seemed very foreign suddenly and full of mystery. How much those walls could tell if they spilled the secrets of two hundred years of history. Still, there was a kind of nobility to the building. It wasn't the fanciest castle, it didn't appear in many guidebooks, it was an emblem of a time that was already passing. How long could families like the Wimbornes survive? Between death duties and women demanding more rights and men coming off the farms and going into businesses and factories, she was living in a changing world. Good lord, she was part of it herself. A generation ago she wouldn't have had a hope of moving to

Paris by herself and embarking on a career. Okay, maybe she still had to write for the women's page, but at least she was doing what she loved, writing, and actually earning a living at it.

As Abby walked toward the fields, breathing in the country air, the clouds shifted and the sun emerged. She lifted her face to the bright light. Birds began singing as though equally pleased to see the sun. She felt as though she had the world to herself but for the birds, who seemed as delighted as she was with the good weather, and a field of docile-looking sheep in the distance.

She skirted the pond, followed a path through the trees, glad to have rubber boots as the ground was soggy, and then emerged on the other side of the wood to farmland. She walked beside newly growing crops of wheat and barley and then noticed a tractor by the side of the gravel path. It seemed to be abandoned there, but as she walked past a man ducked out from behind it. She was so startled she gave a tiny squeak of alarm.

The man looked to be some kind of mechanic; he wore dirt-stained woolen trousers, a shirt with the sleeves rolled up and a flat cap on his head. He had curly black hair, his face was swarthy and there was a look of dissatisfaction about him, she couldn't have explained it any better than that. His gray eyes were cold and seemed to gaze at her with contempt. She had to fight the urge to take a step backward and away from him.

He stared at her insolently and she said, "Good afternoon," in a crisp tone. When she would have continued on her way he muttered, "American" as though it was a curse word.

She turned back, puzzled. She didn't even know this man, why would he be so antagonistic? One part of her knew that she should keep her mouth shut and walk on, but that wasn't the part that had made Abigail Dixon an intrepid journalist. She thought of her idol, intrepid reporter Nellie Bly, being here. Would the woman who had gone undercover in a mental hospital slink off because someone was rude to her? Absolutely not.

So, she stood her ground. Perhaps there was a story here. If there was one thing she had learned in life it was that stories were everywhere if you knew how to look. How to dig. So she responded, "That's right. Don't you like Americans?"

The man turned and spat on the ground. She was revolted, but again refused to run away. When she didn't speak he said, "You and your kind are killing any chance men like me have of a future. So yes, I have a problem with Americans." He pronounced kind so it sounded like *koind* and like became *loik*. She imagined this was the local Somerset accent.

Her sensibilities were slightly battered by his pugnacious attitude but she itched to grab her pencil and notepad, two things she always had with her, only she suspected he would clam up if she tried to get him to go on the record. So she said, as neutrally as she could, "I'm sorry, I don't know what I or my people have done to you. Could you be more specific?"

He looked her up and down, not in the way of a man looking at an attractive woman, more like a farmhand checking to see if a heifer is ready for the market. It was an uncomfortable moment. Then he said, "Do you know anything about farming?"

She didn't know a great deal, but she knew a little bit and she said so.

"Well, in your prosperous country you can afford more mechanization and modern farming practices that we don't have access to here in poor, war-battered England. It's hardly worth growing barley or wheat when we can bring it in cheaper from America, Canada and Australia." He shrugged and she got just a glimpse of the genuine pain of the man behind the belligerent mask. "So, no, I don't like your kind. Soon I'll have to leave this village I've lived in my whole life and find work some-where else. While you prance around like you own the place."

She didn't know what to say. She'd heard something of this, but always from the point of view of America. It had been reported in the *Chicago Post* how well the US economy was doing and how robust its agriculture. The fact that they could not only feed their own country but export crops elsewhere had seemed like a positive thing to Abby. She'd never considered that agricultural laborers might end up out of work in the countries that were importing crops and goods from abroad.

She said, "I'm a journalist. I'd be very happy to talk to you and other people who have been affected by the importation of crops and goods from America. I think it would make a really good story."

He gave a harsh laugh, one she was not tempted to join in with. "And lose my job? I wouldn't be such a fool."

She wanted to say more but she didn't know what. Then glanced behind her and became aware that she could hear footsteps.

"I've got work to do," he said. "You'd better run along."

And having so rudely dismissed her, he bent back down to the tractor.

She turned her head and found Ned Corcoran was striding her way. He was walking as quickly as a man can before breaking into a trot. He was slightly out of breath when he reached her. He gave a quick glance at the man who was now studiously examining the tractor and then back to her face. "Everything all right, Miss Dixon?"

"Yes, thank you. Just fine."

"Smith? Has it broken down again?"

"Aye. It's the front wheel. I can't keep patching it. Needs a new one."

Ned Corcoran looked troubled but nodded. "I know. Do the best you can and patch it one more time. I'll see what I can do." Then he held out his arm to Abby. "May I escort you back to the house?" He said it courteously but she felt that she was trespassing. That maybe she wasn't supposed to be out here in the fields where she could run into a random and very disgruntled farmworker.

"Thank you very much," she replied. She was a guest here and had no interest in making trouble. Still, the idea of a story percolated in her mind.

They headed away from the fields and toward the house and, when she felt that Smith, whoever he was, was no longer in earshot, she remarked, "That man does not like Americans."

Ned Corcoran looked at her very seriously. "Was he rude to you?"

Much as she hadn't liked the man named Smith, she certainly didn't want to get him into trouble. "No. But he heard my accent and let's just say he didn't exactly warm to me."

"You mustn't mind him," said Ned. "He's a very bitter man. Went off to fight the war and when he came back his wife had gone off with another man. George Smith is a proud man. It's not something he's ever recovered from."

She had instant sympathy for the man. "What an awful thing to happen. Has he found anyone since?"

Ned's chuckle was swift and low. "He's never remarried. But I believe he finds female company now and then."

She'd been in the world long enough not to be shocked, but still. And then Lady Constance Harroby's words came back to her. The dead girl, Gladys Trotter, had been caught kissing a laborer named Smith. And the man who'd signed the register at the hotel had used the name Smith. Could he have been foolish enough to sign his real name if he was planning to kill his companion? Or perhaps it wasn't a premeditated crime and the man had grown enraged and killed Gladys in a fit of passion.

"George Smith is a fine mechanic," Ned said. "So, even though he can be a difficult man and occasionally a disruptive influence, we'd miss him a great deal if he left."

"Is he the only person named Smith who works at Darrington?" she asked Ned. He turned to her, looking quite puzzled. "He's got a sister who works in the dairy and his mother and father still live in the village."

Then it seemed quite likely that Gladys Trotter had been discovered kissing that very rude man working on the tractor. And since Ned Corcoran was still gazing at her as though wondering why she was asking about people named Smith, she said, "Mr. Smith had quite an accent. Is that the local Somerset accent?"

"Yes. But although his family are local, I wouldn't say Smith was a Somerset name."

"From your recognition of his skills as a mechanic, I get the feeling that you're pretty handy under the hood yourself."

He grinned at her then. "You've a sharp eye. Automobiles are my passion. There's so much potential. If I had money, I'd spend all my time inventing gadgets that would make driving safer and more pleasant." He laughed and shook his head. "But as the estate manager I've very little time to indulge in my passions. I rely on George Smith to keep the equipment going as best he can. However, as you could see back there, he's hampered by a lack of parts and money in general. Anyway, I mustn't be moaning on to you about the estate's problems. Not on such a beautiful day."

"Did you come rushing out there to rescue me?" she asked.

He shook his head. "I didn't. However, I know this land better than you do and if you'd gone on much further you would have found yourself sinking ankle-deep in mud. We've had enough rain in the last week that those dirt paths will be a quagmire until the land dries out. I propose to take you on a much more enticing walk that goes by the stream."

In truth, since she'd really only wanted to stretch her legs and get some fresh air, she was not sorry to have her footsteps turned in a different direction. Besides, Ned Corcoran was very good company. She found herself reflecting aloud on what

George Smith had said: "I know from reading my own newspaper that our economy in the United States is booming and we've become great exporters of farm crops. But I guess I hadn't realized that farms like this are suffering because of it."

He nodded somewhat grimly. "It's true. We can't compete. Darrington isn't big enough to make the investment in machinery cost effective, and we haven't the money to buy new equipment anyway." He shook his head. "I probably shouldn't be telling you all this, but you're a good listener, Miss Dixon."

"Please, call me Abby."

"The truth is, we've recently had to cut wages. It's the only way to keep many of the people here employed. It wasn't a popular decision, but it was the only thing we could do unless we were willing to take away people's livelihoods altogether."

She began to understand why Smith had looked so angry. "But how are people managing? Prices are on the rise."

He nodded. "They are. Already we're losing young men to the cities. The estate struggles every year to support itself. What the place needs is a big infusion of cash."

She nodded. "At least with Miss Wimborne marrying such a wealthy man, there's hope."

His face went dark and he clenched his jaw. "All the marriage between Miss Wimborne and Reginald Mitchell will do is give Miss Wimborne a future of wealth and ease. It's not like he's planning to invest in the estate. No, the best that can be achieved is that Miss Wimborne's brother Peter goes to America and finds himself a nice, rich bride." He turned to her. "Have you met Peter yet?"

"No. Not yet." She made her tone as cold as possible. Ned must have noticed the ice on her words for he said, "I'm not suggesting you for the position."

"Good. I haven't any money and even if I did, I wouldn't be interested in an arranged marriage."

"Peter's not very interested in women. He's mad about

fishing and hunting. I imagine we'll be able to struggle on until such a time as Lord Wimborne inevitably passes away. It's the death duties that will be the end of the Wimbornes of Darrington Manor if we can't come up with much-needed money."

"Golly, I didn't have any idea it was as bad as that." She'd noticed Ned used the pronoun we rather than they. He clearly felt that he was an intrinsic part of Darrington as much as the Wimbornes were.

"I shouldn't be moaning on to you about it all. And please tell me you won't include any of this in your articles for the newspaper."

She shook her head, knowing full well that even if she wanted to write about disgruntled farmworkers and aristocratic families selling off their art collections to survive, Walter Strutt would cross out every line of prose that didn't rave about the Coco Chanel designed gown, the flowers to be showcased at the wedding, how proud all the parents were, and other such predictable puffery. And yet, there was real drama going on here, belied by the stately grandeur of the Georgian manor house and the gently rolling hills, the village and even the local church which seemed as though it had been there forever and would continue on forever more.

She knew well how quickly things changed, but coming here to this idyllic pastoral landscape it was easy to believe that some things were timeless.

She looked at Ned Corcoran. He was young, well-educated, single, and obviously competent. She had to ask: "Are you one of the young men who are likely to be lost to the big cities?"

He turned to her and his eyes narrowed, and then he glanced away, taking in the manor house and the surrounding countryside she'd just been looking at herself. "If I had any sense I would. But I've lived here nearly all my life. Lord Wimborne pays me what he can, and I have a nice little cottage on the property where I live with my mother. I couldn't take her to the city, she'd be lost there. So, for now at least, I'll carry on."

She and Ned passed two farmworkers who touched their caps as they went by and said, in unison, "Afternoon, Mr. Corcoran. Afternoon, miss." Ned Corcoran returned their greeting and they passed on. She couldn't help but notice how much more deferential these two were than George Smith had been. And yet they must have had their wages cut too if everyone had. Yet George Smith seemed angrier about his lot in life than some of the workers, or at least less able to hide his feelings.

Ned said, "My path takes me this way, but the house is straight ahead."

She could see the way back to Darrington Manor and thanked Ned for escorting her. "My pleasure," he said, and then he grinned. He had a most charming grin. "And if you do know any nice American heiresses for Peter, please send them along. Especially if they are addicted to sport."

She recalled the uncomfortably loud comments Lady Constance had made, suggesting Abby might be such a bride and wondered if the week could possibly get more uncomfortable than the first day of this house visit was turning out to be.

SIX

She quickened her pace realizing the time was getting on and Vivian would be expecting to dress her for dinner. Now she knew Coco Chanel was coming, she was anxious to look her best for Paul Joubert's sake. The two designers were great rivals and Miss Chanel had more than once suggested that Abby might like to wear some of her creations along with Monsieur Joubert's, but Abby was fiercely loyal to the man who called her his muse.

She arrived, slightly out of breath, at the door she'd emerged from only to discover it was locked. She knocked but there was no one in hearing range. She'd have to go around the front. She was certain Adams, Lady Wimborne's very proper butler, would strongly disapprove of her showing up at his front door in muddy boots but she had no other choice. She walked around to the front of the house and discovered a sporty-looking Bentley pulling up. At first she thought Coco Chanel was about to discover her looking mud-splattered and disheveled, but no, there was a man behind the wheel and he was alone in the car.

As she got closer and she could see more clearly, she realized he was distinctly familiar.

Her heart thudded uncomfortably against her ribs as she stood on the gravel drive rooted to the spot, unable to believe her eyes. The way the car jerked to a stop she had a feeling the man who'd now caught sight of her had the same experience. Not taking his eyes off her, he opened the door, got out and took a few steps toward her.

"Mademoiselle Dixon, may I say I'm astonished to find you here."

"No more astonished than I am to see you, Inspector Deschamps."

They stared at each other for a stunned moment. Inspector Deschamps was tall, dark and commanding. He was a figure of authority, and she suspected not only because of his job as a police detective in Paris. She'd heard whispers that he had aristocratic roots, and something about the way he could look down his nose at her with amused detachment made her think it was true. He had dark hair brushed fashionably back off his forehead, beginning to show a few threads of gray, a neat mustache and penetrating gray eyes that seemed to draw the truth out of a person. They were qualities that made him an excellent detective and an unpleasant foe, as she had found to her consternation.

"Are you here about the girl who was murdered?" she asked, but a second's reflection was enough to inform her that a Paris detective would not be required to investigate an English murder.

"No. I read about that unfortunate girl, but I am here on much more pleasant business. The wedding of a close friend's daughter."

"You're a friend of Lord and Lady Wimborne?" And she'd thought this assignment was difficult enough.

"Lord Wimborne and I served together in the Great War." He looked down his aristocratic nose at her. "Is it possible that you are connected with the American car manufacturer?"

She noticed he didn't give the man a name. She said, "If you mean Charles A. Mitchell, then no. I'm here on assignment."

She wished she hadn't said anything. The amusement was in his eyes. "You're going to report on a society wedding?"

She felt flustered and irritated. "It wasn't my choice of assignment, believe me. But Charles A. Mitchell wanted me here and I think he's a man who gets what he wants."

"Naturally. Awkward for the family though. I do not think they are the kind of people who court publicity."

If that was a smack at her profession, she could smack right back at him. "Well, at least you'll be on hand should I be falsely accused of another crime." Feeling that was a perfect exit line she said, "No doubt I'll see you at dinner," and turned away before he could answer.

Fortunately, the butler had already opened the door in anticipation of welcoming Henri Deschamps, so he merely stood to one side and said, "Welcome back, miss."

She held her head high and sailed past him as though she were a duchess in her muddy boots and rain-splashed anorak. "Thank you, Adams."

Then she made for the back of the house as quickly as she could, replacing the boots with her former shoes and removing her outerwear. She ran lightly up the stairs to her room where she found Vivian with the curling iron already warming and an irritated look on her face. "Abby, I was in despair. I have my personal reputation to think of you know. Now that I'm a lady's dresser, all eyes will be on you and I will be judged."

Abby hid her smile. Not only did she have Paul Joubert saying essentially the same words, but her supposed roommate and friend now apparently had a vested interest in making sure she looked the part of the elegant Parisienne. However, she held her amusement to herself, knowing how much she needed Vivian and how important it was for Vivian to fit in here. So she said, "I'm awfully sorry. I just needed to get a breath of air."

Quickly she began undressing and Vivian said, "I drew you a bath. If the water's cold I don't want to hear about it."

She was genuinely grateful for the help. "I'll be so quick you won't believe it," and ran into the bathroom which was fragrant with steam and some kind of potion that Vivian had put into the water. It was probably one of the samples she'd been gifted by her employer who made and sold perfume. It seemed that clothing wasn't the only thing Abby would be representing here in England.

When she came out, fragrant and clean, she noticed Vivian had laid out a drop-waist silk dress in a garnet color. The deep red glowed with bugle beads on the bodice and Paul had been particularly effusive when he'd seen the color against her complexion and dark eyes. In fact he'd clapped his hands and jumped up and down. "If only I could be there to see you wearing this. You will be a triumph."

She said to Vivian, "I thought we were saving that dress for something slightly more glamorous?"

Vivian said, "Trust me, this evening is going to be very glamorous. You won't believe who I saw downstairs."

Since she doubted the inspector had been patrolling the lower level of the manor house, she shook her head in bewilderment.

"Nanette."

This still meant nothing to Abby. "Nanette who?"

Vivian made a tsking sound. Vivian couldn't speak French but her tsk could out-tsk most Parisians. She said, "Nanette. It's just Nanette. She's famous. She's Coco Chanel's dresser. Coco never goes anywhere without her."

"Coco Chanel has arrived?" Even though she was expected, Abby had hoped the socialite designer would have discovered she had more important places to be.

"Well, honey, I don't think her dresser would show up without anybody to dress."

"This is turning into one of those nightmares where people from your past keep showing up and scaring you."

"You're not scared of Coco Chanel, are you?"

"No. But she has a way of looking at me that makes me think I've done it all terribly wrong."

Vivian shook her head. "She's just jealous that Paul Joubert got you first."

She sat Abby in front of the dressing table mirror in the cotton dressing gown and said, "Who else have you seen?"

Her eyes widened in the mirror. "Vivian, you won't believe it. Henri Deschamps is here. Inspector Henri Deschamps."

Vivian's eyes reflected her horror. "The man who tried to have you arrested for murder?"

"The very same. Now you can see why this house visit is feeling like a nightmare."

"But what is Inspector Deschamps doing here?"

"He served in the Great War with Lord Wimborne. He's come for the wedding."

"How awful."

"He didn't look any more happy to see me than I was to see him."

"Oh dear. How awkward. If only I'd had time to have a word with Hazel, that's Cressida's maid, and very helpful she is too. Did you know the maids get together and compare what their mistresses are going to wear so they don't clash? Isn't that a simply stupendous idea?"

"I suppose so, but what's that got to do with the inspector?"

"Well, I know that Cressida was helping her mother arrange the seating for dinner. If I told Cressida's dresser that you had good reason not to want to sit near Inspector Deschamps she could slip a word to Cressida and, just like a Houdini magic trick, you'd be nowhere near him." She put her head to one side. "Unless, of course, Cressida Wimborne had it in for you, and then she'd put you right beside him."

"I don't think she has it in for me."

But she wasn't positive.

Vivian said, "Anyway, it's too late now. You'll have to do your best. Make sure you look pretty while you're doing it."

When Vivian had finished styling Abby's hair and supervised her makeup and then slipped her into the dress and fastened the long string of black jet beads that Paul Joubert had loaned her to wear with the outfit, she stepped into the beaded sandals, also on loan.

She said, "I feel like Cinderella. The only things I'm wearing that are mine are the underwear and the silk stockings."

Vivian put her head to one side. "Maybe you'll meet your Prince Charming."

Abby shuddered. "Miss Wimborne's godmother already suggested me as a bride for Peter Wimborne, but it turns out he needs to marry a fortune. And is more interested in sport than women."

"But you like sports too. Perhaps you two will take one look at each other and fall madly in love."

"You're such a romantic." She shook her head. "Hand me my bag."

Viv did and then clasped her hands in front of her. "Oh, Abby, you look beautiful. I wish Paul could see you. He'd be so proud. Now go downstairs and have a marvelous time."

Abby felt as ready as she'd ever be. She took a deep breath. She hadn't been nervous about covering the wedding of an English lady to an American industrialist's son, but she felt distinctly nervous about social time with Inspector Henri Deschamps.

As though reading her thoughts Vivian said, "I'm sure the inspector's perfectly charming socially. Just make sure you don't get implicated in any more murders."

And on that excellent advice, she headed downstairs to the drawing room where drinks were to be served.

. . .

When the footman opened the door to the drawing room Abby beheld a room that was much more formal than those she'd seen so far. All the grandeur of the Wimborne legacy was on display, from gleaming silver to a glistening and very heavy-looking chandelier to Aubusson carpets and furniture that looked as though it had been hand-polished for a couple of centuries at least. She glanced around at the pictures on the walls, wondering if it was a large oil painting depicting village life that was replacing the sadly hocked Van Dyck, or whether the painting of a man in regimental dress who looked very much like he was about to conquer Napoleon single-handed now took the place of the Lely they'd had to sell.

All this perusal took no more than a couple of seconds and then she turned her attention to the people in the room. There was a man in a wheelchair, a very handsome and distinguished-looking man who had an air of authority about him, Lady Wimborne, Cressida, Mrs. Mildred Mitchell, and a large man wearing an air of importance along with his evening dress. She recognized him from his photograph in newspapers. This had to be Charles A. Mitchell. As Lady Wimborne stepped forward to greet Abigail and introduce her to the people she didn't know, she was forestalled by Charles A. Mitchell who strode forward with both arms held out wide as though he were greeting a long-lost niece.

"Abigail Dixon, I can't tell you how honored I am to meet you," he said, and then pulled her into a bearhug that made her squeak faintly, partly because Paul Joubert would have her head if he saw her dress being treated like this, as would Vivian, but also because he squeezed the air out of her lungs. She rallied as best she could and pulled away.

As he beamed down at her, Lady Wimborne finally made it over. "Abigail Dixon, this is Charles A. Mitchell. We're delighted to welcome Mr. Mitchell's son to our family." And then, taking Abby's hand firmly, she led her to the man in the wheelchair. "I'd like you to meet my husband Alistair. My dear, this is Miss Abigail Dixon, the journalist."

Abby might not have been born and bred in England but she knew enough to address him by his proper title. "It's a pleasure to meet you, Lord Wimborne." She shook his hand and endured a rather thorough scrutiny. "Miss Dixon, I've heard a great deal about you," he said politely.

She had no idea whether it was good or bad and didn't like to press in case it was the latter. All she said was, "Thank you for inviting me, Your Lordship."

He chuckled at that with an edge of sarcasm. "You must call me Alistair. It seems like you're one of the family now."

She hoped his slightly acerbic tone wasn't directed at her so much as at Charles A. Mitchell who'd obviously foisted her onto these people. She'd have loved to apologize and explain that she wanted to be here exactly as much as Lord Wimborne wished her to be, but, as Charles A. Mitchell was listening to every word, she went with, "I'll do my best to make my coverage tasteful." What else could she say?

"And may I present you to my son. Abigail Dixon, Peter."

Peter Wimborne was standing beside his sister. They looked very much alike with the same golden coloring, though looked to be a couple of years younger than Abby. She guessed him to be twenty-two or twenty-three. He was very handsome in evening dress. "How do you do?" he asked her very politely and shook her hand. "May I offer you a cocktail?" he offered. "A martini perhaps, or a champagne cocktail?"

"A champagne cocktail would be perfect," she said, and he turned to the drinks trolley.

She greeted Cressida, who looked gorgeous in midnight blue silk, with a beaded headband that sparkled against her blond bob.

While Peter Wimborne was busy preparing her drink, Inspector Deschamps came into the room, looking dapper in formal wear. She'd seen him before socially and it was always a bit of a shock to witness the transformation from the investigating detective to the debonair man about town. She was interested to note that there was a great deal of affection between Lord Wimborne and Inspector Deschamps.

"My dear old fellow," Lord Wimborne said when the inspector walked in. His rather lined face lit up.

"*Mon ami*," Henri Deschamps said, striding over and taking both Lord Wimborne's hands in his. "I find you well? But I can see I do." However, she noticed he gave the man in the wheelchair a searching look. In her eyes, the inspector had never looked so human.

"Can't complain, can't complain." Then to Abby, standing nearest, Lord Wimborne said, "I would not be here with you today if it weren't for this man. I never saw anything like it. He braved enemy gunfire to pull me out of no man's land. Took a bullet himself in the process."

"Bah." The inspector batted the comment away with one hand. "You'd have done it for me, my friend."

"We recovered in the same hospital. Have been the best of friends ever since. He's an unofficial godfather to Cressida."

"And I was delighted to be invited to Cressida's wedding," he said.

Charles A. Mitchell beamed upon them and said, "Ah, the Great War. I was proud to provide motorcars and ambulances."

In a silky voice Lord Wimborne said, "And you were amply paid for those vehicles too, I believe."

Unoffended, the car king chuckled. "Can't blame a fellow for trying to make a buck. I admit I profited handsomely from the war."

There was an awkward silence. And then fortunately two more people came into the room. They were both about her own age, Abby guessed, mid-twenties, both nice-looking, clean-cut young men of similar height and build with brown hair fashionably brushed back and somehow indefinably American.

Charles A. Mitchell said, "You'll allow me to introduce you to my son, my dear Abby. Reggie, come and meet the young gal who made such a sensation in all the papers when she was wrongly accused of murder."

She couldn't help glancing at Henri Deschamps and was absolutely certain she caught him rolling his eyes.

One of the two young men came forward and shook her hand. "Awfully pleased to meet you, Miss Dixon. My father's a great fan of yours." So this was Reginald Mitchell, the bridegroom. He looked rather pleased with himself, as though life had offered him nothing but treats and he'd enjoyed every one. His face was pleasant without being remarkable in any way. Brown eyes, round cheeks and white teeth that gleamed when he smiled.

She wasn't sure if his statement indicated that he wasn't a fan of hers, or it was just something to say. Then Charles Mitchell said, "And I want you to meet Oliver Platt. These two have been boon companions since they were children. Look at them both. Twenty-five years old, with the world in front of them. When I was their age I was working night and day, making my fortune, and these two will benefit. Oliver's the son I never had. It's a pleasure to have them both part of Mitchell Motors. It's good to know that when I pass on the company will be in such good hands." Then he gave his loud, braying laugh and said, "Not that I have any intention of meeting my maker any time soon. But life's uncertain, as we all know."

Abby shook hands with Oliver Platt. His face was more square than round, his jaw more determined and his eyes were green rather than brown. Otherwise, the two men were very alike.

Peter handed Abby her cocktail and then asked Reggie and

Oliver what they'd like to drink. It was clear he already knew both of them. Though similar in age, she didn't get the impression that Peter was particularly friendly with his soon-to-be brother-in-law. They both asked for a dry martini. Then Charles Mitchell sidled up to Abby and said, "One of the best things about coming to England is getting away from Prohibition." He lowered his voice. "My wife frowns. She's all in favor of banning alcohol, but where's the fun in that?" He raised his glass to hers and clinked the rim.

Abby wasn't a bit surprised that the last to arrive was Coco Chanel. Conversation immediately stopped and all eyes turned to the woman posing by the doorway for a moment before striding into the room. Coco wore a stunningly simple black silk gown with a string of fat pearls. She walked in as though she were a famous actress making her entrance onto a stage.

Before Lady Wimborne had a hope of welcoming her guest, Charles Mitchell had left Abby's side, almost jogging forward to reach the famous designer. "Miss Chanel," he said in reverential tones, "it is an honor to meet you. I so admire your work. I'm Charles Mitchell."

Coco languidly offered him her hand and said, "Monsieur Mitchell. I make my little dresses and you make your little cars, but we do all right, heh?"

He threw his head back and laughed. "We do indeed, Miss Chanel. I look forward to speaking with you often."

Lady Wimborne then took her guest in hand and introduced her to those she didn't know. When she reached Abby, Coco said, "But I know Abigail, of course. We are often seen together in Paris." She spoke pleasantly enough but her eyes were taking in every detail of Abby's outfit. She felt Paul Joubert like an invisible presence reminding her to stand up straight and hold her arms so that the gown would drape to its best advantage. After a long moment when she was afraid to breathe in case she ruined the line of her dress, Abby was relieved to see Coco give a tiny nod. "You look well, Abby."

Peter asked Coco Chanel what she'd like to drink.

"Champagne." She smiled at Charles Mitchell, who was staring at her the way a dog might stare at a juicy steak just out of reach. She said, "I only drink champagne on two occasions. When I am in love. And when I am not in love."

She sipped her sparkling wine and regarded him over the rim of her glass while he laughed heartily.

Then the designer moved to kiss Henri on both cheeks. "But I did not think to find you here, *mon amour*. I suppose you drove down from your so charming house in London."

"I did."

She tsked at him. "You should let me redecorate it for you. Bendor has given me complete *carte blanche* to redecorate his hunting lodge in Scotland and it is *magnifique*."

"Lord Westminster is a lucky man," he said to the designer. Abby knew that the Duke of Westminster, nicknamed Bendor, was also a married man and his association with Coco Chanel was somewhat scandalous. No doubt there had been some awkward moments for Lady Wimborne when she wondered whether Coco might bring her lover along with her, but it seemed good manners had prevailed and she'd arrived alone.

She chuckled deep in her throat. "He is, indeed, and clever enough to know it."

So the inspector had a house in London where he parked his Bentley. She'd known he was from a wealthy family, but not that he was wealthy enough to have a home in London. She suspected he caught criminals for a hobby as he clearly didn't live on his police detective salary.

Reginald Mitchell stood with Cressida, speaking softly, and Abby had a chance to regard the couple together for the first time. They chatted together like old friends.

Oliver Platt moved beside her and followed her gaze. "They make a handsome pair, don't they?"

"Indeed, they do," she replied, watching Cressida's fair head bend to hear something her fiancé whispered in her ear.

"She's a terrific girl. I'm delighted to see my best friend happy," Oliver said. Once more she had the sense that a member of the Mitchell retinue was feeding her copy for her article. The sentiment was nicely expressed and not too long. She could see it in print.

"She's a terrific girl. I'm delighted to see my best friend happy," said Oliver Platt, the groom's oldest friend, as the bridal pair chatted before dinner.

Abby wondered whether Charles A. Mitchell had hired a publicity man to craft these short speeches that were being so obligingly dropped into her ear by Reginald's friends and family. She turned to Oliver Platt and found him blandly smiling at her. She said, "How about you, Mr. Platt? Is there a special woman in your life?" She was certain Mitchell Motors' publicity department wouldn't have prepared Reginald Mitchell's friend with an answer to that. And she felt she received a sincere answer. "I'm afraid I'm married to my work. I dare say I'll end up a crusty old bachelor."

She doubted that would happen but was interested in his answer. "You must be very devoted to Mitchell Motors."

He nodded. "I owe everything to Charles Mitchell. He's the father I never had."

As though those words had summoned him, Charles Mitchell came over and said to Oliver, "Is everything ready?"

Oliver nodded. Then Charles Mitchell walked over and spoke a few quiet words to his son before taking up a position in the middle of the room and booming out, "We've a surprise for you, which is why the two boys were a little late. Lord and Lady

Wimborne, in fact everybody, please come outside. We've got something to show you."

Naturally, all conversation stopped. Abby glanced instinctively at Lady Wimborne, who looked nonplussed. She glanced at her husband who shrugged, and then she said, "Of course. I'll ask cook to put dinner back half an hour."

"Come on outside and see my surprise," Charles Mitchell said.

Lady Wimborne gave a small squeak. "Oh, outside. My goodness." She glanced about her. "We'll need to do something about coats for the ladies."

He shook a meaty hand at her. "No need for all that. It's a fine evening." He was so full of suppressed excitement that Abby couldn't imagine what was waiting for them outside. She had visions of an elephant or a camel or some exotic animal that he'd planned to give these poor people. Her curiosity was definitely piqued.

As they headed out of the drawing room the inspector pushed Lord Wimborne's wheelchair, and as they came abreast of Abigail he said softly, "Do you think it's a giraffe?"

She had to bite down on a burble of laughter. In an equally low voice she replied, "My money's on an elephant."

But when the butler threw open the front doors and they headed outside in procession, the surprise waiting for them on the gravel drive was not a wild animal but somehow equally exotic. Lady Wimborne was the first one to get her voice. "Why, it's an automobile," she gasped.

Charles Mitchell clapped his hands. "I knew you'd be surprised. Not just any automobile, my lady. It's entirely unique. Yes, the only one of its kind in the world. I had it shipped over from America specially for the wedding. I oversaw the production of this baby myself. That color is royal blue. I specifically got them to make it to my specification. I said to the boys on the floor, 'This beaut's going to a genuine Lord and

Lady. I want the color to be as royal as my grandchildren will be.'"

"My goodness," Lady Wimborne said faintly.

It was probably the most enormous vehicle Abby had ever seen outside of a farm. Long and sleek, the vehicle gleamed. And then a figure stepped forward from the shadows. It was Ned Corcoran.

He opened the doors of the vehicle, which immediately lit up inside.

Charles Mitchell said, "It's my gift to the whole family. But, Cressida, you come and sit in it first."

She stepped across the gravel in her pretty shoes and sank into the leather upholstery of the front seat. "Oh my," she said stroking the soft leather. "It's so luxurious."

"Nothing but the best for my new daughter-in-law and her family." Then he chuckled. "I can see Her Ladyship and the butler exchanging glances. Mustn't keep dinner waiting. But tomorrow I'll take you all for a ride." And he said again, "Ain't she a beauty?"

Obviously feeling some thanks was due, a somewhat stunned Lord Wimborne said, "You overwhelm us with your generosity. That is indeed a fine automobile."

He definitely sounded more overwhelmed than grateful.

SEVEN

At dinner, Abby found herself placed next to Oliver Platt on one side and Reginald Mitchell on the other. Inspector Deschamps was seated on the other side of the table between Mrs. Mitchell and Coco Chanel. Coco Chanel seemed to keep him amused while Mrs. Mitchell chatted to Lord Wimborne at the head of the table.

Conversation was mainly about the new car and the upcoming wedding. Abby felt that all of them were on their best behavior. If Charles Mitchell tended to dominate, he was so genuinely pleased with his surprise gift that it was difficult to fault him, though she suspected that a week in his company would be more than enough.

In candlelight and with the family's best china in use, and liveried footmen waiting on them, Darrington Manor and the Wimbornes seemed to be at their best. The soft light disguised any shabbiness in the stately home, while the Wimbornes entertained with an effortless courtesy that must have been bred into them.

After dinner, Lady Wimborne declared, "If the ladies will join me, we'll leave the gentlemen to their port and politics."

Abby was surprised that this ritual still existed, but obediently rose with the other ladies while the gentlemen politely
stood. She followed Lady Wimborne out of the room and back
to the drawing room, where all evidence of their earlier cocktails
had been tidied away. The fire was blazing merrily and with no
formal seating arrangement, the women sat where they pleased.

Cressida settled herself beside Abby on a settee near a
window. "I've been longing to ask you who designed that stunning gown."

Abby sent silent gratitude to Paul Joubert once more and
happily told the woman who would soon be one of the social
leaders in New York that the inimitable Monsieur Joubert
was the only designer for her. She kept her voice low while
she did so as Coco Chanel was not far away and known to
have sharp ears. Cressida, also speaking softly, said, "Reggie
wants to take me to Paris before we sail for New York, so
perhaps I'll pay a visit to Monsieur Joubert." She sighed and
said, "It will be lovely to buy clothes in Paris. I'm devoted to
Miss Chanel, of course, and very grateful that she's designing
my wedding gown, but I shall patronize more than one
couture house."

In the pause that ensued, they could hear Coco Chanel,
who sat beside Lady Wimborne, chatting happily about the
house she was decorating in Scotland. "It is such a pleasure to
me to be able to use my artistic flair for more than simply fashion. This hunting lodge is like a fine woman who deserves to be
gowned properly."

Lady Wimborne made noncommittal noises but looked
rather shocked, and then Cressida leaned closer and said to
Abby, "The house she's talking about belongs to the Duke of
Westminster, her latest lover. Mummy knows his wife. It's very
awkward for her. Fortunately, Bendor didn't even attempt to
spend the week here with Coco. I wonder if she's annoyed that
he wasn't invited? Perhaps that's why she's so eager to tell

Mummy about Bendor's hunting lodge which he's allowed her to redecorate."

Abby knew this but, insatiably curious, which she liked to think was her journalistic nose quivering for a story, replied in an equally low tone, "Her designing your gown puts your mother in an awkward position."

A low laugh greeted her question. "My dear, it's all Charles Mitchell's doing. If that man ever gives up the automobile trade, he'd make an excellent wedding planner. He not only convinced Miss Chanel to design my gown but he'd have paid for it too if Papa had let him."

Abby felt all the difficulties of the impoverished aristocrats coping with the very managing Charles A. Mitchell who was determined that his son's wedding should be as lavish as his own tastes and budget dictated.

When the men had returned from smoking their cigars and drinking their port, the tea tray was brought in and Cressida rose to pour tea.

Charles Mitchell took the now-vacant seat beside Abby and settled in, sitting back and crossing his hands over his ample belly. He smelled of cigar and cologne.

"I can't tell you how pleased I am, Miss Dixon, that you were able to come and be part of this wedding week. When I read your harrowing articles about your ordeal as a friendless young woman unfairly accused of murder, I knew you were exactly the kind of plucky young woman I wanted as a journalist at my son's wedding."

As always, she cringed inwardly at the "plucky" reference. She wasn't entirely sure that he was as keen on her harrowing journalism as he was on the fact that she'd become quite a celebrity in her own right, but she merely smiled and nodded.

"I'm a man who gets what he wants," he went on. "It wasn't always that way. I've come from nothing. When I was a boy, there was more than one night that I went to bed feeling the gnaw of hunger in my belly." He chuckled and patted his expansive midriff. "Of course, I have the opposite problem now. My wife tells me I should be more abstemious at mealtimes, but I enjoy my food. I love the finer things in life and I'm willing to pay for them. However, I expect value for my dollar." He gestured to the suit he was wearing. "For instance, all my suits are handmade on Savile Row. British tailoring is the best in the world. And I get my boots handmade in Milan."

She wondered if he was expecting her to do a profile on him as well as the wedding. He was giving her an awful lot of extraneous information about his likes and dislikes and where his clothes came from. She'd have to ask Walter Strutt if this was part of her mandate for the week. She was fully prepared to gush about the bride and the bridegroom and the dress and the flowers and so on, but was she expected to do a personality profile on Charles A. Mitchell? Although she found him a fascinating character, she rather hoped not.

Still, if only for politeness's sake, she asked, "How do you feel about your son choosing a British bride?"

He chuckled at that. "You won't find a titled young lady in New York, now will you, Miss Dixon?" His eyes twinkled at her. "I've told you I want the best and I'll pay for it. And you can't tell me Miss Wimborne isn't a more fitting bride on the arm of one of the wealthiest young men in America than a mere miss, be she ever so beautiful and well-mannered and charming. No, my son takes after me there. He likes the aristocratic English girls." He glanced over at his wife, who was sitting between Oliver Platt and her son, and added hurriedly, "Millie's a wonderful wife, don't get me wrong, and a fine mother. But when I married her I wasn't the man I am now. My son's in a position to look as high as he likes for a bride."

She felt somewhat embarrassed that he was discussing Cressida Wimborne as though she were an acquisition rather than a person. She said, "Cressida seems like a lovely young woman."

"She's definitely that." He shook his head. "Poor as a church mouse though. It's a good thing we've got plenty of cash, because all that young lady brings to the marriage is her title and her breeding. And she hobnobs with all those other titled young people, so I expect my son will be regularly invited to Buckingham Palace."

"Yes, I'm sure he will."

"I'll be as proud as punch. Why, who's to say I won't get an invitation myself! When Edward's crowned king, you mark my words, young lady, it will be a whole new era. He's young and vibrant and forward thinking. I imagine King Edward VIII and I will do great things together. And it's my son and my daughter-in-law who will introduce us."

"I can see you've thought this through." This man was plotting ahead, and the Honorable Cressida Wimborne, daughter of a Viscount, was a chess piece that would help him win this game of life.

Charles Mitchell heaved himself out of his seat with a groan and barked, "Reggie, Ollie, come on over here." The two young men obligingly came over. "I've just been giving Miss Dixon some background on me and our family. What they call color in the newspapers. The facts that she might not need to use but will help give her an idea of who we really are. Why don't you sit down beside her and tell her a little bit about yourself?"

There was only one seat beside Abby and, with a quick glance at Oliver, Reginald took the place his father had just vacated. Charles clapped Oliver on the back and said, "Come on over here, Ollie. We'll leave these two to talk weddings and you and I will talk business." And the two men retreated into a far corner of the room.

Reginald watched them go and then said, "I don't know what kind of background you could possibly want on me."

Abby didn't know either. But Charles had arranged for her to be here and her editor had made it very clear that she'd better keep the automobile tycoon and advertiser in their newspapers happy, so she said, "I'd like to interview you and Cressida together so I can ask things like how you met and how your courtship has gone, but for now maybe you could tell me a little about your background."

He settled back and she wondered if he even knew how he unconsciously sat exactly like his father. He was a slim, handsome man, but she could imagine in thirty years or so he might look very much like his father did at this moment.

He paused and then began to speak: "Father loves to tell the story of growing up poor. But my life was very different from his. He never wanted me to be short of anything. I've been to the best schools, learned horse riding, fencing, polo and so on from the top instructors. Father made sure I was well-traveled and now I'm ready to settle down. I'm a lucky man, Miss Dixon, and well aware of it."

She smiled at him, admiring his open honesty about his circumstances. "And I understand that Mr. Oliver Platt will be your best man at the wedding."

He nodded. "That's right. Ollie and I go way back. My father's been very good to him. He obviously liked him as my friend, and when Ollie's father died mine stepped in. Over the years he's done everything he could to give him opportunities. Paid for his schooling, paid for him to accompany me on my European travels. He always says Oliver's like a son to him." He stared across the room at the two men who were deep in conversation. Reggie said, "But like a son isn't the same as being a son. Ollie's got no money other than what he earns. Father pays him a pretty good salary, but he can never hope to attain the level of wealth that I've grown up with."

There was a slight undertone and she glanced over at him. "That must be hard for him. Is he ever jealous of you?"

He didn't answer her but his brown eyes stayed steady on hers for a moment. "Oliver is my best friend. And we work together. But it can't be easy for him."

She appreciated that he hadn't said, "Yes, my best friend is jealous of me," but she was left with a strong impression that Oliver would very much like to have the wealth that his best friend's family enjoyed so opulently.

EIGHT

The next morning Abby discovered how much easier it was when a person had a lady's maid and a schedule of events with outfits already prepared for each one. There was no standing there in front of her open wardrobe doors asking aloud, "What shall I wear?"

Vivian had a complete itinerary of what outfit went with what activity, which accessories, which hat, which shoes, which coat. It was absolutely remarkable. Abby would have felt like royalty if it wasn't Vivian helping her to dress while cracking jokes and feeding her the gossip from downstairs. And there was plenty of it.

"The cook threw an absolute fit last night when you were late for dinner. Do you have any idea how precisely they had timed the cream soup? And then she was worried about burning the vol-au-vents." Vivian laughed mischievously.

"I can only imagine." Abby smiled. "You should have seen poor Lady Wimborne's face when Charles Mitchell decided we should all go outside. He wouldn't even let us get coats. Not that it was a cold night, but I could see Lady Constance shivering in her silks."

"That automobile is the talk of the house. I took a peek and I think it's splendid, but downstairs they're calling it vulgar. And you know that can only have come from upstairs. That's an upstairs opinion."

"I'm inclined to agree that it is a little vulgar. And, worse, Charles Mitchell's put the Wimbornes in a terrible position. After dinner last night, as I was going to bed, I overheard Lady Wimborne saying to her husband that they would now have to reciprocate with an expensive gift of their own."

As she summarized the scene for Viv, Abby could hear the exchange she'd overheard last night.

Lady Wimborne had sounded truly distressed. "And there's so little left of value. Must it be the Turner?"

"Absolutely not, my dear," came the tones of Lord Wimborne, sounding tired. "That was my wedding gift to you. No matter what happens, we'll never sell it. I'll have to think of something else."

"That wretched man. I know he meant well, but it's so very awkward."

"I couldn't agree more."

Then Lady Wimborne chuckled. "And can you imagine us motoring through the country lanes in a royal blue car as though we were Prince Edward himself?"

When she'd repeated the gist of the conversation to Vivian, her friend nodded. "It's true, they really are quite poor. The servants haven't had a pay raise in two years and meanwhile everything gets more expensive. Jerry says he's going to London as soon as he can get the money together." She sent Abby a coquettish glance in the mirror. "Or Paris."

"Oh, Viv. You'd better make sure he's the real thing before he follows you to Paris."

"Oh, Abby, he's dreamy. So different from American and French men. I can tell he really likes me. We went to the pub last night. You mustn't tell anyone because it wasn't his evening off, but he told Adams that you'd specially asked him to show me the local sights and what could Adams do but let him go?"

Abby was a little shocked. "I only hope Adams doesn't have it in for me now," she said, thinking the butler was not a man she wanted for an enemy.

"Of course not. They all think you're perfectly wonderful. I think they treat me extra nicely because I'm your maid. They sit me beside Nanette, Coco Chanel's dresser, at meals—and because she despises the English servants so dreadfully, she talks to me. She's rude about everyone except her mistress, but she does have good gossip. She despises the Mitchells. Apparently, Reggie got hold of Miss Chanel as he wanted her to make a coat for Cressie as a present. He gave her the measurements and she created an exquisite thing of great beauty, only when she got here, she could see he'd got the measurements all wrong and the coat is too big. Coco's being very sweet to Reggie about it, but apparently she's furious as it will have to be remade. It seems he didn't mention it was for his bride whose measurements Coco has, so she assumed she was making a coat for his mother."

"But it's a coat. Can't she just wear a sweater under it if it's too big?"

Vivian's shudder was as dramatic as Coco Chanel or Paul Joubert could have wished. "Abigail, this isn't a winter coat you get at the five and dime. It's a couture creation meant to fit like a second skin."

Then she saw Abby's grin and laughed. "Oh, you're teasing. Of course you understand."

Abby was pleased that Vivian was getting on so well, and slightly curious. "What's the local pub like?"

"It was very picturesque, with a big fire burning and a long bar where the men stood talking to each other and drinking beer. There's a separate room where gentlemen can sit with ladies. That's where Jerry and I sat. I drank a local ale, which wasn't very nice, if I'm honest. But Jerry is such good fun I didn't mind."

"Were people gossiping about the girl who was strangled?"

"Probably, but I didn't really pay attention." Of course not; she'd been too busy flirting with Jerry. Viv's eyes widened as she recalled something: "You'll never guess who walked in."

Abby was tempted to say, "Jerry's wife?" but as Viv wasn't looking distraught, she suspected something else had occurred so she just said, "Do tell."

"Reginald Mitchell came in with his friend. I knew who it was immediately, of course, because he was pointed out to me, but he didn't know me. Well, they had a beer and seemed to be enjoying themselves when this horrible man came up and bumped into the pair of them so their drinks spilled. He was quite fierce. There was a frightful row. Jerry said we'd better beat it before the local police were called."

"Oh, Viv. How awful."

"It turned out fine. Mr. Reginald's friend smoothed things over, but I said to Jerry that I wanted to get back anyway and so we left." She shook her head. "Jerry said it's not usually so exciting at the Darrington Arms but George Smith has a chip on his shoulder. He hates Americans."

On hearing that name, Abby felt her eyes widen. "George Smith? Is he a thickset fellow with curly black hair and gray eyes?"

Vivian nodded, looking astonished. "You know this man?"

"I've met him." Briefly she told Viv about their conversation over the broken-down tractor and how scathing he'd been about Americans.

"I hope you don't run into him again," Vivian said. "In fact, I hope neither of us do."

Abby then went down for breakfast to find she was among the earlier risers. Henri was there enjoying coffee and so was Lord Wimborne. They were obviously talking over old times and she felt as though she'd intruded. In fact, she was hovering on the threshold wondering whether to beat a hasty retreat when His Lordship glanced up and said, "Ah, good morning, my dear. I trust you slept well."

"Perfectly, thank you. It's so quiet here after Paris."

"Come and sit beside me," he said, waving her to the chair next to him. "We're not formal at breakfast."

The butler came forward and asked, "Tea, miss, or would you prefer coffee?"

Even though she knew the British loved their tea, since Henri had already opted for coffee she felt better about asking for some herself. If she had to get through another day at the house party of the landed gentry, at least she ought to be fueled by coffee.

Coco Chanel came in next. "*Ma mignonne*," she said. "You look delightful this morning. I see my friend Paul Joubert has attempted a British tweed, but you should really let me have the dressing of you in England. It is I who spends so much time here and understand the climate."

Since she was under absolutely the strictest orders never to let Coco design so much as a hair tie for her, she merely smiled and said thank you. Coco herself was arrayed in a masculine style jacket and skirt in checked tweed, but in Abby's opinion her own outfit was every bit as stylish.

Coco said, "I understand there's to be fishing one day this week. I am a keen fisherwoman."

Lord Wimborne smiled at her. "So I've heard. My friend Winston Churchill speaks most admiringly of your skill with a rod."

She laughed in delight. "Dear Winston. He was quite chagrined when I caught a twenty-pound salmon in Scotland. And all he could manage was a seven pounder."

Everyone laughed at this anecdote.

Abby walked over to the breakfast, which was laid out

buffet style, and admired the presentation. Everything from bacon, eggs and sausages to kippers and smoked salmon graced the spread. She happily helped herself to eggs and bacon, some fried mushrooms and toast and butter. She gazed at the black pudding but decided to pass on that.

Over the next half hour the rest of the party wandered in for breakfast.

Reggie and Cressida came in together chatting away and looking as much like lovebirds as Abby had seen them so far. He had obviously said something that had made her laugh and she looked relaxed and very pretty that morning wearing a soft pink dress that really complimented her coloring. Abby saw both the mothers look on approvingly as their children made such a joyful entrance into the breakfast room.

While Cressida settled between her mother and Coco Chanel to enjoy a cup of tea, Reggie said, "I'm starving," and went straight for the buffet of breakfast foods. Oliver came in then and joined his friend at the buffet.

"And are you excited, my little one?" Coco Chanel turned to Cressida. "Your final fitting this morning. Your wedding dress will be talked of for months, copied, *bien sûr*, and how many young women will dream of being you? Walking down the aisle with the most eligible man on your arm, an acknowledged future as a chatelaine of fashion and a leader of society."

Cressida giggled nervously. "My goodness, you make it sound like I'll be an ambassador or something."

Very seriously the French designer replied, "My dear, that's exactly what you will be. You will be an ambassador for your country, for my designs, for young women beginning married life." Then her seriousness dissolved into her most charming smile. "But, of course, it begins with the dress."

She didn't have to say what Abby imagined they were all thinking, which was that when you began your married life in a gown designed and fitted by the most famous of dress designers, it was a pretty good start.

While Oliver and Reggie brought their heaping plates of breakfast food to the table, Cressida went to get hers. She helped herself sparingly to scrambled eggs with a slice of toast. Abby recalled her own experiences with Paul Joubert and the measuring tape and could only imagine that Coco Chanel would be most exacting with her measurements. And woe betide the bride who had gained an extra pound or two between the first fitting and the last.

Breakfast was a much more casual affair than dinner and conversation was general and good-humored. Everyone seemed to be in a good mood, which was nice after the slight strains Abby had noticed the night before.

Reggie suddenly said, "That fellow Ned Corcoran's very good, isn't he? Quite a dab hand with the automobile. He spent ages last night with the hood up, poking around at the engine and seeing how it all works."

Charles Mitchell clapped his hands. "I'm glad you mentioned the automobile, son. After breakfast, she'll have her maiden voyage. Everyone must take a ride." Abby looked at him, glowing with pride. It occurred to her now that he had dressed to match the car in a deep blue suit and cravat.

He said to the assembled company, "I call her the Mitchell 925. And that model number is no coincidence. I see the twinkle in your eye, Lord Wimborne. You know as well as I do that that is the number that signifies sterling silver. Nothing but the best for my son and my new daughter. I don't mean to boast, but the Mitchell 925 is one of the finest vehicles available. It was crafted to my own specifications by expert coachbuilders. It's got an elongated hood and a spacious passenger compartment, as you'll soon find out when you go for a ride on wire-spoke wheels with whitewall tires."

Cressida's brother Peter seemed to be the only one who

could find something to say in response other than offering vacuous compliments. He stepped forward and said, "What's her horsepower?"

Charles Mitchell beamed at him. "Excellent question, young man. The Mitchell 925 is powered by a 357.8 cubic inch straight-eight engine. Now in horsepower she'll give you eighty-five to ninety."

Peter gave a low whistle. "That's a lot of power."

"You wait till you get her on the road. You'll never find a smoother ride." Then he stood up and looked at them all. "I offer myself as today's chauffeur. May I suggest that the soon-to-be-newlyweds and Lord and Lady Wimborne take the first ride?"

Lord and Lady Wimborne exchanged a glance that Abby couldn't read but suspected contained a wealth of meaning between the long-married couple. "I'm looking forward to it. My goodness, this will make the old Rolls feel like a farm cart," Lord Wimborne commented drily.

After the wave of polite laughter had subsided, Charles Mitchell said, "That Rolls-Royce is a fine vehicle. You British make some excellent automobiles. But I'm curious to see what you think of this one. I'm very proud of her."

It was clear to everybody that this vehicle he'd designed and had made specially for his son on his wedding and had shipped all the way from America was his pride and joy.

Cressie said, "I'll go and get my coat." And that seemed the signal for everyone to get up from the breakfast table. "Are you certain, Alistair, that you're well enough for a ride?" Lady Wimborne asked her husband gently.

"Yes, yes," he said, sounding impatient. "My man can pop me in and out of the vehicle. He's accustomed to moving me about." Abby felt that Lord Wimborne was drawing attention to his inability to get in and out of the Mitchell 925 on his own so as to forestall anyone else commenting on it.

Abby wished the photographer was present, but she felt she could begin her coverage of the wedding festivities with an article about the car. No doubt Charles Mitchell could provide the newspaper with a sketch if not an actual photograph of the automobile.

She had her notebook open and pen in hand when Charles Mitchell came out with his son and Cressie. Lord and Lady Wimborne followed behind, Lord Wimborne's valet, whom he called Winslow, pushing the wheelchair.

Coco Chanel and Henri came out of the front door together, then Mildred Mitchell wearing a mink coat, and Peter and Oliver bringing up the rear.

Ned Corcoran was once more standing beside the vehicle, which glowed deep blue in the morning sunshine.

Then Charles Mitchell opened the front car door and invited everyone to peer inside. "That's the finest leather you can buy on the upholstery, the wood trim is mahogany with some beautiful inlays. Do you notice the initials? M. and W. Mitchell and Wimborne, together forever."

Reginald and Cressida sat in the front seat, Cressie between the two Mitchell men, and Mrs. Mitchell joined Lord and Lady Wimborne in the back seat.

Before he left, Charles Mitchell turned to Abby and said, "Don't you go anywhere, young lady. You'll be the next person I chauffeur. You have to experience the smoothness of the ride to be able to report it correctly."

The ride took about half an hour and when everyone got out of the car they commented on how comfortable the ride had been.

"Come along then, Miss Dixon," Charles Mitchell called to her. Abby was invited to go out along with Peter. Henri Deschamps was invited but he declined the treat and Oliver said he had work to do. Charles Mitchell then invited Ned to join them. She was quite surprised as Ned seemed more employee than guest, but as Charles Mitchell explained, the young man had been kind enough to polish up the vehicle and had shown an enormous amount of interest in her.

As they got in and the car pulled away, she couldn't help but admire the low purr of the engine and the smooth ride as they cruised down the drive toward the road which led to the village.

"What do you think of her so far?" Charles Mitchell asked, barely waiting for them to settle into the admittedly luxurious seats.

"I've never sat in a more comfortable automobile in my life," Abby said truthfully.

"I'll bet you can get some speed out of her, with all those horses under the hood," said Peter.

Charles A. Mitchell chuckled. "Couldn't I just. But best not horrify the locals. Plenty of interest we gathered driving around the village earlier. You'll see." He invited them to make themselves comfortable. "Unroll the windows and let a little of the spring sunshine in. Or perhaps you'd like to put down the footrests."

Yes, there were footrests. To Abby's amusement, there was even a vase with fresh flowers. It was indeed a beautiful vehicle.

Charles motioned to Ned in the back. "I thought we'd never be ready in time. Not content with polishing her up after the journey, Ned had his head in the engine all morning."

Ned chuckled. "I'm interested in engines. As the person who needs to keep the old Rolls-Royce going, it's a pleasure to see the newest innovations in technology."

They drove to the end of the private drive and then turned left onto the main road. Farms and fields gave way to the small village of Darrington, and with practiced familiarity Charles Mitchell drove in a stately manner down the main thorough-fare. Abby was fairly certain this was the same route he'd taken earlier. He could just as easily have driven them farther out on the country roads, but she got the impression that he quite liked the stir he was causing in the village. Boys ran from all corners as though inaudibly summoned to hang over garden gates and stare. Women pegging their washing out stopped to gaze as the fine automobile cruised past like a luxury liner. It was that unexpected. One man pulled off his cap and stood to attention as though he thought perhaps royalty was passing through the village.

Then she spotted two men, one of whom had a notebook out. At first she thought he was a fellow reporter. But then she looked more carefully. The pair were walking up the path of a small cottage that appeared completely shut up and devoid of life. Not reporters, she realized, but police. Ned, obviously seeing the same sight, commented, "That's the Trotter home. Where poor Gladys lived."

The police officers knocked on the door and it opened to reveal a woman wearing all black. Even if Ned hadn't informed them that this was Gladys's mother, she'd have known it. Tragedy enveloped the woman along with her black dress.

"Sad business," Charles Mitchell said, as they drove by.

Abby turned to watch as the two policemen entered the house and then the door shut behind them. She wondered why they were there and what questions they were asking Gladys Trotter's mother.

And could she somehow find a way to convince Walter Strutt to let her report on this?

Two boys whooped as the vehicle drove by and a dog barked and wagged its tail. Charles Mitchell seemed to lap it all up. She recalled him telling her proudly that he had come from nothing. He was enjoying his status as a millionaire automobile magnate. There was a kind of childlike enthusiasm to the way he showed off his latest toy.

As they cruised past the local pub, the Darrington Arms, she caught sight of George Smith and another farmworker.

They both stared at the Mitchell 925 and the look in George Smith's eyes wasn't one of admiration. After the car had passed, he spat on the road.

When the royal blue automobile pulled up in front of Darrington Manor, Abby thanked Charles Mitchell very much for the treat. It was Peter who opened her door for her and helped her out, while Ned continued on with Charles Mitchell to put the vehicle away and perhaps discuss the finer points of its transmission at greater length than they already had.

Peter stared after them and said, "I wish Charles A. Mitchell had a marriageable daughter as well as a son. I wouldn't mind a high-powered sedan as a wedding present."

She chuckled. "And Charles A. Mitchell as a father-in-law?"

He let out a low whistle. "Well, he's got heaps of American dollars, and those wouldn't go amiss. It's really me who must marry the money, you know, not Cressie."

She felt slightly embarrassed that he should be telling her this, even though she already knew it.

He said, "The trouble is, I'm not interested in dancing and parties and making up to rich girls. I just want to stay at home and fish and enjoy my home as all my ancestors have been able to do before me. Seems terribly unfair that this government should have introduced death duties. It's like they're trying to destroy this country, and certainly pull apart the ruling class."

As an American, she didn't entirely favor the idea of birth equaling destiny, that simply because his father was rich and titled and his father before him was rich and titled, Peter too should be rich and titled. She was from a country that valued hard work, where a man like Charles A. Mitchell, who'd come from nothing, could build himself a fortune and the fanciest house in town if he so chose. However, she kept that opinion to herself and nodded sympathetically.

Then Peter looked at her and grinned. "I don't suppose you're rich, are you?"

She burst out laughing. "Lady Constance already asked about that—and at great length. I'm sorry to tell you that no, I'm as poor as a church mouse. I have to earn my living."

"Good for you. I like you modern young women with your typewriters and tape measures and your shops. The world's changing." He stopped to gaze at the manor house and the land around it. "The trouble is, I don't wish to change with it."

NINE

Abby retired to her room and her portable Underwood typewriter in order to write up the first of her articles about the upcoming wedding. She'd feature the Mitchell 925, of course, as well as describe Darrington Manor and all the excitement felt by everyone at the house party.

She clacked away on her typewriter keys, adding a few quotes from the principal players in the wedding. She had 800 words, which was a respectable number for the first article. She teased the piece she'd write tomorrow, her interview with the bride and groom and a sidebar piece featuring Coco Chanel.

She could telephone in her article or send it as a wire. Either would be expensive, but if she used the telegraph office no one could overhear her words and rewrite her piece, which she suspected Charles Mitchell might attempt to do. Besides, a walk to the village would stretch her legs and perhaps she could interview a few locals about their feelings on the upcoming wedding. Though she'd make sure to steer clear of George Smith.

When she got downstairs, Lady Wimborne invited her for a

light luncheon. Abby put off walking to the village until after lunch.

Lunch wasn't a formal affair. The same group who'd been present at breakfast helped themselves to breads and cold meat and cheese. They were able to discuss again the various merits of the car that Charles A. Mitchell had gifted the family.

"My wedding suit is arriving today by train," Reggie said. "I thought I'd take the new car out for a spin down to the station. Cressie? Why don't you join me? Then we'll take a drive around the countryside. Just the two of us. What do you say?"

Cressida glanced up and said, "Oh. When were you thinking of going?"

"As soon as we finish lunch."

She glanced slightly nervously at Coco Chanel, who answered for her. "*Mais absolument pas*, I'm doing your final fitting this afternoon. There is no possibility of changing it. If anything needs to be altered, it must be done immediately. No, no, no. You may go for a drive later."

Cressida glanced helplessly back at Reggie, who said, "But I need to meet the train. Can't you do the fitting later?"

Coco Chanel looked very seriously at him. "Young man, if you wish to have a most beautiful bride by your side at the altar, you will go to the station on your own. Later, when we have finished our fitting, you may take her for a drive then."

He made a comical grimace of fear and threw up his hands. "All right, I consider myself beaten on all points. Cressida, darling, will you do me the honor of driving out with me later this afternoon when you have no further engagements?"

She laughed at that. "I'd be delighted."

"Good. In the meantime I'll motor on down to the station and pick up my suit."

Lady Wimborne looked slightly sheepishly toward Abby and said, "I had hoped to have more time to spend with you, but

I can't resist being present at the final fitting of my daughter's wedding gown."

Abby was most happy to have some time on her own and said, "Please don't worry about me. I'll walk into the village. I have some business to attend to." She felt foolish telling them she was sending her first article as she suspected at least one person at this table would want to read it first and she'd already stretched her journalistic ethics as far as she was going to for Charles Mitchell.

"Care for a lift?" Reggie asked her.

"No. Thank you, but I need the exercise." The truth was she was far too athletic to be cooped up inside all day long. She'd always enjoyed pursuits like tennis, skiing and country walks.

Henri and Lord Wimborne were discussing a new hunting rifle that His Lordship had purchased. Abby discovered that even from his wheelchair Cressie's father was an avid marksman, and it seemed it was an interest the two men shared.

Oliver said to Reggie, "I'd drive with you but—"

Charles A. Mitchell interrupted, "Don't be ridiculous. My boy can drive to the station and back by himself. I need you on the call to New York." Then he turned to the ladies and said, "I never get a holiday, no matter how hard I try. Business follows me all around the globe."

His wife shook her head at him. "That's because you let it, Charles my dear." She glanced over at Lady Wimborne and said, "The truth is he lives for his work. He loves his cars like they're family."

Her husband nodded. "Millie's quite right. I'm involved in every aspect of production. My shop floor is the first thing I think of when I wake up in the morning and the last thought I have when I go to bed at night. Automobiles have made me a very rich man, but even if they hadn't I think I would still have the passion."

He patted his pockets and drew out a notebook. "Always carry a book around to record my ideas. They come to me day and night. Many's the time I've woken Millie scribbling away with a new design." He chuckled but his wife said, "Really, Charles," as though mentioning being in bed were unseemly in front of aristocrats.

But he only laughed and patted his pockets once more. "I'll show you," he said, then to Oliver, "Lend me your pen, will you, Ollie? I'm forever forgetting to bring something along to write with." Oliver reached into his pocket and brought out a beautiful gold pen which he handed to Charles Mitchell.

As he uncapped the pen, Charles said, "I bought Oliver this when he graduated from Yale. Sent Reggie to Oxford, but Oliver studied business at Yale. When you buy a young man a very nice pen, you'll find he doesn't lose it." He shook his head. "Unlike me."

"It's my most prized possession," Oliver said. "I keep it with me always." Then, as though embarrassed that he'd revealed so much, he said in a lighter tone, "Lucky for you, Charles, as I've never known a man to lose so many pens and pencils."

Then Charles Mitchell opened his notebook, found a blank page and rapidly sketched the outline of an automobile. It looked very like the Mitchell 925 but the front was even more elongated. He said, almost to himself, "I've been wondering if we can't make the front end more streamlined. Was thinking about ocean liners last night in bed."

These seemingly cryptic utterances made sense to Oliver. He leaned forward and scrutinized the sketch. "Yes, I see what you mean. Gives a very elegant line."

Mildred said, "I'm sure that's enough business for now, my dear," and Charles immediately returned the pen to Oliver and put away his notebook. "Quite right, my darling."

Abby noted how carefully Oliver returned the pen to his pocket.

After lunch, she fetched her hat and coat and changed into walking shoes. She'd go to the village via the path through the woods rather than following the long drive.

She needed to stretch her legs and tramp over fields and jump across streams and follow whatever meandering trails were to be found on the Wimborne's property.

While she was in her room changing, Vivian was airing out Abby's ball gown. There was more involved in being a lady's maid than Abby had ever known.

"When do you have to start writing about this wedding anyway?" Viv wanted to know.

"I'm going to send my first story from the telegraph office in the village," she admitted. "I've already booked the affianced couple for an interview this evening. Paul Joubert won't be happy, but obviously I'll need to interview Coco Chanel about the wedding gown."

She let out a sigh. "I'm absolutely convinced that Charles A. Mitchell will have a few words he would like to see printed in the *Chicago Post* and the *Chicago International Post*. The Wimbornes would no doubt be quite happy simply to be photographed, or perhaps they'll try to find a reason to stay out of the newspaper. This publicity is clearly very trying for them."

Leaving Viv to get on with her duties, Abby was only too happy to head out and enjoy the spring sunshine. As she came back down the stairs she saw Oliver and Charles Mitchell making their way to Lord Wimborne's office. Reggie was standing in the hall wearing his driving cap and holding a pair of leather gloves in his hand.

"You sure you don't need me, Pa?" he asked.

"No, no. You make sure you do all that's proper for the wedding. That's your strength, my son, being a pillar of society. Oliver's the one with the head for business."

Reggie looked as though he would have said something but thought better of it. "I'll see you later."

He watched the two men disappear into the office and shut the door with a curious expression on his face. One she would have been hard put to identify. Fondness? Chagrin, perhaps. Then he gave a small shrug and turned toward the door which the butler immediately stepped forward to open for him. He was pulling on his gloves as the door shut behind him.

Abby slipped to the rear of the house where she had previously discovered the door out to the back of the property. It was a beautiful spring day and her mood lifted just being outside. Not that her mood had been down, but it was so nice to be outside. The English countryside was rich with the sounds of birds and full of sights that were both comfortingly familiar and completely different to what she was used to. She'd seen plenty of cows and sheep grazing in fields, but never penned in by drystone walls before, and the antiquity of the property was evidenced by an old well and the ancient-looking stone church where the wedding couple would exchange their vows.

The manicured lawns gave way to wilderness and Abby headed for the stream and the woods that ran alongside it. She was aware that her path ran roughly parallel to the long private drive leading to the main road into the village and the train station at the end of it. The roar of an automobile engine caused her to glance up and through the trees she caught the gleam of the royal blue sedan. Then the car shot past in a flash of blue. Mr. Mitchell Jr was driving the Mitchell 925 at a much faster speed than his father had earlier.

The drive sloped down toward the road for quite some time and she imagined Reggie would enjoy the speed.

As she walked, Abby found her mind drifting to thoughts of love. Was it love that had brought Cressida and Reggie together? Clearly, there was a joining of dynasties of a sort, one an American business dynasty and the other belonging to the

British aristocracy. Had they come together through mutual regard? Or had there been manipulation and coercion from the families? Or maybe it was a bit of both.

Abby was twenty-five years old and wondering if she'd ever fall in love. She suspected she might be too practical. Besides, if she were to marry, Walter Strutt would immediately tell her there was no place for married women in a newspaper. And her current passion was definitely her profession. Not that there was any struggle within her. No man had proposed and she'd yet to meet one whom she felt enough fondness for that she'd consider giving up her work. She was much more interested in becoming a news reporter than a wife. Perhaps one day her feelings would change—or perhaps they wouldn't.

She crossed the stream on a whim, getting her shoes wet and surprising a young deer who bounded off. It was so pleasant to walk among the trees and flowering bushes.

She was pulled sharply from her reverie by the sound of a terrific crash.

TEN

It felt as though for a moment the birds stopped singing and the leaves stopped fluttering in the trees. She wasn't entirely sure where the sound had come from but instinctively she crossed the stream again and headed for the road, breaking into a run. What on earth had happened?

When she got to the private carriage drive she glanced both ways and then saw, much further down the drive, that the beautiful royal blue sedan had crashed into one of the noble, ancient beech trees that lined the avenue.

It was very still and very quiet, and there was no sign of Reggie Mitchell. Abby began to sprint.

She was out of breath and panting when she reached the car. When she grew close enough, she saw Reggie slumped over the steering wheel. A trickle of blood dripped onto the gleaming dashboard. Her heart clutched in her chest to see him so still.

"Reggie?" she cried. She wrenched open the driver's side door and to her enormous relief he lifted his head and looked at her, dazed. There was a gash on his forehead and blood trickled down into his eyebrows.

"I don't know what happened. I think I crashed the car."

"Don't worry about that now. How are you feeling?" she asked hurriedly.

"I was trying to brake, coming around that corner. I was probably going a little too fast, just trying out the engine, you know? Listening to the pistons and enjoying the smoothness of the ride. And then when I tried to brake, nothing happened. I was helpless." His voice began to rise.

She felt certain that the best thing for him was to stay calm so she said, as soothingly as she could, "Never mind that now. Is anything broken?"

He put a hand gingerly to his forehead. "Just my head, I think."

She noticed both the windows were open. He must have been enjoying the April breeze just as she had. A quick scan of the vehicle showed the hood had folded in around the tree but the main passenger compartment seemed undamaged. The windshield had broken and there was glass everywhere.

She held out her hand. "Hold my hand. Let's get you out of the car."

He put one foot on the ground and then the other and turned his body slowly and then, grasping her hand, pulled himself to his feet. He looked pale and shaken. She took her own handkerchief and dabbed the blood away before it fell into his eyes. He winced.

"Are you able to walk? Or shall I run back to the house and get help?"

He looked back at the car. "This will break Pa's heart."

She said, "Your father will just be happy that you're unhurt."

"I won't sit here like an invalid," he said with a grimace. "If you don't mind giving me your arm, I can make it back."

They walked slowly back toward the manor house. Fortunately, they hadn't gone more than a hundred yards when the old Rolls-Royce came slowly toward them. No doubt it would have stopped anyway, given the view of the Mitchell 925 buckled against a tree trunk, and Reggie tottering down the drive on her arm, but just to make certain Abby waved her arms to get the driver to stop.

As the car drew up, Ned Corcoran looked at them with alarm. "Are you all right?" he asked Reggie, who clearly wasn't all right.

Reggie shook his head and then winced. Since he seemed to be having trouble speaking, Abby said, "There's been an accident. The car went off the road and hit a tree. Do you think you could give us a lift back to the house?"

"Of course." Ned jumped out of the Rolls and they both helped Reggie into the back seat and then Abby got in beside him.

He dabbed at his forehead with her handkerchief, muttering, "I don't know what Pa will say."

She was sorry to see him so upset about letting his father down, but could imagine that where his cars were concerned Charles A. Mitchell might be quite fierce.

It didn't take long to return to Darrington Manor.

Between them, Abby and Ned supported Reggie into the front door of the manor house. The butler looked understandably surprised to see this extraordinary sight and as soon as they were inside Ned said, "We need a doctor."

Adams nodded once. "Of course. I'll see to it. Shall I call your man, sir?"

"Please do," Reggie said. "I've a devilish headache."

She and Ned exchanged a glance. She had no idea what kind of head injury Reggie might have sustained or whether it could be serious.

Hearing the commotion, Charles A. Mitchell came storming out of the office. "What is going on? A man can't hear himself—" And then he stared at his son. "Reggie! What have you done to your head?"

"I had an automobile accident, Pa."

"Oh my God. Not the royal blue sedan?" His son nodded and then moaned, putting a hand to his forehead, where blood was once again trickling from the wound.

"Is it badly damaged?"

Charles Mitchell looked to Ned, who said gently, "I'm sure it can be repaired. But we should get a doctor to your son as soon as possible."

Then Charles A. Mitchell pulled himself together and looked around at the people assembled in the hallway. "Yes. Naturally. Has a doctor been called? He must see a doctor."

The butler said, "I was just about to see to it, sir."

"Well look lively, man."

Reggie's valet appeared at that moment and let out a cry of distress seeing his master in such a state.

"Badger, take me upstairs. I've an awful headache."

"Of course, sir, lean on me."

Abby hung back while Ned and Badger between them supported the injured man up the stairs which led to the bedrooms. They hadn't gone far when Henri Deschamps came striding down the hallway. "I heard raised voices. Is everything all right?" He turned instinctively to Abby with his eyebrows raised. Briefly she told him what had happened. He walked straight toward the injured man and said, "You say you've a headache?"

"Yes," Reggie said testily.

Deschamps held up two fingers and said, "How many fingers am I holding in front of your face?"

"What kind of a bloody stupid question is that to ask a man? I need to lie down."

"It would help to ascertain the nature of your injury."

Reggie squinted at him. "Two, I think."

Henri turned to the butler. "Has a doctor been called?"

"I'll do it now, sir." The butler made his stately way toward the back of the house.

Charles A. Mitchell turned to Deschamps. "You've a knowledge of medicine?"

Henri gave a grim smile. "Years on the battlefield. I've seen many a head injury. I'd guess this man has a concussion. Hopefully nothing more serious than that." To the valet he said, "Make sure he doesn't fall asleep. That's the most important thing you can do. Keep asking him things like his name, his birthday, who the president of the United States is—those sorts of things. Hopefully the doctor won't be too long."

As the three men walked slowly up the stairs, the inspector came over to her. "You've blood on your hands." His keen gaze swept over her. "Were you in the car when it crashed?"

She looked down and sure enough her fingers were streaked with blood. They were also trembling from the shock of seeing the man slumped over the wheel and fearing the worst. "No. I wasn't in the car. It's Reggie's blood, not mine." She didn't have her handkerchief, Reggie still had that. If she wasn't careful, she'd ruin the coat she was wearing. She held her hands out rather helplessly.

Henri pulled out his own linen handkerchief and methodically cleaned her hands. Though he was seemingly unaware of it, the matter-of-fact way he handled her helped steady Abby. His hands were strong and there was a solidity about him that made her suddenly glad he was staying at Darrington Manor.

Lord Wimborne came down the corridor in his wheelchair, his face creased with worry. "Adams is phoning the doctor now. I do trust Reggie's not seriously hurt?" he asked, looking to Henri.

Before Henri could answer, Charles Mitchell cut in: "I don't understand what's going on. The boy seems to have had an accident with the new car. But he's an excellent driver. He wasn't drunk, surely?"

It was eleven o'clock in the morning. Abby couldn't imagine that Reggie had partaken of alcohol between breakfast and going for a drive. But it was Henri who answered: "There was no smell of alcohol on his breath." So, he'd thought that was a possibility too then. She wondered if that was partly why he'd engaged the young man in dialogue.

Charles Mitchell was in a state, red in the face and breathing shallowly. Abby was certain he was very worried about his son, but he was also clearly agitated about the state of his beloved car that he'd shipped all the way from America. "There's nothing I can do here," he said. "I must go and see to the Mitchell 925."

At that moment Oliver Platt appeared. "I had to end the call to New York, Charles. The butler needed to phone a doctor. He says Reggie's been hurt. I'll go up and see if there's anything I can do."

"He's got his man with him and a doctor on the way," Charles Mitchell said testily. "I need you with me. You know the Mitchell 925 better than anyone other than myself. Come along." He headed for the front door.

Henri said, "My car is outside. I shall drive you."

Mitchell nodded briskly. "Good, good. And you, young lady, you know where this accident occurred?" Abby agreed that she did. "Well, you'd better come along with us then—no point driving all over the place looking for the wreck."

She didn't think that it would be easy to miss, but she was curious to go back to the scene of the accident herself. She'd been rather shaken up by the whole experience and worried about Reggie. Now she couldn't help wondering how such an experienced driver had managed to crash into a tree while driving down a quiet country lane. Had something distracted him? He'd mentioned something about the brakes failing, which seemed ominous. Had the car king designed a car with faulty brakes?

Abby excused herself to quickly wash her hands, then ran outside to join them.

She got into the back of Henri's Bentley after he courteously opened the door for her and then Charles Mitchell got into the front seat and sat beside the driver, while Oliver settled in beside her and they headed off down the gravel road.

Charles Mitchell looked through the front windshield and the side windows, swiveling his head. "I can't understand it. It's incomprehensible to me that the boy could crash the car on a beautiful sunny day like this. It's not like there's ice on the road or heavy rain."

"It does seem curious," Henri said in his quiet way.

Abby didn't need to direct Henri to the crash site, beyond telling him to follow the lane as it sloped down toward the main road. The moment they rounded the corner, they came upon the blue sedan exactly where she'd last seen it, with its nose pushed into a tree. Charles Mitchell gave a cry that sounded like grief. Henri had barely pulled up when he was opening the door and jumping out, running toward the beautiful car. The rest of them alighted more slowly. The inspector stood back and looked all around before approaching the car.

Charles Mitchell was beside himself. "He must have been going at quite some speed. The windshield's broken, and that's good American steel in the front of the car that's been dented in. I tell you, I'm flabbergasted. Simply flabbergasted."

Then he shook his head. "Well, we can't leave it here. I shall have to make inquiries, see if someone can fix her." As he spoke, he stroked his hand along the side of the car as though it were a racing horse or a well-loved pet who was injured. "Oliver, you get in the driver's seat and see if the engine will start." Oliver did as he was asked, careful to brush the broken glass out of the way. The engine started right away. "Well that's a blessing anyway," Charles Mitchell said. "Now, back it up."

They all watched as Oliver put the car into reverse and

pressed on the gas. Abby found herself cringing at the sound. Metal crunched and both tree and car moved as though the automobile had wrapped around the tree, giving it a hug, and didn't want to let go.

"Put on some more gas," Charles Mitchell ordered.

Oliver did. The engine grew louder and then suddenly the car jerked backwards. He fought the wheel a little and brought the car back onto the drive. He left the engine running and looked toward Charles Mitchell for guidance.

"Turn it off," he ordered. "I don't want you driving it if moving it will make anything worse. Let's see if there's any damage under the hood."

Oliver obediently turned off the engine and got out of the car and went round to the hood. He wrestled with it for a while, trying to get it open, but it was hopeless. His shoulders bunching with the strain, he finally gave up. "I'll need proper tools to get the hood open. But I'll have a look underneath and see if I can spot anything."

For some reason Abby felt a clench of anxiety as the young man lay down on the road and shimmied himself underneath the front of the car. They all watched as he studied the inner workings of the vehicle or whatever he could see from underneath it. Abby didn't know enough about cars to have a clue what he was doing, but after a few minutes of tinkering he slid himself out from under the car and stood up. There were bits of stone and twig clinging to his trousers and a dab of oil on his hands. But this time when he pulled on the hood of the car he was able to get it open.

Charles Mitchell rushed in to peer under the hood alongside Oliver. "Sir, look at this," Oliver said. It sounded as though whatever he'd seen had shaken him.

"Well, I'll be danged." The tone of utter amazement in Charles's voice had both Abby and Henri edging closer. Abby looked down and saw the inner workings of an automobile engine. It was all chunks of metal and snaking tubes. And then Oliver reached forward and lifted one of the tubes, which was clearly split in two.

"The brake line is split in two," he gasped.

Charles A. Mitchell turned to them, very red in the face, and said, "Not split in any kind of accidental way. That line's been cut, and deliberately."

Abby was shocked. "Mr. Mitchell, what are you saying?"

He looked at her and there was fury in his eyes. "I'm saying, young lady, that somebody tried to murder my son."

ELEVEN

Once Charles Mitchell had thrown out the suggestion of murder, the word echoed around them, seeming to rustle through the trees as though the leaves were whispering to each other, "Murder, murder, murder." A crow shrieked somewhere nearby and Abby jumped. There were goosebumps on her arms and the cold came from somewhere deep within her, from the knowledge that someone had deliberately tried to hurt a seemingly harmless young man who was about to be married. Who would do such a thing? And why?

She glanced at Henri to see how he had taken the startling news but his face, as usual, revealed nothing of his thoughts. He stepped closer. "May I see the split brake line?"

Oliver lifted the two pieces and she could see that his hand shook slightly. "I don't think there can be any doubt that this was deliberate sabotage. It's impossible to imagine such a thing happening by accident."

"I see."

"Well, the 925's not drivable," Charles Mitchell said, stating the obvious. "It will have to be dragged back. Or perhaps taken to a garage somewhere nearby."

He took a handkerchief out of his pocket and dabbed his brow and she saw that it was wet with sweat.

Henri spoke again, in cool, measured tones. Pretty much the way he always spoke. "I think, sir, you will have to inform the local police. If what you say is true, and someone has attempted to harm your son, then this is a police matter."

She noticed that he didn't use the word murder. And Charles A. Mitchell noticed too.

"*Harm*? What do you mean *harm*? It was a miracle my son wasn't killed. If he wasn't a fine driver who'd grown up around the automobile, it would have ended up much worse." He pointed to where the steep drive merged with the road leading to the village. "Why, he'd have shot through the gates onto the main road without being able to stop. Anything coming..." He shuddered, unable to finish the sentence. But she pictured what he wasn't saying. A truck or large farm vehicle traveling down the road at speed could have caused a terrible accident.

"That is why you should alert the local authorities," Henri reiterated.

Charles Mitchell pondered and then said, "Still. I don't like it. I don't like the idea of some local plodding policeman poking his nose into our business."

"Nevertheless, if someone has deliberately tried to harm your son, it would be well to investigate the crime. At the very least, someone is responsible for destroying your beautiful automobile."

She wondered if that was it. Was the intended victim not really a person at all, but that car? But again, who would do such a thing.

Charles Mitchell seemed as puzzled as she was. "Are you suggesting that someone deliberately wanted to hurt this beautiful marvel of engineering? This beauty I had specially shipped over from the United States of America?"

Henri lifted his shoulders in a Gallic shrug. "It is a

suggestion only. Until this is investigated, it is impossible to be able to tell what happened here today. Or who is responsible."

Abby looked at the three men. It occurred to her that whoever had done this terrible thing must be a resident or a guest of Darlington Manor. And now she realized the source of the gooseflesh. When she walked back into that manor house, she would be in the vicinity of someone who had planned terrible harm to another person, if not murder.

They stood there and then Oliver said quietly, "I think he's right, Charles. The local police should definitely be called."

Charles Mitchell puffed out his cheeks. "Take me back to the house. I must think on this. I will consult with Lord Wimborne. See what he has to say on the matter. It was his car, after all, that was damaged."

They left the beautiful royal blue wreck on the road and drove slowly back to Darrington Manor.

Charles Mitchell and Oliver got out of the car, Oliver politely holding the door so that she could alight from the back. But Henri didn't turn off the engine, nor did it seem like he was about to park.

Instead of following them into the house, she gazed at him through his open side window. "You're going back, aren't you?"

He didn't smile but his face softened and smile lines fanned around his eyes. "I am, in fact, an investigator. One cannot help one's instincts."

She walked around the front of the car and got in beside him. "Then I'm going with you."

He raised his eyebrows at that. "Are you a trained investigator now?"

"No. I am a journalist and this is news."

He shook his head at her. "Very well. But don't get in my way."

They drove slowly back to where the sedan sat abandoned

on the drive. He pulled over to the side a hundred yards or so behind the car and then they both got out.

"What are you looking for?" she asked him.

"Clues as to what really happened. Weather and people driving up and down this lane will soon obscure any hints we may have as to how this accident occurred." He paced the area around the car and then pointed to a place where the gravel had been disturbed. "That is where he tried to brake, coming around the corner. I expect he was going too fast. He was a young man driving on his own, a man, as his father said, who has grown up around the automobile. He'd be very confident. Possibly realizing he was going a little too quickly, he puts on the brake and then nothing happens." He stepped forward and stared at the ground. "Here, does he lose control? Or does he make a decision? As his father said, if he kept going, he would have plunged into the road, risking a worse accident. Does he make the decision to turn the wheel and take his chances with the tree? Or is the decision taken away from him when the speed is too much and he can't control the car?"

Since she didn't have an answer, Abby remained silent. Presumably he was thinking aloud and didn't expect her to contribute.

He walked to where the tree showed signs of the collision. There was glass on the ground and bits of tree bark. He came back and opened the driver's side door. Since he didn't tell her not to, she went around to the other side and opened the passenger door. She didn't sit, as there were shards of glass everywhere. She noticed blood on the steering wheel and on the luxurious leather seat.

"The windows are both open. Do you recall whether they were open when you first came across the accident?" he asked.

"Yes," she said. "I noticed that. It was such a beautiful day, he must have rolled down both windows to enjoy the cross-breeze."

He ran the edge of his finger around the steering wheel thoughtfully.

"What are you thinking?" she asked curiously.

"I am thinking what a tragedy it is that such a beautiful car should be damaged on her maiden voyage. But how very fortunate that Reginald Mitchell wasn't hurt any more badly than he was."

He got out of the car, took a few steps back and gazed over the scene for another minute or two. She followed suit, trying to visualize the scene through his eyes. What clues was he picking up that she couldn't spot? She knew him well enough to know he wouldn't tell her so she gathered her own impressions. She could also see where the tire marks showed a sudden swerve. No skid marks because he hadn't been able to brake. She suspected the gardeners had swept and repaired the gravel drive in preparation for the wedding so the S shape of tire tread marks was easy to spot.

He turned a slow circle and seemed to study the trees, then asked, "Where were you when the accident occurred?"

She pointed to where the path meandered along the stream. "I was walking toward the village by the path through the woods. I saw a glimpse of the automobile as it passed and then heard the crash."

His eyes narrowed and she felt all at once as though the woods were full of dark things. "Do you think someone was watching to see if their act of sabotage worked?" she asked him.

"It's possible. Perhaps they wanted to watch the crash, or perhaps..." His words trailed off but she thought she could guess where he was going.

"Or perhaps, if I hadn't come running toward the car so soon after the accident, they could have done worse?" She pictured some horrible person sneaking up to the vehicle with a stone; it would have been so easy to strike the unconscious man through the open window.

In a small voice she said, "I'm very glad I came along when I did."

"And you walked the injured man back to the manor house?"

"No. Luckily, Ned Corcoran was driving down the lane in the Rolls. He drove Reggie and me back."

"I see. Are you now ready to return to the manor house?"

"Yes," she said, and they got back into his Bentley. Once he started up the engine, she asked him, "Do you think Charles Mitchell could be right? Could someone be trying to murder Reginald?"

"I think it's one possibility," he mused.

"But if that's true, it has to be someone at the manor house."

He turned to her. "You think so?"

"Who else would want to hurt Reginald Mitchell?" Her mind scampered over everyone she'd socialized with, eaten meals with. "Who would do such a terrible thing?"

He shook his head. "That I do not know, yet."

She looked sideways at him. "You're going to help with the investigation, aren't you?"

"That will be up to Lord Wimborne and the English detectives assigned to this case. I would not like to intrude where I'm not wanted."

She didn't believe him for a minute. She knew darn well that he'd be poking his nose all over the place trying to figure out what had happened. Partly because he was Lord Wimborne's friend and houseguest, but mostly because it was in his nature.

She was very much afraid that she'd be doing a fair amount of poking her nose where it didn't belong as well. Abby had a feeling that investigative reporting was in her nature too. Walter Strutt could try all he liked to keep assigning her to the women's page, but her forte was hard news. And now, through most unfortunate circumstances, she was being offered a scoop.

TWELVE

They had barely pulled up before the front doors of the manor house when a battered old sedan lumbered up beside them. A man emerged wearing a dark suit and carrying a medical bag. The doctor had arrived.

By unspoken agreement, Abby and Henri sat in the car and waited for the doctor to be admitted to the house before following him. Things had calmed down since she had first arrived with the injured Reginald, but there was a sense of suppressed alarm in the air as she walked in this time. She saw the butler escorting the doctor upstairs, presumably to Reginald's bedroom.

Lady Wimborne was hovering at the bottom of the staircase as they came in. "Oh, my dears, what a terrible shock. And poor you, Abigail, to have been the first one on the scene. Are you all right, my dear? I'm sure you should sit down and have a cup of tea for the shock. Perhaps some whiskey. I'm not a great one for drinking in the day myself, but after such a traumatic event I think perhaps a glass of whiskey might be medicinal."

Abby shook her head. "I certainly don't need whiskey this early in the day, thank you. But a cup of tea would be nice."

It wasn't that she needed the tea so much as she felt that Lady Wimborne needed something to do. She seemed almost relieved to be able to say, "I'll ring for some."

Then Cressida came running lightly down the stairs. "I was sitting with Reggie, but the doctor told me I had to leave." There were tear smudges on her cheeks and she looked dreadfully upset. "I can't believe it, I was just having my wedding dress fitting and nearly lost my fiancé."

Lady Wimborne gently ushered her daughter into the sitting room. "I've rung for tea, dear. I think we all need some."

Coco Chanel came down the stairs more slowly. "What a good thing I insisted you have your dress fitting as planned, or you'd have been in that car with him."

It was true. In the drama of Reginald's accident, Abby had completely forgotten that he'd invited his fiancée to drive with him.

Lady Wimborne went so pale Abby stepped forward, thinking she might faint. In a shaking voice she said, "My love, you could have been hurt."

After tea, Abby remembered she still had her article to send to the paper. She'd phone Walter Strutt when things calmed down and tell him the news about the crash, but for now she had to file her story.

For the second time that day, Abby prepared to walk into town, but this time she succeeded without any dramatic events preventing her.

Her article was all about love and weddings, but her thoughts were much darker. A local girl had been murdered, a bridegroom injured and an automobile sabotaged. And she, a trained reporter, had been assigned to write about nothing more violent than cupid's arrow striking a young lover's heart.

After she'd sent the copy of her scintillating article off to Walter Strutt, Abby walked into Darrington village. She didn't consciously choose her route, but somehow she found herself outside the home of the poor murdered girl, Gladys Trotter.

Gladys's mother was weeding the front garden with some vigor. Abby could feel the woman's grief as she yanked out weeds with such violence that clumps of dirt flew about. Abby suspected she wasn't too worried whether she was pulling weed or flower. Weeding gave her something to do and a way to get rid of some of her terrible energy.

Abby hadn't intended to stand and stare, but perhaps she paused a moment too long, for the woman glanced up as if she'd felt her gaze upon her. There was a blank, shuttered look about her face. And then she rose and dusted off her hands.

"Can I help you with something, miss?" she asked warily.

Abby was almost tempted to say, "No thank you," and move on, but she'd suffered the grief of losing both her parents, and also, despite what Walter Strutt had said about keeping her nose out of hard news, she was on the scene.

She stepped forward, "Mrs. Trotter?"

The woman's face seemed to harden. "Aye."

Abby couldn't seriously contemplate a career in hard news if she couldn't step forward into another person's pain. So, even as she shied away from causing Mrs. Trotter any further discomfort, she felt she had to introduce herself. "My name is Abigail Dixon. I'm a reporter for the *Chicago Post*. I was very sorry to hear about your daughter. If you'd like to talk about her, I'd be more than happy to listen."

Mrs. Trotter wrung her hands and seemed undecided whether to tell Abby to go throw herself in the closest lake or to speak with her. Finally she said, "Are you going to make my daughter out to be some kind of harlot like the other newspapers have?" The jaw jutted out belligerently now.

Abby shook her head slowly. "I thought we might speak, woman to woman, and you could tell me more about her," she offered gently before continuing, "I can't promise it will be published, but I'd like to write a profile piece. I was accused of murder myself last year and I know how terrible it can be to find yourself in the glare of public scrutiny."

Then the woman's face seemed to crumple and she put her apron to her eyes. "Bad enough to have lost my precious babe. But the things they're saying—"

Abby didn't stop to think, she unlatched the gate and walked into the small front garden and rubbed a hand up and down the woman's back. After a moment Mrs. Trotter pulled herself together and said, "Come inside. I'll make us a cup of tea."

She took Abby into a painfully neat front room that looked as if it was only used on special occasions. It smelled closed up and unused, and yet everything gleamed. Mrs. Trotter was a fine housewife, that was clear. When she came back with the tea, in her finest china, she'd removed her apron and tidied herself up a bit. And then she sat down, sipped, and began to talk. Abby took out her pencil and notebook, but as Mrs. Trotter began to speak, she barely took any notes at all. The woman's words were almost volcanic in nature, as though they'd been held in as long as they could be and now they needed to pour forth, hot and immediate and angry. She told Abby how pretty her baby girl had been, and how funny.

"She always liked nice things. Even when she was little, always wanted a frill or a bow on everything. Well, she was my baby, so I indulged her. Spoiled her some might say. But she was such a sweet, bright, little thing. And when she grew up and said she'd marry a duke or become a ballerina, I never checked her. It seemed so harmless." Her tears were flowing freely now and she swallowed hard before continuing with a sob in her voice. "Perhaps I should have. I should have let her know that she'd be lucky to get a place in service and maybe in time would marry the butcher's son or a farmer's son and have a life like mine." She gave a bitter laugh. "Our kind don't marry dukes, and they don't end up on the stage, Miss Dixon."

"Did she seem more than usually happy recently?" Abigail inquired.

"Not so much happy, excited more like. She glowed like she had a secret."

"But she didn't confide in you?"

She sniffed. "No. And how I wish she had. Mayhap I could have stopped her." She shook her head in dismay. "London—what was she doing in London?"

Abby nodded, feeling so much sympathy for this woman. She felt she had done a kind deed but doubted that there would be any news story forthcoming. Then Mrs. Trotter looked up and said, "Would you like to see her room?"

"Yes. Thank you."

"Course, she was the last of my children living here. The rest are all married and moved away." As she spoke, she led Abby upstairs to a small bedroom with a pink quilted cover. It was simply furnished but the stamp of Gladys Trotter was all over it. Pictures of film stars smiled down at Abby. "Oh, she loved that Rudolf Valentino," Mrs. Trotter told Abby. "Saw every film she could."

Abby knew the police would have searched the room, but still she asked if she might look at Gladys's clothes.

"I suppose so."

There was a sober-looking skirt and blouse that looked like what the servants at Darrington Manor wore, and then two dresses that were cheap copies of the latest fashions. One blue and one black. There were no silk stockings in the room. She recalled Vivian reporting that Gladys had "swanned around" in a too-tight red dress.

"She left here wearing clothes suitable for working at Darrington Manor. That's why I never suspected. But she had that red dress with her." Mrs. Trotter wiped her eyes. "They found it, the police did. In her room."

"I'm so sorry."

"Thank you. You're kinder than those newspaper men who came here with their sharp pencils and their sharp eyes and sharp questions."

"Was there anyone she might have told who she was meeting, or why she was going to London?"

Mrs. Trotter's mouth pursed and then she said, "Mary in the butcher's, I suppose. I never approved of their friendship. That Mary's no better than she should be, but Gladys would never hear a word against her." She sighed then. "Gladys did hint that she wouldn't be working at Darrington Manor much longer, but she wouldn't say where she hoped to find another position. I thought perhaps she could become a lady's maid. She did love clothes so." Her voice became choked with emotion, and she shook her head. "Look, I found this. She was already writing a letter telling them she was resigning. Bless her."

She went to a drawer and opened it. From it she withdrew a sheet of paper. *Dear Miss Wimborne* was written in careful rounded letters that a schoolgirl would have learned. Then she'd crossed that out and beneath it written *Dear Lord Wimborne*, then finally, *Dear Lady Wimborne*. The body of the letter began, *I regret to inform you*, and then stopped. Mrs. Trotter pointed to the letter and said, "She didn't know which of them she was meant to write to. I could have told her to address her letter to the housekeeper, not the family. She was that young."

Somehow that childlike writing filled Abby with determination. She would do everything in her power to find the culprit who had taken this naïve young woman's life. Perhaps her newspaper articles would keep the story alive and that would encourage the police to continue their investigation into the murder of an obscure country girl.

When she left, Mrs. Trotter thanked her. "It's helped me a little to speak of my Gladys. And I know you'll do right by her."

Abby clasped the woman's hand and said she'd do her best.

Then Abby headed for the butcher's. When she walked in, a woman of about twenty came from the back wearing a brown apron. Above a dissatisfied-looking countenance was a mop of curly red hair. She wore bright lipstick, unfortunately the color of blood.

There were carcasses hanging from the ceiling that gave off an unpleasant odor. It seemed the perfect location to talk about death.

"Can I help you, miss?"

"Are you Mary?"

A guarded look came into her eyes. "Why do you want to know?"

Abby explained who she was and told her that Mrs. Trotter had thought Mary might know why Gladys had gone to London.

The young woman looked both excited and trepidatious. "You'll have to buy something," she said in a rapid undertone. "I'm not allowed to stand about gossiping."

"I understand." But what could Abby purchase at a butcher's when she was staying at Darrington Manor? Surely the cook wouldn't appreciate Abby giving her a dozen sausages. Then she thought of the dogs she'd seen in the village. She was certain there'd be a hungry stray among them. "Could I buy a meaty bone for a dog?"

"S'pose so."

The girl went into the back and Abby heard her say, "Rich woman out front wants a meaty bone for her dog." There was some discussion Abby couldn't hear, then Mary emerged with a very meaty-looking bone.

"It will cost a penny," she said.

Abby had no idea how much a bone should cost, but that

seemed rather high. However, she took out her purse while Mary spoke softly.

"I don't know who it was she was meeting, honest I don't. All Gladys said was that he was a theatrical agent and she'd got an audition."

"But how did she get this audition?"

While Mary wrapped the bone in brown paper and tied it with string she shook her head. "Dunno. She said a special friend had arranged it all. She was so excited. I admit I was a bit jealous. She was going to be on the stage and I'm stuck here with blood on my apron. And then look what happened to her."

"Did you ever see her with George Smith?"

Mary looked up, her mouth opening. "George Smith? Course I did. He used to take her out on a Sunday sometimes. But she never really fancied him."

"Do you think he might have taken her to London?"

"To London?" she made a sound like a snort and a laugh combined. "Not him. Why would he?"

Why indeed?

"Can you think of anyone else she associated with who might know more?"

"There's a footman at Darrington, Jerry. They were thick as thieves. He had big ideas, too. And an eye for the girls. I told her to be careful, but she never listened. She thought he might take her to his home in Devon to meet his family, but I told her it wasn't marriage he had in mind. Not that one."

"Mary?" a gruff voice called from the back. "You come back here and stuff these sausages."

"I must go," she said, and Abby barely had time to thank her before she disappeared into the back.

After making a hungry-looking dog very happy, Abby made her way back to Darrington Manor. She needed to speak to Jerry.

THIRTEEN

The time remaining before dinner passed with a kind of breathless dread, like waiting for a threatened hurricane to arrive. Abby felt jumpy, as though every time she turned around in the old and slightly creaky manor house she might bump into a saboteur, or worse, a murderer. She knew she was being fanciful, but her recent experiences with murder had left her with wounds that had yet to heal.

She and Vivian debated what she should wear to dinner that night and chose the most sedate of her evening gowns. It was a midnight blue silk with little embellishment. After she bathed, Vivian styled her hair and naturally fell into conversation about the dramatic crash.

"It's just so awful what happened to Reggie," Vivian said. "None of us can believe it."

"What are they saying below stairs?"

"That Reginald Mitchell is a spoiled young rich boy from America. No doubt he annoyed a local. Jerry told me in confidence that Reggie likes to go to the local pub and flirt with the girls. Oliver's usually with him, so I suppose if Cressida ever asks he'll say he's keeping his friend company."

There was a sense of suppressed excitement about Vivian as she helped Abby dress. Her eyes were glowing and there was a little smile playing around her lips. For a girl who had been suffering heartbreak so recently, Abby was surprised at her rapid recovery. When she mentioned the footman, Abby saw her lips curve.

As Vivian slipped a string of jet beads over her neck, Abby said, "It seems like Jerry and you are getting on."

"Oh, yes. It's amazing how different it is being downstairs with all the servants," Vivian replied, her cheeks coloring slightly.

Their gazes met in the mirror. "You don't mind? It feels quite wrong that you're not sitting beside me at the dining room table."

Vivian waved that off. "It's much more interesting below stairs, believe me. Jerry is ever so entertaining. He loves my American accent. He said he thinks I'm the most glamorous girl he's ever seen."

Abby couldn't help but recall her visit to the butcher. "Vivian, we're only here for a week. You barely know Jerry, be careful, all right?"

Vivian tossed her head so her blond curls danced. "I'm always careful, Abigail."

"I suppose so. He's not married, is he?"

"No. But I can tell you he's very ambitious. He has big plans. He's working as a footman here, and then he hopes to work in a shop. Perhaps one of the lovely men's shops in London." She met Abby's eyes in the mirror and hers were twinkling. "Or Paris."

Abby picked up her lipstick and before she applied it said, "Just don't break your heart."

"I won't. But would you mind terribly if I wasn't here to undress you this evening? He's invited me to the local pub again. They're quite liberal here, you know. Lord and Lady

Wimborne are perfectly happy for the staff to enjoy their time off so long as they're here when they're needed. And he did ask me specially if I would go with him. Our time together is running out."

Abby had to laugh. "You know I don't need you to undress me, silly. I feel awkward to have you dressing me at all, though I'm awfully glad you're here. And you remember ever so much better than I do which shoes go with which outfit."

Vivian was obviously pleased by the compliment. "You'd be lost without me. But I agree, you really don't need me to undress you and put you to bed. You need me before you go downstairs so I can check and make sure that you're wearing the correct outfit with the correct jewelry and hat and shoes and accessories, and that you haven't got a thread hanging or a bit of lint attached to your elbow from where you've been leaning on the bedspread writing or something."

Abby smiled. "I admit I'm not much of a clothes horse, though I do love these beautiful outfits Paul sent along."

"Well, you'd better keep them in good shape, or he'll stop designing for you."

"I promise."

Abby didn't know what she would have done if she didn't have her friend with her acting as her lady's maid. Vivian was the person she could pour her heart out to and with whom she could share her worries.

Vivian had been there when she'd been accused of murder and knew what Abby had been through. The minute Abby told her about the accident and how she'd rushed up to the wreck thinking the worst, she said, "Oh poor you. Imagine being the first one to come upon Reggie Mitchell. It must have been simply terrible."

Abby shuddered. "It was. I wasn't even certain he was alive. He was slumped over the steering wheel, jagged pieces of broken glass everywhere, and that beautiful car smashed."

"I can tell you, Reggie's man was in a terrible way downstairs earlier. No one likes Badger much. He's very full of himself and how much better everything is in New York, but you couldn't help feeling for him. He was worried Reggie might not make it through the night. Fortunately, the doctor seems to have reassured him."

"That's good. Are Reggie's injuries very serious?"

"According to Badger, the doctor said he was lucky. He's got a concussion but the wound on his head didn't even need stitches. It sounds like the car is in worse shape than he is."

"His father's pretty broken up too. I wasn't sure whether Charles A. Mitchell was more concerned for his son or his beloved automobile."

When she was gowned, and had been able to share everything she was feeling with Vivian, Abby felt better able to face what was bound to be an awkward dinner.

She picked up her beaded evening bag, already packed with her notebook and pencils. She'd intended to sit with the bridal couple and conduct an interview. Now she wasn't sure what to do.

She was early for dinner and on impulse asked Adams if she could make a phone call. He showed her to Lord Wimborne's office and she put through a call to Walter Strutt. She told him she was hot on the trail of a hard news story and when he heard what it was Walter stopped her as devastatingly as that tree had stopped the Mitchell 925.

"Abigail Dixon, you are not reporting one negative word about this wedding, so get that right out of your pretty little head."

She was utterly shocked. "But, Walter, it's news."

"Do I have to repeat myself? You don't report hard news. You're on the women's page. I want copy about how much in love those two are, what Reginald Mitchell has to say about English girls and England, and what does Walter A. Mitchell say about combining his newfound wealth with a historic family name? I want to hear from the Wimbornes and Coco Chanel, and I want to know what everybody's wearing, what the flowers will be, what they're going to eat at the wedding lunch." With every sentence his voice rose.

"I understand all that, but I'm right here in the middle of a news story."

He said sharply, "It's not a news story until I say it is."

"Did you know that a girl from this village was murdered? Strangled with her own silk stocking?"

"Yeah, I read about it on the wire. Was she a guest at this wedding?" His tone was laden with sarcasm.

"No, but she worked casually at Darrington Manor. I talked to her mother today and—"

"No."

"But—"

"If I decide it's a news story worthy of reporting to the readers of the *Chicago International Post*, I will assign a news reporter to cover it. Do I make myself clear?"

"Crystal," she said with a sigh and ended the call.

Now she headed for pre-dinner cocktails with her notebook and pencils and wondered what on earth she was going to write about for the women's page that would be sufficiently upbeat. The bridegroom was unlikely to appear, having suffered a head injury, his bride was probably not thinking of clothes and wedding luncheons and flowers when she had nearly become widowed before she even got married. And what would Charles A. Mitchell have to say about England when it had smashed up his prized automobile?

Still, she had a job to do. She'd have to figure out something. Perhaps she could interview Coco Chanel about the dress and squeeze a few comments out of the bride and her mother. That would have to do. Photographs would take care of the rest.

It was a desultory group who sat in the library before

dinner. The cocktail hour was very different from the one the night before. Charles A. Mitchell was drinking whiskey like it was water and he was in the middle of the desert. Lady Wimborne tried a few topics of conversation and Lady Constance Harroby supported her as best she could, but it was hard going. Mrs. Mitchell was upstairs sitting with her son and so, presumably, was Oliver. Cressida sat beside her father, with the colorless Beatrice on her other side. Even Coco Chanel didn't bother making an entrance. She walked in with Inspector Deschamps, speaking in French. They immediately switched to English when they entered the room, but Abby noted the flirtatious nature of the designer's tone. Even though she was involved with the Duke of Westminster, she seemed very happy to flirt with an attractive Frenchman.

Abby was seated beside Peter Wimborne. A champagne cocktail had seemed too frivolous so tonight she sipped a gin and tonic. While Lady Wimborne and Lady Harroby talked about the lightest of society gossip, as though nothing unpleasant had occurred, Peter asked, in a low voice, "How are you holding up? Must have been a dreadful shock to find Reggie like that."

"It was." She glanced over to where Cressida rested her head against the back of the sofa like a wilted flower. Beside her, Lord Wimborne appeared tired and a worried frown creased his forehead. "But the shock was much worse for Cressie."

"It was. When she found out the brake line had been cut she went so pale I thought she was going to faint. She's not got Mother's strength. Look at her going on about how much Lord and Lady Thisby enjoyed their trip on the Orient Express— you'd never know there's an injured bridegroom upstairs. Cressie doesn't have that steadiness of character. She's nervy. Always has been."

"In fairness, her fiancé was nearly killed." Abigail felt

herself defending Cressida's perfectly natural response to the shocking situation.

"You should have seen Mother when Father was brought home from the battlefield. He was in a military hospital for months and I'm convinced she was the one who pulled him through."

Abby turned to Lady Wimborne and imagined her using all her will and love to help her husband recover from his injuries. Yes, her manner might be soft but there was a core of steel beneath. Abby felt there was nothing she wouldn't do for her family and those she loved.

Oliver Platt came in and apologized for being late. He went over to Charles Mitchell and sat beside him. From the little she overheard, it seemed Oliver hadn't been visiting Reggie but trying to find a place to have the Mitchell 925 repaired.

There was a stir a few minutes later when Reginald entered the room on the arm of his valet.

Cressida jumped up and ran toward him. "Reggie! You should be in bed."

He had a bandage across his forehead and was wearing a dressing gown over his trousers. He smiled wanly and said, "I don't want to lie in bed like some invalid. The doctor gave me something for the headache. It's better to be down here with you all than having Badger keep asking me every five minutes what day it is and what my name is."

Abby glanced at Badger, knowing from Vivian how worried he'd been about his master. He had the impassive countenance of the perfect servant, but she could see how keenly he watched as Cressida steered Reggie to the seat beside hers, which Beatrice obligingly vacated. Cressie brought him a footstool for his feet, a cushion for his head and then sat beside him. "You're all right, aren't you? I've been so worried."

"Take more than a bang on the head to keep me from your side, my dear."

Everyone cheered up having him back in their midst. He accepted a glass of whiskey and Cressida's mother pretended she didn't notice that they held hands.

The butler came in and Abby got ready to rise, assuming he was announcing dinner. But instead of looking at Lady Wimborne, he gave his attention to her husband. In sepulchral tones, he announced, "There is a Sergeant Kelston to see you, my lord."

It was as though an electric current zapped through the room. The law was here, and for a very good reason. It was yet another reminder that a crime had taken place at Darrington Manor earlier in the day.

"He'll want to speak to everyone," Lord Wimborne announced, glancing around the assembled company. "May I invite him in here?"

"Oh really, my dear, must we have a policeman in the library? Can't he wait until we've dined?" Lady Wimborne asked in a harassed tone.

It was Inspector Deschamps who replied: "It will be easiest, Lady Wimborne, if he meets us all at once. It will be simpler for you in the long run." He didn't respond to her suggestion that the police might wait until the family had dined before bothering them.

She sighed and said, "Oh very well."

The butler withdrew and returned moments later with the detective. "Sergeant Kelston, my lord," he announced, and then withdrew.

Sergeant Kelston was a solid-looking man of average height with a large nose, protuberant eyes and curly, dark hair cropped close to his head. He wore an overcoat and held a notebook and pencil in his hand, something similar to what Abby had in her evening bag, though of course he wasn't here to report on the society wedding.

He glanced around the room and said, "I understand there's been some trouble today."

Charles Mitchell made a rude noise. "I call it more than trouble when my son is nearly killed and the beautiful automobile I had made specially is all but destroyed. Yes, indeed, I call that more than a bit of trouble."

The sergeant turned to him, clearly noting the half-full glass of whiskey and the flushed cheeks of a man who'd had too much to drink. "And who might you be?"

No doubt he knew.

Charles Mitchell drew himself up to an impressive height even though he was sitting down. His torso alone could proclaim he was the great man. "I am Charles A. Mitchell of Detroit, Michigan, in the United States of America. It was my son who was nearly killed today."

"And you are the owner of the vehicle?"

"In point of fact, I have given the vehicle as a gift to the Wimborne family."

"And a very nice automobile it is, sir. You drove it through the village today, caused quite a stir it did. My wife burned the toast running out to stare over the fence at the fancy sedan going by. It's been the talk of the town."

He sounded almost sarcastic as he related the effect on the village.

Lord Wimborne, who'd been listening intently, said, "Sergeant Kelston, we believe the brake cable was cut and the car sabotaged. Are you perchance suggesting that someone in the village might have done this?"

The sergeant narrowed his gaze as he looked down at the man in the wheelchair. "I'm not saying anything, sir. I'm merely gathering facts. However, it occurs to me that not everyone in the village might appreciate seeing so much wealth pass through their midst. Some of them are having a hard time. Crops haven't been so good this year. A lot of men didn't come back from the war, leaving hardship. I don't say we harbor radicals, mind, but there's grumblings."

Charles A. Mitchell looked like he might explode. "You're saying some lout from the village deliberately sabotaged my beautiful car?"

"As I said, sir, I'm merely gathering facts. Now"—he turned to Reginald—"I'm guessing, sir, being as I'm an investigator, that you must be the man who suffered the accident."

Reginald Mitchell chuckled at the heavy humor and said yes, he was. Sergeant Kelston poised pencil over paper. "I'd like you to go through exactly what happened, step by step, for me."

Reginald obligingly went through a recital of how his father had taken first the Wimbornes and then some of their house-guests for a drive, which the sergeant clearly already knew, and then everyone had lunch, after which he'd taken the car out to pick up a package from the station. The sergeant took very few notes, mainly listening, watching his subject's face carefully. At the end of the recital he said, "And you announced your intention to go to the station in this very room?"

"Yes."

He glanced around the room. "And every one of these people heard you?"

"Yes. But good God, man, you can't be suggesting—"

"Mr. Mitchell," the sergeant interrupted, "do you have any enemies?"

FOURTEEN

There was a slight pause and then Charles A. Mitchell exploded.

"What!" he shouted, getting to his feet and pointing a stubby finger at the sergeant. "Of course, my son doesn't have any enemies. Why would he? Anyway, this isn't even his country. I think you solved the case yourself, my man. It's clearly disenfranchised locals who are jealous that such a beautiful vehicle should be in their midst. Perhaps they're anarchists or people who don't believe in aristocracy. If anyone has enemies here, it's likely to be the Wimbornes."

"My dear," Mildred Mitchell said in a soothing tone. "I'm sure the Wimbornes don't have enemies any more than Reggie does."

Realizing perhaps how insulting he'd been to his hosts, Mitchell spluttered, "Well, somebody cut the brake cable and my son could have been killed. I insist you get to the bottom of this."

"That is why I'm here, sir," Sergeant Kelston said impatiently. "Now, if you'd let me continue my inquiries, perhaps I can find the culprit."

Charles Mitchell glared at him but grudgingly sat down and took another slurp of whiskey.

The sergeant asked a few more questions and wanted to know where everyone had been after Reggie had announced his intention to go to the station in the car.

He began with Lord Wimborne, and Abby thought that the social hierarchy seemed to matter to Sergeant Kelston. His Lordship had been in his room. He appeared extremely uncomfortable as he explained he did exercises every day with the help of his valet.

Lady Wimborne had been in the garden.

Reggie said, "Well, Cressie and Mademoiselle Chanel were together having a dress fitting. I know, because I invited Cressida to come with me on the drive and she couldn't."

"You never said that before, sir."

Charles Mitchell pointed that stubby finger again, this time from his seated position. "Don't you go asking if she's got any enemies. I've never heard such rubbish in my life. Beautiful young woman like that? Who would have it in for her?"

"Perhaps it's you, sir, who has the enemies," the sergeant suggested. "You're a very wealthy man, and powerful and American. Could there be enemies of yours who are trying to get at you through your son?"

"I think this man is a fantasist," Charles Mitchell announced. Abby noticed that he slurred the word fantasist. "Sure, I've got enemies, and plenty of them, but if they want to get back at me they do it through commerce. Industrial espionage, that's what I worry about, not some fool cutting my brake cable."

There was an uneasy silence after this. Then Inspector Deschamps said in his calm way, "If this is an attempted murder investigation, Sergeant, I wonder if Scotland Yard should be called in?"

"That's the first sensible thing I've heard this evening,"

huffed Mitchell. "Why didn't I think of that? Scotland Yard must be called in—"

"Pa, please," Reginald said. He was looking pale and Abby suspected his head was paining him. "It was probably just a prank. Apart from a sore head and a bit of bodywork to be done on the car, we shouldn't let this get in the way of our week of wedding festivities."

Lady Wimborne smiled at him as though, in her opinion, that was the most sensible thing that had been said all evening.

The sergeant asked Abby to recite her movements and describe finding the damaged vehicle and Reggie.

When she'd finished, Lord Wimborne glanced around. "It's been a trying day for all of us. May I suggest, Sergeant, that you continue your inquiries tomorrow?"

"And make sure you're here bright and early," Charles Mitchell insisted.

With great dignity and not a little pride, the sergeant said, "I'm involved in a murder investigation at the moment, sir, and I'm afraid that takes priority."

Before Charles Mitchell could explode again, Lady Wimborne exclaimed, "Oh, yes, poor Gladys Trotter. Do the police have any idea who did it yet, Sergeant?"

"It's a great tragedy, indeed, Your Ladyship," the sergeant agreed. "We are following up every lead, please be assured of that."

"Murdered with her own silk stocking, I read," Oliver Platt spoke up.

"That's right, sir. We have traced the stocking in question. It was purchased locally."

"In Darrington?" Lady Wimborne sounded quite shocked.

"In Frome, Your Ladyship. There is no establishment in Darrington where one could purchase silk stockings."

"Of course. I see. How dreadful to think it could be someone who knew her here."

"We'll see you as soon as is convenient then, Sergeant," Lord Wimborne said, ending a conversation that was clearly uncomfortable.

The police officer put away his notepad. "Very well. I will be back tomorrow, sir. An unpleasant business. A very unpleasant business." And then he left the room.

Charles Mitchell was growing quite red in the face. "I demand that Scotland Yard be brought in. I can't have my family in danger."

Lord Wimborne said, "Yes. I fear you're correct. It grieves me to think that anyone here in this house, employed on the estate or even in the village would do such a thing. But someone obviously did." He turned to Cressida and said, "I'm terribly sorry, my dear. This isn't what you would have chosen on your wedding week, but above all I must ensure your safety. You could have been in that car."

His voice held strong but there was a note at the end when the tone went suddenly soft. And Lady Wimborne cried out, "Please, I can hardly bear to think about it. You must know people at the Yard?" she said to her husband.

"I expect it's our friend here, Henri, who has the most current association with the Yard."

"I can certainly make a call and suggest they send someone to investigate."

Cressida turned to her fiancé. "Poor Reggie. You're looking wretchedly pale. Come on, my dear, let me help you upstairs. You're not well enough to dine with us. I shall bring you a tray myself. It will be like a picnic."

"No, Cressie," he said. "I'm too heavy for you. Call my man. Badger can take care of me."

She smiled at him. "If I'm to be your wife, you must become accustomed to me telling you what to do." There was gentle teasing in the tone and he smiled adoringly at her.

"You see that, Pa? I'm being henpecked already."

The jokiness had the desired effect and Charles Mitchell subsided into a weak grin. "Never mind that—none of your lip. You get up those stairs with Cressie and do as you're told."

But it was Oliver who stood and helped his friend to his feet, and the three of them headed toward the door.

Once they'd left, Coco Chanel remarked, "This is all so very exciting. I had planned to go to London tomorrow but I think I shall stay. This is the most thrilling drama."

Thrilling and possibly deadly, Abigail thought.

After a subdued dinner, with both Reggie and Cressida missing, the party returned to the library. During dinner, conversation had been kept deliberately light, but once they were settled in the library afterwards, Henri said to Lord Wimborne, "The sergeant's questions were inept, perhaps, and badly put, but could there be any truth in it? Have there been any stirrings of unrest on the estate or in the village?"

Lord Wimborne looked suddenly much older. "The world's changing so rapidly, Henri, I can barely keep up. I fear that the world I grew up in and fought a war for, lost my legs for, is on its way out." He let out a sigh, then rallied himself. "Oh, perhaps it's not all bad. It allows young women like Abigail here to seek employment just as though she were a man. And women are smoking and driving and I don't know what. But there's always a certain amount of unrest, particularly among the young men. I think some of them do want the old guard gone. They see people like me as relics, taking up space, contributing nothing. I was brought up to believe I had a duty to my people and to the land, and an obligation to hold the estate so that I could pass it on to my son, and he to his sons, but the truth is we're barely hanging on as it is. Once I'm gone, the death duties will cripple the family. I'm not sure I've got much of anything to leave Peter but my name. So, do I think it's possible that locals may have come at us in this unorthodox manner? Yes, in fact I do. Not that I could name one man whom I would suspect. I've known most of these people and their families all my life."

"There are some new people moving into the area," Lady Wimborne pointed out in her gentle manner. "People who didn't grow up here and have never known our ways. They're bitter after the war. Their prospects aren't as good as one would hope. Perhaps it was one of them?"

"Father, none of this is your fault," Peter said in a reassuring tone. "You've been an excellent steward for the land and you've cared about the people who live here. I don't care what happens, I intend to follow in your footsteps as best I can." And then he offered up a wry grin. "Even if it means I have to marry an heiress to do it."

That lightened the mood and even Lord Wimborne managed a small smile. "You'll have to learn to like women more than your fishing rod and your hunting rifle then," he said.

Cressida returned saying Badger was preparing Reggie for bed. Coco Chanel patted her on the hand and then disappeared.

A few minutes later, Mademoiselle Chanel returned looking like one of her own advertisements in her evening dress, her hair in classic waves. In her hand was a bottle of Chanel No. 5.

Abby immediately recognized the square bottle with its light golden perfume inside. It might be a lovely scent, but since her stepmother had sprayed herself top to toe in the stuff, she always associated the scent with the woman who'd destroyed her family.

With her mischievous smile, Coco walked over to Cressida Wimborne as she sat chatting quietly to her mother.

"*Mignonne*, here is a little present from me to you. To cheer you on this gloomy evening. My signature fragrance. When you go to New York, I want all the other young ladies and all the young men to say, 'What is that beautiful perfume you are wearing?' and you can tell them you wear Chanel No. 5."

Cressida accepted the gift looking slightly alarmed. And Charles A. Mitchell burst out laughing.

"Miss Chanel, I admire you. I admire your business acumen and your nose for opportunities." And then he rose out of his chair and stuck his hand out, shaking Chanel's slim hand heartily. "And I'll make sure my daughter-in-law wears your perfume. You see if I don't."

Her sharp eyes flickered, resenting the insinuation that Cressida would need to be convinced to wear her signature fragrance. Then the designer came over and sat beside Abby. "I do not wish to make a fuss, but you know you have only to ask and I will happily gift you my fragrance as well."

Abby said, "As grateful as I am, I'm already wearing perfume."

The woman beside her nodded, her nostrils quivering slightly. "Of course, I have an excellent nose. Your perfume hasn't the complexity of my scent, because your *parfumier* sticks to a strong, single note. A classic perfume, but not mine."

Since Vivian's boss had also hoped that Abby would be inundated by requests to know what she was wearing, she said, "No. This scent is called Paris Evening. It's by Maison Chapelle on the Champs-Élysées."

Coco didn't seem upset by Abby's steadfast refusal to wear her perfume. She glanced over her outfit and said, "You also dress very well. Give Paul Joubert my compliments. The beaded decoration on your hem is quite inspired."

She knew that such a compliment could only be genuine. Coco had such an amazing eye that she recognized a fellow couture genius when she saw one. She added, with a rueful smile, "However, it would make me very happy if you would at least let me offer you some of my sportswear. Paul Joubert doesn't do that nearly as well as I do, my dear."

That might or might not be true, but Abby wasn't going to turn her back even the slightest bit on the man who had given her so much. She said, "Paul Joubert would have to agree first."

Coco Chanel made a noise that sounded like "Pah" and said, "And that he will never do. He, like me, is an *egoiste*."

She had to laugh. "But, he's a talented one. As are you."

Since they were sitting side by side, Abby took the opportunity to interview Coco Chanel about the gown she was designing. Coco obligingly raved about the beauty of Cressida Wimborne, her beautiful fair complexion, "So utterly English." And then, in great detail, she described her inspiration for the dress.

Lady Wimborne rose and said, "I think young Reggie isn't the only one who's worn out from the excitement today. If you'll excuse us, I'll settle my husband for bed now."

That was the sign for the party to break up. Everyone began to get to their feet, it had indeed been a long day.

Coco was a savvy and very successful businesswoman who'd been featured often in the papers and magazines, so she knew exactly how to talk to a reporter. It should have been a gift to Abby, and it was, but she felt irritable as she bashed out her article on the typewriter in her room. She was talking about covered buttons and silk chemises when she wanted to be talking about political unrest and attempted murder.

She was the only reporter on the scene of a crime and she'd been told to sit on her scoop.

Instead of writing about car crashes and vandalism, Abby wrote about silk and pearls. When she'd finished she pulled the typing paper out of the machine and read over her work.

Coco Chanel Designs Bridal Gown for Wedding of the Year
Union of Elegance and Innovation

"To be a bride is a beautiful thing, and to design the gown for a wedding is a great honor," the legendary designer Coco Chanel said. Miss Chanel has created an original gown for the Honorable Cressida Wimborne, the English debutante soon to marry Reginald Mitchell, son of American car king Charles A. Mitchell.

The dress, crafted in the finest silk, features a demure bateau neckline and a fluid, straight-line cut that redefines traditional bridal wear. "A young woman does not want to be restricted on her wedding day," the couture designer said. "She wants to have the freedom to move and express herself."

Abby continued on in this vein for five hundred words, feeling like the worst kind of hack.

However, as she lost herself in describing the fine details of bridal gowns and couture, the terrible sound of the Mitchell 925 crash which had taken up residency in her head began to subside.

The next morning a current of unease permeated the house. Abby felt it even over the breakfast cups, looking around wondering if someone here, either one of the servants or even worse one of the people sitting around this very table, had tried to harm Reggie or perhaps Charles Mitchell through damaging his car and his son.

The day's schedule included rabbit shooting as it was too early in the season for game birds and clearly Charles Mitchell wanted to take part in a proper British shoot. So Peter had suggested they shoot the rabbits that ravaged the crops. Viv had shuddered when she heard about the day's regimen, but Abby had grown up near enough to the country to accept that an overabundance of rabbits required a cull. Cressie was country born and used to the practice and Coco Chanel thought she might take part if time permitted. She was a keen hunter and fisher.

Lord Wimborne promised them fishing after lunch. "There's excellent sport fishing to be had on the river that traverses our land. Brown trout make a wily opponent." He sounded much better than he had the night before and quite enthused. As though he caught her unasked question, he said, "I love to fish. Been doing it since I was a boy. Naturally, I need help these days, but it's something I can still manage, at any rate."

The men arrived for breakfast already wearing hunting gear. Reggie was the last to arrive, but he wore a navy-blue sweater with his university crest on it over woolen slacks.

Charles Mitchell was arguing the merits of his Remington rifle with Peter Wimborne, who preferred his Enfield. Lord Wimborne nodded. "We all shoot with the Enfield at Darrington. Used them in the war." As though it were a patriotic act to take them out for sport.

Charles Mitchell glanced at his son. "Not hunting rabbits, Reggie?"

"I've still got a wretched headache. Think I'll save my strength for the fishing later. You know I'm a much better angler than a shot."

"Nonsense, boy. You're an excellent shot. I taught you myself."

Oliver laughed then and turned to his friend. "Remember, Reggie? He'd reward whichever of us hit the most soda bottles with a silver dollar. We were awfully competitive."

Charles Mitchell grinned. "For the cost of a few silver dollars, I turned you both into fine marksmen."

Lady Wimborne spoke up. "I think you're very wise to stay away from shooting this morning, Reginald. Those guns are so loud, my dear, they give me a headache. With you still recovering from concussion, you really ought to rest."

"Oh, I shan't do that," he said. "I'll walk out to take a look at the Mitchell 925. Have the police finished with it yet?"

"I believe so," Lord Wimborne said.

"Then we ought to get somebody to fix that brake cable, otherwise it's no use at all."

Charles Mitchell looked up from his bacon and eggs. "I've got one of my men flying over. He'll fix it all right and tight."

"Flying over?" Lord Wimborne said the words as though he suspected whoever was coming would flap their wings to cross the Atlantic. "But we've perfectly good car mechanics here."

Charles Mitchell shook his head. "Wouldn't let one of the local boys touch my pride and joy. No offense, Alistair, but she was designed and built by my people. I want her repaired by someone who knows her as well as you know this manor house of yours." He put down his knife and fork. "Once we've gone, naturally you'll use your local mechanics for maintenance and so forth, but I want that car as good as new before I leave here. I wouldn't feel right in myself if I didn't."

"I see," Lord Wimborne replied. "Very generous of you."

"Not at all. We're family now. Or we will be, once the knot is tied. I hope I know how to look after my family."

"Indeed," Lord Wimborne said faintly.

Charles Mitchell spoke to Reggie with approval. "But, yes, good idea, son. See that the Mitchell 925 is properly stored and that the local constabulary haven't made a mess of her."

"I'll do that, Pa. I warn you, though, that when I'm back in the pink of health, I shall expect to go out shooting."

"Wait until the fall," Peter said. "That's when the good shooting begins. Pheasant, grouse—we'll keep you busy, don't you worry." He was more animated than Abby had seen him since she'd arrived. She could see clearly that this was what Peter lived for: working the land, and hunting and fishing.

"Rabbits are good sport and they must be culled. The mess they make of the crops is shocking."

None of the ladies were going on the hunt. Even Coco Chanel had declined, saying, "I shall join you fishing, and perhaps I shall catch enough for dinner." Everyone laughed politely.

Ned Corcoran came into the breakfast room at that moment, declined coffee, and said he'd take whoever was shooting to the gun room to get them kitted out.

Ned pushed Lord Wimborne's wheelchair and the shooting party left the breakfast room.

"If you two are both free, I'd like to interview you for an article about your upcoming wedding," Abby said quietly to Cressida and Reggie.

Reggie looked humorously at the recently closed door. "I should have escaped when I could!" But at Cressida's nudge, he submitted to be interviewed.

Jerry the footman Vivian was so keen on arrived to check the buffet and see if anything else was wanted. On seeing him, Lady Wimborne said, "Ah, Jerry. How is your mother?"

"She's much better, thank you, Your Ladyship."

Abby was impressed that Lady Wimborne took such an interest in her servants' lives as well as the people in the village. "I'm very pleased to hear it. No doubt your visit helped immensely."

"I believe it did, Your Ladyship."

"Whereabouts in Devon is your family located?"

"Near Bideford, Your Ladyship."

She nodded graciously, making Abby think she'd either never been to Bideford or could think of nothing nice to say about the place.

Abby felt as though she'd sat on a pin, she jumped so in her seat. Jerry left the room and she debated following him, but her first priority was Vivian.

She asked the affianced couple to meet her in the library in thirty minutes and then dashed upstairs. As she'd hoped, Vivian was checking over her outfit for that evening. When Abby burst into the room she jumped. "Abby, whatever is the matter? You startled me. Heavens, you look quite wild."

"Viv, I don't want you to be alone with Jerry any more."

"What are you talking about? I like him. Has he said something to offend you? I know he can be a bit cheeky, but he doesn't mean anything by it," Vivian responded, looking startled and hurt.

"No. It's not that. Oh, I've been such a fool. Remember when we first arrived and Jerry arrived on the same train as us?"

"Well, I never saw him, but that's what you said, sure."

"It was definitely him on our train and, when I asked him, he said he'd been visiting his family as his mother was sick."

"Yes, I do recall that."

"Viv, I just heard Lady Wimborne ask how his mother is and they talked about where he's from. His family lives in Devon."

"Do they?" Viv asked, clearly confused.

"Vivian, Devon is in the opposite direction. Jerry would not have been on our train if he'd been visiting his mother. He lied to Lady Wimborne and he lied to us."

"Well, maybe he had a good reason," Viv offered, but she did look perturbed.

"There's more." Abby pushed her hand through her hair. "A police sergeant was here last night asking questions about the car accident and Lady Wimborne asked how the murder investigation was going. Turns out the silk stocking that killed Gladys Trotter was purchased in Frome. That's the nearest town to Darrington where a local person could buy lady's undergarments."

Viv sat on Abby's bed. It wasn't as though she'd meant to, more that she dropped down when her legs gave out. "Abigail Dixon. You cannot seriously suspect Jerry of murdering Gladys Trotter?"

Abby paced to the window and back. "I don't know. There's no evidence—but, Viv, he was on the train from London, and she was killed near Paddington station. You said yourself that we could have walked right past the murderer. He knew Gladys, and he said she stopped being friendly with him. Maybe he was angry."

"So he went to Frome and bought her silk stockings?" Viv sounded somewhat scornful of Abby's half-baked theory.

"No. He would have bought her the silk stockings before. I wonder if he even bought her that red dress."

"No. She showed off the dress after. When they weren't so friendly anymore."

"Gosh, Viv. I'm not saying he killed her, but it's possible. She sounds like the kind of girl who liked to get presents from men. Maybe he bought her some silk stockings. And then she threw him over."

"But why kill her in London? Why not strangle her here?"

"Because it was too close to home. London's big and anonymous. She told everyone she was going there, so he could have followed her. Maybe he was in love with Gladys and wanted her back. But it all went wrong and he killed her."

"That sounds like the plot of one of those lurid cheap paperbacks!" Viv protested. "Jerry's nice, Abby. He wouldn't do that."

"Maybe not, and I have absolutely no evidence, but please, Viv. Promise me you'll be careful. Don't go anywhere alone with him." She sat on the bed and hugged her friend. "I can't manage my buttons without you."

It was enough to pull the tense look off Vivian's face and replace it with a half-hearted grin.

Abby knew Viv might not like what she'd heard, but at least she'd be careful around Jerry.

. . .

Abby wasn't in the mood for talking about romance when she walked into the library to interview Reggie and Cressida. Still, she got out her notepad and pencil. She sat in a leather armchair and the engaged couple settled side by side on the sofa opposite. "Let's start at the beginning. Tell me how you met."

Reggie turned his head and regarded Cressida. He gave a little laugh and said, "It seems such a long time I've known you, it's hard to remember exactly."

Cressida leaned her shoulder into his. "Oh, I remember it perfectly. You were at Oxford and I'd come up for a party. We talked for ever such a long time, and then you took me out punting the next day, and to my surprise you'd had your man prepare a picnic." She turned to Abby and said, "It was awfully romantic. There was a plaid blanket and a proper hamper with champagne and ham and cheese and bread and strawberries. Most delightful."

Reggie looked a bit embarrassed but said, "My father always told me if you want to impress a girl, go big."

Cressida laughed and waved her engagement finger where an enormous diamond sparkled. "You can see he followed his father's advice." She was smiling, but was there a slight edge of sarcasm? Did she consider the blinding diamond ring to be vulgar? The moment passed so quickly Abby couldn't be sure. She heard about their courtship, how he had pursued her and then invited her to Detroit for Christmas to meet his family.

"I had to make a transatlantic call to Lord Wimborne to ask permission for his daughter's hand, which I'm happy to say he gave. I'd had the ring specially designed by Cartier so I'd have everything in place. And then on Christmas Eve I popped the question." He turned to his bride-to-be and said, "You were awfully surprised."

She gazed down at her diamond ring and said, "I was. Of course, everyone in Reggie's family knew, including the servants, so when we came back from our walk there was a big party to celebrate."

"Not a party, Cressie," Reggie argued. "It was just that Pa was so pleased he invited a few of his closest family and friends to share the good news with us." He held her hand in his and said, "Getting Cressie to agree to marry me was the best Christmas present I've ever had."

He smiled at her and she ducked her head, pinkening slightly. Abby resolved to mention that in her article. It was the kind of detail that Walter Strutt clearly wanted. Unlike the facts of Reggie nearly being killed only days before his wedding. No, he wanted to know what kind of flowers Cressida would be carrying in her bouquet. It was most annoying, here was Abby, sitting on quite the scoop, and unable to do her job as a reporter and report the news.

"It's a good thing Cressida said yes," Abby said, thinking how humiliating it would have been to return from the walk to a party if he'd been turned down.

Reggie looked half stunned by the remark then laughed. "You know, I never even thought of that." He reached for Cressie's hand. "It's a good thing you said yes. But you had to know I was mad about you, after all those bouquets I had delivered to Darrington Manor. All the love letters I wrote to you."

"I suppose I did."

"I don't think you'd have come to meet the family if you weren't serious too," he continued.

"No. I suppose not," Cressida said softly.

There was a short pause.

"I understand that after the wedding you'll be moving to America. How does that feel, Cressida? To travel so far from your family?"

For just a second Abby witnessed an expression of bleak despair in Cressida's eyes, and then she blinked and said, "Obviously, it will take some getting used to. I'll miss my family and my friends, and my home."

Reggie jumped in. "But you'll have new family and new friends. And a new home. The builders are hard at work on a mansion for us. You'll be the mistress of your own home with your own servants, and one day, God willing, your own family. We won't even live in Detroit. We'll be in New York and you'll be the toast of the town," he promised her. "And we'll come back and visit."

To Abby's surprise, Cressida's eyes filled with tears, which she blinked rapidly away. "I know. It's just that I'm a little worried I'll be homesick."

Reggie patted her hand. "I'll be there. We'll be together and you'll be fine."

His patronizing tone was slightly grating to Abby's ears, but Cressida just nodded and said, "I'm sure you're right."

Abby gave her a moment to compose herself, then she said, "The rest of the questions I'm afraid I have to ask Cressida alone. Details of the dress and so on."

"Then I'll take advantage of the time to change my clothes," Reggie said. "I hope to be able to join you for fishing this afternoon." He leaned over and kissed Cressida on the cheek. "See you at lunch, darling."

He left the room and then Cressida settled down once more to share details of her bridesmaids and the flowers and a few details about the dress. The photographer would of course take photographs of the happy couple, but in the meantime Coco Chanel was providing a sketch of her design to be published in the newspaper. And Reggie Mitchell was under strict instructions not to read the *Chicago International Post* so he couldn't accidentally glimpse so much as a sketch of Cressida's gown before the wedding. When so ordered, he'd waved his hands in the air and said, "I've never read that paper in my life, I promise."

While the interview was fresh in her mind, Abby decided to type up the article and send it by wire to Walter Strutt. As she headed upstairs to her bedroom, it struck her how was quiet it was. The only person in sight was a maid carrying a stack of fresh towels, who curtseyed as she went past. "Good morning," Abby greeted her cheerfully.

"Morning, miss."

Her room was tidied, the bed made. Then she settled down at the small table by the window where her typewriter sat waiting. Abby glanced out of the window to a blustery day and, as though the steel gray clouds gave her inspiration, she began to type.

FIFTEEN

There were times when a journalist wrote with courage and passion about a story she was burning to tell. And there were times when a journalist did what she was told if she wanted to keep her job.

Transatlantic Ties Tighten with the Union of Miss Cressida Wimborne to American Industrialist Heir Reginald Mitchell

Somerset, April 24 1925 — In a splendid affair that promises to blend traditional British aristocracy with the dazzling modernity of American industry, the upcoming nuptials of the Honorable Cressida Wimborne and Mr. Reginald Mitchell, Esq. are the talk of both continents.

She paused, read over what she'd written. Her journalism professor would be horrified by such flowery prose but Abby had her orders. She sighed, checked her notes and soon the clack of the typewriter keys filled the air once more.

The Honorable Cressida Wimborne, 20, the graceful and

accomplished daughter of the esteemed Lord and Lady
Wimborne of Darrington Manor, is set to exchange vows with
Mr. Mitchell (25), the dashing son of Mr. Charles A. Mitchell,
universally known as the "Car King of Detroit," in what is antic-
ipated to be one of the most splendid events of the season.

Abby had intended to mention the creation of the Mitchell
925 and the excitement of the Wimborne family when the automobile was presented to them as a gift by the car king himself,
but due to the unfortunate crash and subsequent discovery of
the vandalism of said car, she left that out of her article.

The ceremony will be held at the historic St. George's Chapel
on the Darrington Manor property. St. George's has witnessed
three hundred years of Wimborne nuptials, but Mr. Mitchell
will be the first American to exchange vows in the
picturesque Georgian chapel. The wedding promises an
exquisite blend of old-world charm and contemporary
elegance. Esteemed guests, including nobility, diplomats, and
luminaries from the world of business and the arts, are
expected to grace the occasion. Miss Coco Chanel has
designed the bridal gown and will lend her stylish presence to
the wedding.

Abby had a list of dignitaries who were expected but had
decided to wait until the wedding day to mention who'd actually turned up.

Miss Wimborne, known for her refined beauty and sharp wit, is
an alumna of the prestigious Cheltenham Ladies' College and
has been a radiant presence in the social scenes of London and
Paris. Her humanitarian work, particularly with war orphans,
has garnered admiration and respect far beyond the elite circles
of British society.

She reread the paragraph and deleted "and sharp wit." Cressie had many good qualities but no one but her godmother had referred to her wit. It was Mrs. Mitchell who'd told Abby about Cressie's charitable work and Lady Wimborne who'd confirmed the fact, though she did so hesitantly. "It's really nothing extraordinary, you know. One has a duty to look after the people of the parish, including the war orphans."

Still, knowing how much Walter Strutt would expect this kind of gushing, Abby left the rest of the paragraph as it was. She continued in the same vein:

Mr. Mitchell, who attended Oxford University, exemplifies the ambitious spirit of the New World. He met his bride-to-be at Oxford and their first date was a punting expedition complete with a proper English picnic. "It was so romantic," Cressida said, gazing at her fiancé with a slight blush tinging her cheeks.

The match, said to be a love match with a fairy-tale twist, also signifies a strengthening of transatlantic ties. According to the groom's father, Charles A. Mitchell, the union is "a harmonious blend of tradition and progress, with Miss Wimborne bringing her ancestral heritage and Reginald infusing the dynamism of American enterprise."

Abby added Charles's quote with a cynical curl to her lip. She knew how much the industrialist would enjoy reading his own words in the newspaper. She stood up to take a break and stretched her arms over her head, enjoying the view out of her window. She saw Reginald Mitchell walk along the path that led to the outbuilding where the Mitchell 925 was being stored. She recalled him saying he'd visit the automobile and only hoped he found it none the worse for having been looked over by the local police. He was dressed for sport in an eye-catching jacket of green tweed with a distinctive plaid design. As he walked, she stiffened slightly, recognizing the figure walking toward him. The tight black curls under the flat cap had to belong to George Smith. Would the pugnacious Smith cause trouble? But even as she had the thought, the two men passed each other and Smith raised his cap, while Reggie nodded briefly and walked on. At least in front of the manor house, the two men remembered their manners. She wondered briefly who the young woman in the pub had been. She hoped for Cressida's sake that Reggie was only there so Oliver could meet local girls. With a sigh, she went back to her typewriter.

The couple plan to reside in New York, where they will undoubtedly be at the forefront of social and philanthropic endeavors. As they embark on this exciting new chapter, the eyes of society on both sides of the Atlantic eagerly await the dawning of this illustrious union.

The sound of voices and laughter caused Abby to glance out of the window and she saw the shooting party returning. Ned Corcoran held his rifle under one arm while pushing Lord Wimborne's wheelchair. His Lordship was looking much better after his excursion, his own gun settled across his lap. Oliver and Charles Mitchell were deep in conversation. Peter brought up the rear, with Henri a tall figure by his side and a collie following at their heels.

Reggie came toward them, and joined the group of men heading toward the manor house.

If they were back, lunch would soon be served. Abby decided her article was quite long enough and signed off: *Reporting by Abigail Dixon.* She was tempted to add: *Special correspondent*, but decided to let Walter Strutt give her whatever special title he chose, or none at all.

Getting up from her typewriter, she glimpsed Jerry the footman crossing the grass and wondered how she could find out more about him, his relationship with Gladys Trotter and his movements in London. She'd been tempted to ask Adams about him, but immediately stopped herself. Adams did not gossip with the guests and what could he really tell her?

Viv might be able to glean more from the other servants, but she was clearly smitten with the young man and not inclined to snoop on him. Abby decided to lay her concerns before Henri. He would be the best person to advise her.

With that decision made, she went down for lunch.

The atmosphere as the men came in was joyous. They had obviously enjoyed their morning and Lord Wimborne informed his wife there'd be plenty of rabbits in stewpots in the village that evening. After the ominous atmosphere of the morning it was good to see the ease and camaraderie among the hunting party.

Reggie came in, his head bent, listening to something Oliver was saying to him. Then he laughed, clapping his friend on the back.

"Come and sit down wherever you like," Lady Wimborne said. "There's no formality at luncheon."

Reggie held a chair for Cressida to sit and then reached for his own. As he did, he stumbled and had to hold on to the back of his chair with both hands. His eyes were closed and Abby felt like jumping up to steady him, as he was clearly fighting a spell of dizziness.

Abby suspected he'd tired himself out this morning and was far from well enough for a fishing expedition. She kept her opinion to herself, but his fiancée didn't.

"Reggie, you can't possibly go fishing in your condition."

"Nonsense, my dear," he said with an attempt at a jaunty smile. "I'm looking forward to it."

Lady Wimborne added her voice to her daughter's, suggesting he'd be much wiser to stay home and rest.

Charles Mitchell glanced from his son to Lady Wimborne

and cast his vote with Her Ladyship. "She's right, son. I admire your pluck, and in a day or two you'll be right as rain. But we don't want to risk you getting worse right before your wedding."

Reggie wasn't as pale as he had been yesterday and the bandage had been replaced by a sticking plaster. However, he was clearly far from recovered. He argued that he was well enough to fish but, between his fiancée, his mother-in-law-to-be and his father, he was outnumbered and acknowledged the fact. Holding his hands up, he said, "All right. I give in. I'll be a very good boy and rest this afternoon."

When they rose from the table Charles Mitchell said to Oliver, "What have you done to your jacket, boy? There's a great tear in your pocket. Whatever will Lord Wimborne think of you, going fishing in that disreputable thing?"

Oliver looked down at his jacket, surprised, "I have no idea how that happened. Well, I shall manage."

Reggie said, "I'm not going fishing. You can borrow mine."

Oliver looked reluctant but when Charles Mitchell said, "I don't want the locals thinking I don't pay you enough to afford a decent sporting jacket," he subsided and accepted his friend's jacket. It was a striking design of green tweed with a brown leather belt and brown leather patches on the pockets. It looked more like something one might see in an advertisement for men's sporting fashion than something one would expect to see out in the wild, but perhaps that was unkind. Reggie must have bought the coat specially for this trip.

Oliver slipped off his own coat and put on Reggie's. They were similar in build so it fit perfectly. "This is too fine to wear trout fishing. I'm sure they'll see it and swim away," he joked.

"It needs breaking in," Coco Chanel stated. Then she looked critically at Oliver. "But it is very well on you. The fabric brings out the green in your eyes."

This did not seem to be great news to Oliver, who looked longingly at his own shabby tweed with the torn pocket.

Reginald got up slowly, holding his chair again to steady himself. Oliver was quick to move to his side. He had his own coat draped over his arm. "Come on, old sport. I'll see you to your room," he said.

"I hate to be so weak, it's just this devilish headache." He glanced at Cressida. "Can you make sure nobody comes into my room to dust or anything. I didn't have a very good night. I'll try to get an hour's sleep."

"Of course. I'll make sure you're not disturbed."

When they'd left the room, his mother wondered aloud whether the doctor should be called in again.

She looked to Charles as she said this and he shook his head. "A concussion gives a man a headache. No point you all cosseting him. Leave him alone to rest. It's a shame he's not well enough for fishing, but I can tell you, I'm looking forward to it."

Lord Wimborne looked tired but happy. "I doubt you'll find better fishing in this country, Charles, but I'm curious to see how the sport compares with what you get in America. No doubt the rivers and streams are teeming with fish the like of which we've never seen."

Charles Mitchell chuckled at that. "We've got fine fishing, Alistair, I won't pretend otherwise, but I'm sure there's excellent sport to be had here. I look forward to experiencing it myself. Yes, it's rare for me to take a day off from work, but it does me good."

Abby was mildly tempted to join the fishing party but had to file her story first. Heaven help her if the riveting story about the upcoming nuptials of Miss Cressida Wimborne and Reginald Mitchell didn't make that evening's edition of the *Chicago International Post*.

Since Ned was busy taking Lord Wimborne fishing, he wouldn't be able to drive her. Abby said she'd walk to the post office in the village to send her wire but, to her surprise, Cressida said she'd be happy to drive Abby.

They set off in the old Rolls-Royce and Abby soon relaxed, realizing that Cressida was an excellent driver. When she remarked on this, Cressie said, "Ned taught me to drive. With no chauffeur it seemed silly for the Rolls to be sitting gathering dust when I'm perfectly capable."

She rattled down the lane and, instinctively, both women turned to look at the tree still showing the recent impact of the Mitchell 925. "Ned's worried that tree will have to come down," Cressida said, then gasped and turned to Abby. "But please don't print that in the newspaper, or, indeed, mention it to anyone. I shouldn't have spoken."

Abby felt all the awkwardness of her position. She wasn't a real guest, though she was being treated like one, and it troubled her to think that the Wimborne family was being careful what they said around her. After assuring Cressida that she wouldn't repeat what she'd heard, she wondered again about the damage to the sedan. Clearly someone must have been disgruntled to have tampered with the brake line.

While she filed her story, Cressida picked up a hat she'd had made in the village and then the two returned to Darrington Manor.

"What would you like to do this afternoon?" Cressida asked, very much the society hostess.

"I thought I might go and observe the fishing expedition," said Abby.

"What a good idea. I'll change my clothes and come with you."

As Abby and Cressida walked down to check on the progress of the fishing, Cressida kept her conversation light and superficial, but Abby could feel there was tension beneath her words. "It was funny this morning, thinking back to when I met Reggie." Cressida gazed around her, taking in the view of green lawns and fields in the distance. "What a long time ago that seems."

There was a wistfulness in her tone, but Abby reminded herself that it was not her place to dig into whether Cressida was completely happy about her upcoming nuptials. Walter could not have made it more clear that Abby was here entirely to write glowing and positive articles about everything from the dress to the flowers to the couple and their respective sets of parents. No darkness could intrude, in spite of the fact that the groom-to-be had nearly died in a very suspicious automobile crash, and the dark circles she spied under Cressida Wimborne's eyes suggested worry and sleepless nights rather than the bliss of a young woman dreaming of her wedding day.

In spite of her best intentions not to interfere, after a moment she said gently, "I know it can be difficult to move to another country."

Cressida turned to her with a startled look on her face, almost as though she'd been thinking of something else. Then she faltered in her steps. "Of course, you've done that, haven't you? Only the opposite way, I suppose. You left your home in the United States and moved to Paris. Was it difficult for you?"

Abby thought back. It was the tragic events that had occurred in her home that had precipitated her move, not a new beginning with a new husband. Still, it hadn't been easy to start her life over in Paris and she didn't want to give Cressida a false idea of how easy a transcontinental move could be. "I think you have to balance the excitement of living somewhere new with the loss of what you leave behind," she said.

To her shock, Cressida's eyes filled with tears. She blinked them rapidly away. "I'm sorry, how silly of me." She turned her head and fumbled for a handkerchief. "It's just that everything I've ever known and loved is here. My parents, my brother, my home, my friends. In America it will all be so new and so different."

"I do understand. But I'm sure you'll be the toast of New York," Abby offered.

A brittle laugh stopped her from continuing. "I've no interest in being the toast of New York or anywhere else. I merely want a happy life with the man I love."

"Well, at least you'll have the man you love by your side. Surely that will make everything better."

There was a long pause and then Cressida said sadly, "Yes. Yes, of course."

Then, changing the subject and in a much brighter tone, she went on, "I do hope they've caught plenty of fish. I expect Cook is counting on them for our dinner. Oh, no doubt there will be lots of other delicacies, but she's quite well known for her way with brown trout."

As the path headed toward the river, they saw Lord Wimborne and Ned. Cressida's father was leaning forward and she could see the strain on the line as a fish pulled against the line. Ned was standing by with the net. Instinctively, both Abby and Cressida remained silent, watching the struggle until, with a shout of satisfaction, Lord Wimborne pulled a brown and glistening trout into the air. Ned was quick with the net. "Well done, Papa," Cressida said, warmly heading forward and patting her father on the shoulder.

"Cook will be pleased," said her father, turning in his chair. He was trying to look modest and not succeeding.

"It's at least a seven pounder, sir," Ned said excitedly.

Not wishing to witness the demise of the trout, Abby and Cressida carried on walking.

The path followed the river and it was pleasant enough, though rather gray. Charles Mitchell sat on a flat-topped boulder. A fishing line hung over the water but Mr. Mitchell seemed distracted. Perhaps he was dreaming up the next Mitchell motorcar.

They passed Coco Chanel, who was casting her rod with an expertise that impressed Abby. She reminded herself never to underestimate the designer.

Not wishing to disturb her, they continued on the path. Abby's attention was caught by a carpet of bluebells that seemed to glow blue beneath the trees. Cressida, no doubt accustomed to the sight, walked ahead.

Abby tried to think of the lines of the poem by Emily Brontë. It took her a moment and then she quoted softly: "The bluebell is the sweetest flower That waves in summer air; Its blossoms have the mightiest power To soothe my spirit's care."

She was thinking how true it was that nature could soothe a troubled spirit, and was thinking of Lord Wimborne so happy being outdoors on his land, when Cressida let out a terrible scream.

SIXTEEN

Abby jumped and clutched her chest in panic. She ran forward and followed Cressida's pointing finger as the woman beside her screamed, "Reggie. It's Reggie. My God. He's dead."

Sure enough, a man was floating face down, his tweed jacket billowing slightly.

"We don't know he's dead," Abby breathed as she strode into the stream, barely noticing the cold water creeping over her boots and up her calves. Cressida was moaning and sobbing, her arms wrapped around herself. Abby shouted, "Don't just stand there, come and help me."

She had the wild idea that perhaps he hadn't been in the water very long and might still be alive. Behind her, Cressida seemed unable to move.

The man bobbed up and down in the current, his arms floating over his head, and she was reminded of times as a child, swimming, when she'd opened her eyes while floating in the water to better see the undersea world below her. But something about the man's bearing told her he wasn't engrossed by the view underwater. His hair swayed almost as though a breeze were blowing through it.

Abby reached the man and as she did so immediately realized her efforts to save him were too late. He was utterly cold to the touch. Still, she turned him over, knowing that it would be easier in the water and she could more efficiently drag him to shore. She bent down, really soaking herself now, and managed to get her hands under him and flip him with the aid of the water.

Cressida was crying, "Reggie, Reggie, oh no, let it not be so."

But it wasn't Reggie. The man staring sightlessly up at her with a surprised expression on his face was Oliver.

She was bending over and grasping the poor dead man under his shoulders when she heard splashing behind her. Had Cressida finally come to her senses? But she glanced up to find Henri pushing her out of the way.

"I'll take him," he said urgently. He took her place and heaved the body up onto the bank. She followed, panting from her efforts and shivering as the cold grabbed at her. He glanced up and said, "There's nothing more to be done for him. You'd better see to Cressida."

Cressida was bent over now and looked as if she was about to faint.

Abby rushed to her side. She was shaking with both cold and shock, but Cressida was beside herself. Close to hysterics. Abby firmly placed her hands either side of Cressida's face and in a cool, commanding tone said, "Cressida, it's not Reggie who's dead. It's Oliver. Oliver."

Cressida seemed hardly able to take it in but her sobs subsided for a moment as she glanced up. "What are you talking about? I saw him." Tears were streaming down her face.

"No. You saw his coat and the back of his head. They changed coats this morning. Remember? Reggie's napping in his room. He's perfectly safe."

She took Cressida's hands in hers and then the woman pulled away. "You're so cold. And wet."

Behind her Henri said, "Take Cressida up to the house and get yourself warmed up and into dry clothes. And send Peter and Ned down here. Try to keep everyone else away."

She nodded, realizing that even though Henri must be as cold as she was, he would stay with the body and try to keep the others from seeing the terrible sight of one of the houseguests dead.

She put her arm around Cressida, wet though she was, and urged her, "Come along now, let's get you home."

Supporting the half-fainting girl kept her mind off her own misery as they made their slow way back to the house. She led Cressida to the back door, which was fortunately unlocked. As they entered, she called out for help. Lady Wimborne must have been close by for she ran in, took one look at her daughter and rushed forward with her arms out.

"Cressida, my darling, whatever's happened?"

"Oh, Mummy, it was so dreadful."

Then she spied Abby. "My dear, look at you, you're soaking wet. Whatever's happened?"

Through chattering teeth, Abby told her, "Cressida's in shock. She needs some hot tea, then she'll tell you all about it. But I must go upstairs and change into something dry."

"Yes, of course, my dear. I'll send your maid up to you."

By the time Abby got to her room the shivering had set in and she felt as though her very bones were shaking. It wasn't just the cold; it was the shock. She'd been able to hold herself together while Cressida had needed her, but now that Cressida had her mother to lean on Abby could process the horror of what she had witnessed.

The scene played like a film reel in front of her eyes. The river, the people fishing, and then the man floating face down in the river. When Cressida had screamed out Reggie's name, Abby had assumed it was Reggie lying dead and cold while sunlight danced off the surface of the water in a way that seemed obscene. She'd run into the river barely thinking what she was doing. There had always been a chance that he was alive, but she'd very quickly realized there was no life in the body bobbing on the surface.

When had she realized it wasn't Reggie?

For some reason, this seemed important to work out. Perhaps she instinctively knew that using her logical brain would help keep the emotions at bay.

Looking back, she believed she'd noted the physical differences quite soon. The hair was wrong, the shape of the head. Somehow she'd known before she'd reached the body that it wasn't Reggie. But not until she had turned him over and seen his face had she realized it was Oliver. Poor Oliver. He had been Reggie's best friend, helper, partner in business, and now he had died wearing his friend's coat.

She was trying to pull off her wet clothes with hands that were trembling and a body that was shaking and teeth that were chattering when Vivian rushed into the room saying, "Oh, my poor darling. Abby, I can't believe it! And look at you, you're shaking with cold." She scolded and chattered like a mother, and it was all that Abby could do not to subside into her arms weeping the way Cressida had subsided into Lady Wimborne's arms. But she was made of stronger stuff and was determined to remain as calm as possible. This was not the time to fall apart.

A man had died and she'd been the first to get to him. She was certain she'd be required to answer questions from the local police. Perhaps Sergeant Kelston would expect her to make a statement. No. She couldn't give in to her emotions. Not yet.

However, she let Vivian fuss over her and thankfully her friend and current lady's maid didn't require any answers or conversation, she just chattered on, casting frequent glances at Abby's face. Once she had Abby's clothes off, tossed into the corner in a sodden heap, she wrapped her friend in a robe.

She said, "I'm running you a bath right now. And you're getting straight into it to warm up. I've told them to send up tea. Maybe you'll want some whiskey or some brandy, I don't know, but you'll have your tea first. With lots of sugar in it. I've heard that's good for shock." She dashed into the bathroom and soon Abby could hear the sound of the faucets pouring water into the tub. Normally their pretend relationship of lady and her maid was restricted to Vivian laying out garments and helping her with buttons and zips and that right glove that was very difficult to get on once she already had her left glove on. But now all pretensions to modesty were gone.

As soon as the bath was run she helped Abby into the tub and then Abby sank deep and tilted her head back against the edge of the tub and waited for the warmth to seep into her cold, cold bones.

Vivian said, "Do you want me to sit with you? Or would you rather be alone?"

Abby gazed at her friend's worried face through a gauzy curtain of steam, but then she said, "I think I need a few minutes. Thank you for doing all this for me, Vivian."

"That's what friends are for. I'll be right outside if you need me. Don't stay in too long, don't let that water get cold. I'll have your tea ready when you get out."

Vivian turned at the bathroom door, but must have been satisfied that Abby would be all right if left alone for she gave a small nod and exited the room, closing the bathroom door softly behind her.

Abby let the bath do its work, warming her muscles and bones. And as she lay there, breathing in the steamy air scented with flowery bath oil, she thought of a man who'd died in cold water today. Questions floated across the surface of her mind like soap bubbles across the surface of the bath.

Oliver Platt had died while out fishing in a shallow river. How had that happened? Had he somehow fallen in and drowned? She recalled Lord Wimborne fighting with the trout on the end of his line. He'd had Ned standing by to help. Had Oliver been struggling with a fish and lost his footing? But he was an athletic and healthy young man. Had he hit his head perhaps?

As tragic as that would be, Abby hoped he'd fallen and hit his head, drowning accidentally. Because the alternative was so much worse.

In light of the sabotage to the Mitchell 925 and Reggie's injury, she had to ask herself if Oliver had been a victim of foul play.

As the shock wore off, Abby's reporter instincts kicked in, as did her natural curiosity. Soon she was climbing out of the bath and toweling herself off vigorously. When she emerged into the bedroom, wrapped in her robe once more, Vivian greeted her with a look of relief.

"That's more like it. Now you look like yourself. There's color in your cheeks and expression in your eyes. You looked like a ghost when I walked in and saw you cold and shivering."

"It was awful," she admitted. "Simply awful."

Vivian handed her a cup of tea and the two of them sat.

Vivian poured her own tea, moving smoothly from the role of maid to that of friend. "I even managed to squeeze a few oatmeal cookies out of the cook," she said. "She called them flapjacks."

Whatever they were, they were sweet and crunchy and went wonderfully with the tea, and right now Abby needed both.

There was silence as both women sipped tea and nibbled on the sweet biscuits. She felt that Vivian deserved to know what had happened in proper detail and perhaps she needed to talk through her experience to help make sense of it.

"How much do you know?" she asked carefully.

"Only that Oliver is dead and you dragged him from the river. Lady Wimborne had no time for more. Cressida was in hysterics," Vivian replied anxiously.

"It was dreadful for her, poor girl. You see, she thought it was Reggie."

Vivian looked utterly confused. "I think you need to start at the beginning and tell me everything."

Abby tried to straighten her jumbled thoughts and impressions into some kind of logical order. To think like a reporter and give the most important facts in the correct order. Vivian already had the headline: *Oliver Platt Found Dead While Fishing.* Now she filled in the background. "Cressida and I were walking by the river, checking up on how the fishing was going. Everyone seemed to be enjoying themselves, but they were spread out in different spots."

Vivian nodded, her gaze fixed on Abby's face.

She thought back to their stroll along the river, admiring the bluebells. One moment rhapsodizing about nature and the next facing death.

"It was Cressida who saw him first. She pointed and screamed, 'Reggie!' That's when I saw the man floating face down in the water. And for a split second I thought it was Reginald. But it wasn't. It was Oliver." She thought she'd already said all this to Vivian, but perhaps she hadn't completely overcome her shock yet. She seemed to need to repeat the story in order to make sense of it. It still felt more like a bad dream than something that had actually happened. "They were similar in build and coloring, but it was the coat, you see. That's why we thought it was Reggie."

"The coat?"

Then Abby explained how Reggie had lent Oliver his coat.

Vivian said, "Did he somehow fall in and drown? Did he hit his head?"

"I've been wondering the same things. He was an athletic young man. I suppose he could have had a fish on the line and, as it pulled, his feet slipped out from under him and he hit his head, knocking himself unconscious, and then drowned. But it seems very unlikely."

"It does."

"And if that were the case, wouldn't he have landed face up in the water?" She stood and mimed fishing and her feet slipping and every time she did it she let go of the rod and her feet slipped out from under her and she went backwards.

Vivian said, "Could the fish have been vigorous enough that it would have pulled him forward?"

"I suppose so." But her tone was doubtful.

Having finished her tea, and with her body warm once more, Abby felt much better. Vivian suggested she might want to lie down on her bed for a little while, but Abby said no. It was better for her to be downstairs with the others. Besides, as one of the two people who had found Oliver, no doubt the family would want to hear the story, and she didn't think that Cressida was in a fit state to describe what had happened.

Henri was probably engaged in overseeing the removal of the body to somewhere safe until the police arrived.

"Very well. I'll find something warm for you to wear." She helped Abby dress in a soft tweed skirt and a wool sweater, then insisted she brush Abby's hair and freshen her makeup. "I don't care how bad the shock," she said with a half-smile, "I have my professional reputation, and Paul Joubert's to think of."

Vivian picked up the bundle of wet clothes and said she'd see what could be done about saving them, though Abby doubted she'd ever wear that outfit again.

When Abby reached the bottom of the stairs, she found

Adams waiting for her. "The family is in the library, miss," he said and, walking ahead of her, opened the door.

It was a somber group sitting in the library when she entered. Lady Wimborne and Cressida were missing, most likely in Cressida's bedroom. She very much hoped that Cressida wouldn't suffer too badly. The shock had been terrible for her. But having her mother nearby would be the best thing.

Lord Wimborne was there though, looking deeply troubled. Charles A. Mitchell was like a man stunned. "Like a son to me he was," he kept repeating over and over again. Mrs. Mitchell was dabbing at her eyes with a damp handkerchief.

Coco Chanel sat apart with an odd expression on her face. Where the others all showed grief or shock it took her a moment to see that Miss Chanel looked annoyed. Was she that shallow? Could she really be put out because her fishing had been spoiled?

Reggie was there, looking positively ill. He was in his dressing gown, his face pale and heavy-eyed. "I should have been with him. I said I was going, didn't I? And you all stopped me." He looked around accusingly as though the group in the library had prevented him from joining the fishing expedition. "We'd have been together. He and I always fished together. And then I could have saved him. I could have stopped whatever happened."

When he spied Abby standing just inside the door, Reggie rose and said to her eagerly, "You were there. Tell me, how did it happen? Oliver was an experienced fisherman. I cannot understand how he could have fallen in and drowned."

She nodded gravely. "I've been thinking the very same thing. He looked very athletic and seemed quite sure-footed. I can't understand myself how it could have happened."

Lord Wimborne spoke then. "It must have been a terrible shock for you, my dear. Come and sit down beside me. What can I get you? With my wife being absent, I will have to stand in for Her Ladyship. Shall I ring for tea?"

He spoke with a lightness that wasn't humorous exactly but made her feel better. He was treating her the way she imagined he'd have handled a daughter or beloved niece who'd suffered a shock. She was happy to sit beside him and explained that she'd already had some tea.

He said, "Well, I hope you don't mind, my dear, but I could use something stronger."

Peter walked in then, looking as stunned as the rest of them. "I've been helping Henri," he said. "Putting the poor fellow in a safe place until the police arrive." Then he glanced around at the shelves of books as though searching for some etiquette book that would tell him how to behave in this dreadful situation.

Lord Wimborne, perhaps sensing that his son needed something to take his mind off thoughts of Oliver, suggested, "Peter, can you see who wants a drink?"

"Of course, Papa."

Relieved at having a task, Peter busied himself pouring generous shots of whiskey. Abby allowed herself a small glass. The tea had been lovely, but like Lord Wimborne she felt she needed something stronger. The fiery liquid burned its way down her throat.

It wasn't long before the man she'd been unconsciously waiting for walked in. Henri had a very grim look about him. It reminded her of the first time she'd ever met him, when he'd been investigating a murder, a murder that she had discovered, and one that he had initially believed she had committed.

"I was so sorry to leave you like that," she said to him.

He looked at her and his eyes lightened. "Your task was much more important. There was nothing to be done for Oliver, but it was vital to get Cressida back to the house."

She knew he was right, but still it had seemed unfeeling to

leave him alone with a corpse. Even though he must be accustomed to death in his line of work.

Reggie looked up. "You're just the man I've been wanting to see. I've been racking my brains, trying to understand how Oliver could have slipped like that and drowned. Did he hit his head?"

Henri stood in the middle of the room and his very silence drew every eye toward him. There was a deathly quiet when he uttered the words, "I'm very sorry to inform you that Oliver Platt did not die by accident. He was murdered."

SEVENTEEN

Abby let out an audible gasp. And then Charles Mitchell yelled, "What?"

"No..." Reggie began, his voice breaking as he continued. "That's not possible."

Lord Wimborne said nothing, only sighed, a sound that was almost worse than the cries of distress coming from the others. In a low voice he said, "Not another promising young man dead before his time." And she had a feeling he was thinking back to his time in the war. She barely knew him, but she reached out and put her hand over his. It was cold and trembled slightly.

Finally, Charles Mitchell said, "How can you be sure Oliver was murdered? I'm not saying you're wrong, but he could just as easily have hit his head on a rock when he fell."

Henri shook his head and his eyes were cold. "He did not die from a blow to the head. Oliver Platt was shot in the back. If the bullet didn't immediately kill him, then drowning would have."

Once more there was a terrible silence in the room as they all absorbed this new information.

Charles Mitchell, who was given to bombastic outbursts in

a loud voice said, in the quietest tone she'd ever heard, "Murdered? You mean killed deliberately? But why?"

"That is what we must find out," Henri said.

"But it makes no sense," Peter cried. "Why would anyone want to hurt Oliver? He seemed such a nice chap. We were shooting rabbits this morning; perhaps one of the gamekeepers shot him by accident." He glanced around and could see no one was convinced by his argument. "I suppose it's unlikely, but it could have happened. Seems more believable than that someone would deliberately shoot a man in the back. And he wasn't even in his own country."

"On top of someone sabotaging my beautiful car, too. It's like some evil has followed us from Detroit," Charles Mitchell said woefully.

It was shocking to hear a man so businesslike and practical talk of evil creeping along behind him, but Abby could understand how he felt.

Slowly, because she was still trying to feel her way to the truth, Abby posed the question: "What if Oliver wasn't the intended victim?"

She had everyone's attention now. She colored faintly, wondering if soon they would mock her, in particular the cool-eyed French inspector. But at this stage she felt that any theory was worth putting forth, no matter how absurd.

"We know that the brake cable was cut before Reggie took the wheel of the Mitchell 925 yesterday. And when we first saw poor Oliver lying there in the water, Cressida pointed to him and screamed out 'Reggie!'" She glanced around at the assembled company. "Cressida of all people would know her fiancé. But it was the jacket—Oliver was wearing Reginald's jacket. They have similar build and coloring. It would be easy to mistake one for the other, certainly from behind."

Reggie stared at her, almost transfixed. Charles Mitchell

said finally, "Are you suggesting that Oliver's death was a case of mistaken identity? And the intended victim was my son?"

"Yes. That's what I'm saying. I don't know if it's true, I'm simply proposing a theory."

Henri seemed to weigh her words and then said, "It is a compelling argument." He turned to Reggie. "But again one must ask, what enemies do you have in this country?"

Reginald shrugged his shoulders. "None, as far as I know. With all due respect, Miss Dixon, I can't believe this is true. The sabotaging of the car was surely locals in the village letting it be known they were angry and upset to see such displays of wealth. I'm convinced there was no intention that anyone would be killed, least of all me. And as for Oliver, Peter must be right. No doubt an over-enthusiastic gamekeeper saw movement near the water. Oliver could have been bent over, adjusting a fly or, I don't know, doing up his boots, any one of a number of things. Bent over like that, he makes a movement..." His words petered off. Even he must see that finishing the sentence was impossible. No matter what Oliver might have been doing, he could not have been mistaken for a rabbit.

Charles Mitchell stood up slowly. He appeared to Abby as though he had aged at least a decade. He said, "Peter, if you'll show me where Oliver is lying, I should like to sit with him for a bit."

Reggie looked up, startled. It was obvious it hadn't occurred to him to pay such respects to his dearest friend. He stood up too and said, "I'll come with you, Pa."

But Henri shook his head. "I'm sorry, but until the police have seen him, I cannot allow you near the body."

She waited for Charles Mitchell to explode but oddly he didn't. Instead he nodded sadly. "A horrible business, but I understand what you mean. Mustn't disturb anything until the officials have studied everything. You'll let me know when I might be allowed to sit with him for a little? Say my goodbyes?"

Henri merely nodded.

"I think I shall go to my room for a little while," Mr. Mitchell said wearily. "Call me if—" He let out a great sigh. "Well, call me if I'm needed." His footsteps sounded heavy as he left the library.

They sat in silence for a moment, as though waiting to be told what to do. Lady Wimborne was usually the one who kept conversation flowing and reminded her guests of whatever was on the agenda, but in her absence no one had any appetite for chatter. Clearly, the wedding festivities were on hold. The group in the library were in a kind of limbo. Waiting. Abby knew she was waiting for the police to arrive.

Lady Wimborne came in a little later. "My poor little lamb," she said. "She's finally dropped off to sleep. I gave her a sedative. She's so overwrought, poor child." And then she turned to Reggie with a wan smile. "She kept saying, 'I thought it was Reggie.' She's very fond of you. Believing, even briefly, that you were dead has left her quite overwrought."

He smiled somewhat mechanically. "Poor Cressie. What a shocking thing she should have been the first one to stumble upon poor old Oliver. And then to think it was me, which according to Miss Dixon here, it should have been."

Lady Wimborne, who hadn't heard this theory until now, jumped, and her eyebrows rose almost to her hairline.

"It was the jacket, you see," Abby said.

And then Lady Wimborne nodded. "Oh, of course, I see. Yes. Oliver was wearing Reggie's jacket, wasn't he? I suppose everyone in the house saw Reggie in that jacket, and only those of us who were present at breakfast knew they had swapped coats."

But Peter said, "No. Don't you recall, Mama, he said he'd been out to see the car before breakfast. Anyone on the estate might have seen him."

"That's right, I did," Reggie confirmed. He squinted his eyes and tilted his head back, then said, "Though I don't remember noticing anyone in particular. The household staff, I suppose. A few of the locals and Ned. Can't recall anyone sinister hanging about."

Lady Wimborne let out a sigh. "Cook's in a quandary about what to do about dinner. But, even with this tragedy upon us, I suppose we must eat. I'll have dinner put forward half an hour. We won't have cocktails before. It would seem too festive somehow."

Henri said gravely, "I'm very pleased you should say that Lady Wimborne. I've put a call through to my colleague in Scotland Yard. There will be someone on their way."

She looked surprised but resigned. "I suppose they must intrude on our grief, even though it seems rather unseemly."

Then she moved to sit beside Mrs. Mitchell in the chair recently vacated by her husband. "I wouldn't have had anything so dreadful happen for all the world. One cannot help thinking there's some kind of darkness lurking at Darrington Manor. The car, Oliver being killed like that. Even poor Gladys Trotter."

It was so similar to what Charles Mitchell had said that the hair on the back of Abby's neck rose. Both Charles Mitchell and Lady Wimborne seemed to feel they were cursed. Could it possibly be true?

"At any rate," Lady Wimborne went on, "there's no question of going ahead with the wedding. I wouldn't have my daughter's nuptials overshadowed by such a terrible tragedy."

Mrs. Mitchell stared at her as though it hadn't even occurred to her to postpone the wedding. "I don't know what to say. Everything's arranged. I wonder what Oliver would have wished? I must consult with my husband. Poor Oliver would never have wanted to upset Reggie. They were the dearest of friends." And then she sobbed into her handkerchief. It was so creased and damp that Lady Wimborne offered the distraught woman her own white handkerchief edged with lace. Mrs. Mitchell took it with a muffled word of thanks.

Abby glanced at Reggie and saw him looking at Lady Wimborne most earnestly.

"Is this Cressida's wish? Does she prefer to postpone our wedding?"

She looked at him kindly. "Cressida was in no state to make any rational decisions. But she did cry out more than once, 'The wedding cannot go forward.' Still, I'd have made the same decision anyway. No young woman should begin her married life under a cloud of tragedy. In a few months' time, we will be better able to celebrate your wedding."

"What dashed rotten timing," Peter said. Then looking guilty he said, "Forgive me, ladies. But when I think of the effort my parents have put into this week it beggars belief. Are you absolutely certain there isn't a plausible explanation that this could be an accidental death?" he said, turning to Henri.

The French inspector made a motion that only Frenchmen can make. Part shrug, part spreading of the hands, with a certain raising of the chin and drooping of the mouth. "It is possible. But it will be up to Scotland Yard to investigate most thoroughly."

"Even so, my love," Lady Wimborne said to her son, "this tragic death means the wedding ought to be postponed. I feel it's the right thing to do out of respect for Mr. Platt."

Lord Wimborne said, "In the meantime, is there anything we can do to help in this investigation? My lovely wife is correct. A pall of darkness and guilt hangs over this house until we can resolve how this dreadful thing happened. If one of my gamekeepers shot that man by accident, they will be found and punished. And, if the most appalling possibility turns out to be correct, and someone connected with Darrington Manor or with the village is responsible, again, we will make sure they are punished to the full extent of the law. That I promise you."

As daunting as his speech was, Abby was pleased to see Lord Wimborne had lost the terrible faraway look he'd assumed when he first learned of the murder. He seemed to have taken back his mantle of authority as head of the household.

"Thank you, my lord," said Henri. "I have taken the liberty of gathering everyone who was on the property earlier today, especially those who were involved in hunting rabbits. They are all below stairs awaiting a visit from Scotland Yard."

Lord Wimborne nodded. "Excellent. Very sensible. I'm afraid, my assembled guests, that the entertainment isn't quite what we had planned for this week, and for that I apologize." He turned to Mrs. Mitchell. "And, on behalf of my family, I extend our deepest condolences and sorrow that we must postpone the union of my daughter and your son."

"I understand, of course. In a few weeks, months perhaps, we will celebrate the wedding of our children. But in the meantime, I do see your logic. No young couple wants to start married life with a cloud hanging over them."

Reginald nodded sorrowfully and said, "And much as I love and honor my future bride, I must mourn my dearest friend."

Abby was on her way to dress for dinner, wondering whether Vivian had found anything in her wardrobe that was sufficiently somber, when a voice called her name. "Miss Dixon? Telephone for you."

It was Jerry, the footman. She nodded, thinking Walter Strutt must have heard the news, and he'd expect her first impressions. She tried to arrange her thoughts sensibly, ordering the facts the way a decent reporter should.

When they reached the office, Abby hurried toward the desk. It was only when she reached for the phone that she realized the receiver hadn't been lifted. She turned to see that Jerry had quietly entered the room behind her and shut the door. The two of them were alone.

She glanced up at him, already edging toward the fireplace where a brass poker leaned against the stone. She'd been so busy thinking of writing an article, she'd forgotten she'd warned Vivian not to be alone with Jerry. And now she'd fallen into his trap. Before she could speak, he said, in an urgent tone, "I'm not a murderer."

"I beg your pardon?"

The footman's discomfort was palpable. She edged closer to the poker, wishing she had her handgun with her. Never would she travel without it again, she promised herself.

If she screamed, would anyone hear her? She was hopeful they would.

"I never touched Gladys Trotter. That's to say, not after she told me she wasn't interested. After I gave her the silk stockings."

She quelled her gasp with an effort. How she wished she could take everything he was saying down in shorthand. She'd try to remember every word. "You admit you bought her silk stockings?"

"Yes. In Frome. She said if I wanted to..." He went quite red in the face. "She'd made me promises. Said if I bought her a pair of silk stockings then she'd... let me take liberties with her."

"I think I understand." Abby was getting a picture of Gladys who traded her favors for gifts. Had Jerry felt he hadn't received enough favors in return for the stockings? "So you followed her to London?"

"No! I went to London because I was interviewing for a position." His face clouded. "I didn't get it. Didn't have enough experience to work on Savile Row. That's what they told me. So I came back here. I lied about where I was going because I didn't want the Wimbornes to know I was looking for another job. See, miss, I know it looks bad for me. But I never even saw Gladys. Didn't know she was in London."

He looked hot and frightened. She didn't say anything.

He went on. "They'll remember me, at Dunville and Savvy. My appointment was at four o'clock."

She shook her head. "That won't help you. Gladys Trotter was killed that night. Where were you all night Jerry?"

"I went to the pictures. And then a dance hall."

"Alone?"

He nodded, miserable.

"If what you're saying is true, perhaps someone will remember you. Now, you've kept me long enough. I must dress for dinner."

"There's something else."

"What is it?"

"I saw him there."

"Who?"

"Mr. Platt. The one who got killed. I didn't know who he was until I came here, but I remember the automobile. He was driving it and looked like he had everything in the world he could ever want. I envied him. Funny that."

"It's not surprising you would see him. He and his friend drove from London to Darrington. There was no secrecy."

"But he wasn't with his friend. He was alone. What was he doing near Paddington station?"

"What time was this?"

"Late. I missed the last train so I had to find a cheap place to stay. Then, in the morning, I thought, how often do I get to London? So I had a look around. Then I got the train back."

She didn't know whether she believed him or not, and her indecision must have showed.

"Please, miss. Please don't say anything. I'll lose my position here if they find out I lied."

"I can make no promises. You must tell the police that it was you who bought those stockings. They'll find out anyway, you know. And it will look much better for you if you come forward voluntarily."

Dinner was an understandably dreary affair. Lady Wimborne had rearranged the usual seating plan, but still the absence of Oliver was keenly felt. Perhaps he didn't sit like Banquo, a ghost at the dinner table, but his absence was a tangible thing among them, constraining conversation and adding gloom to what had previously been a joyous gathering.

In the place where he'd always sat, Lady Wimborne had placed the hapless Beatrice, who appeared more brow-beaten than usual. As though she were sharing her chair with a ghost, she started every so often and turned around. She barely ate anything and took no part in the conversation.

Cressida was also absent and as soon as dinner was over Lady Wimborne made her excuses to go and check on her daughter.

The butler came in to suggest they all adjourn to the library for coffee. There was no question of leaving the men to their port. Obediently, they settled themselves back in the library. It was very clear they were making a pretense of small talk, but every single one of them was waiting for the arrival of whatever investigators Scotland Yard would be sending.

Abby's keen ears heard the crunching of wheels on gravel and then the commotion that announced arrivals at the front door. Very soon the butler opened the door and said, "Inspector Grenville, my lord."

The man who entered surprised Abby. After the stolid sergeant who'd come around investigating the car accident, this man was so polished and urbane he could easily have passed for one of the guests at Lord and Lady Wimborne's daughter's wedding. He wore a beautifully cut suit and his hair was most fashionably cut and greased back. A thin mustache graced his upper lip. When he spoke, she had her suspicions confirmed. He spoke as beautifully as Peter. Henri rose at his entrance and it was clear the two men knew each other.

Henri said, "Digby, good of you to come."

"Not at all." He turned to the assembled company and said, "I'm very sorry to intrude on you this evening, my lord, but I hear you have had some trouble. Perhaps you'd like to tell me exactly what's happened."

Abby found his manner fascinating. He was talking in that smooth, cultured way as though this really were a social visit, but she didn't miss the way his sharp eyes took in every single person in the room. What kind of judgments was he making about them? And what clues or emotions were each of them giving off that he was picking up?

"It's been the most shocking tragedy," Lord Wimborne said, before continuing. "It was Miss Abigail Dixon here who first discovered the dead man, in company with my daughter Cressida, who is suffering deeply from shock. She has taken to her bed."

Inspector Grenville nodded. "I'm very sorry to hear that. I shall look forward to speaking to your daughter tomorrow." Then he turned toward Abby. "In the meantime, in your own words, perhaps you could tell me what happened?"

Abby's throat suddenly felt dry and she swallowed. Even though she had expected to be questioned, somehow looking at this tall, elegant figure, knowing that another tall, elegant figure was also listening to every word, was unnerving. Her thoughts felt they were all jumbled up and she needed to take a moment to recite clearly and dispassionately exactly what she had seen.

She was about to do so when Charles A. Mitchell broke in and said, "I think you need to begin with what happened with the car. If you ask me, that's where it all began."

Only the faintest hint of irritation crossed the smooth

complexion of Inspector Digby Grenville. He turned to Charles Mitchell and said, "Mr. Mitchell, I recognize you of course from the newspapers. Why don't you begin the proceedings then?"

For some reason she'd imagined that he would take each of them into a small room and interrogate them separately. Perhaps because that had been her experience when she was accused of murdering her stepmother. But evidently he had his own way of doing things. She wondered whether he and Henri would somehow work in tandem so that he might ask questions and Henri might look for stumbled-over sentences or alibis that didn't make sense. Either way, this would mean that she would be able to hear what everyone had to say.

Charles A. Mitchell described the beautiful automobile that he had painstakingly designed, envisioned, and then had overseen the production of, then shipped to Darrington Manor only to have it sabotaged and his son nearly killed.

The inspector turned to Reggie and said, "I am a little puzzled. I have heard this story, and indeed spoken to the sergeant who first investigated this crime. The roadway going away from the manor house drops toward the main road, but it is not a precipitous drop. I'm confused as to how so much damage was done to the automobile."

Reginald looked quite sheepish. He glanced at his father and back to the inspector before admitting, "You're right, of course. It was my own damned— Excuse me, ladies. My own dashed fault. She's a beautiful engine, with nearly a hundred horses under the hood. And she'd never been properly opened up. I saw my chance, a beautiful straight stretch of road, no other vehicles upon it, and I'm afraid I put my foot on the gas."

"I thought so," his father said, with what Abby thought was grudging pride. "Did you get up to a good speed?"

"Pa, I had her up to sixty miles an hour."

"If we might come back to the matter at hand," the inspector reminded them gently.

"Of course. Sorry," Reggie said. "Anyway, I was going on at a very good clip, and then obviously had to slow down before I got onto the main road leading to the village. I put the brakes on and nothing happened. The more I tried, the more clear it was that the brakes weren't engaging, and meanwhile the vehicle was gaining speed. As you know, the road slopes going down toward the main road, and then there's the weight of the car itself, so I was trying to maintain control and work out what to do, and that's when the car fishtailed and... well, next thing I knew Miss Abby Dixon was calling my name and asking if I was all right."

"And I understand—" He stopped speaking, for somewhere outside the library a woman screamed.

EIGHTEEN

Abby jumped. It was fair to say that everyone was startled in their own way. They were in the middle of talking about death and attempted murder and cars going out of control, and a piercing scream had filled the room.

"Cressie," Lord Wimborne cried out, trying unsuccessfully to get out of his wheelchair.

Henri was already at the door, throwing it open and rushing into the hallway.

She was right behind him and saw a young woman, one of the servants of the house, with a hand to her chest. "I'm awfully sorry, sir, it's just he startled me so."

And standing foolishly in the middle of the stairs with a small bouquet of flowers in his hand was Ned Corcoran.

"And what do you think you're doing?" Henri demanded.

The young man looked both mortified and pugnacious at the same time. "I was worried about Miss Wimborne. I merely wanted to make sure that she was recovering after the terrible shock she suffered today."

By this time, Abby wasn't the only one out in the hallway.

Charles Mitchell was breathing heavily behind her. "And what gives you the right to inquire about Miss Wimborne's health? What were you planning to do with that miserable little posy? Walk into a young lady's bedroom?" His disgust and shock were apparent.

Ned colored and said, "No. I was trying to find her lady's maid. I just wanted to know that she was all right. I would never enter her bedroom."

"And who is this young man?" The cool tones of Inspector Digby Grenville cut through all the other voices like a knife through soft white bread.

"I'm the estate manager," Ned said with what dignity he could muster. He was very red in the face. "My name is Ned Corcoran."

The inspector said, "I think you'd better come in and join us, young man."

Just as he was about to hand the flowers to the young chambermaid who'd screamed, Charles Mitchell said, "You keep your miserable wildflowers. You'll not be bothering my future daughter-in-law with a bundle of weeds."

His contempt was punishing, and so Ned came into the library still clutching his humble bouquet.

Coco Chanel sauntered into the room shortly after Ned Corcoran walked in. For a woman who always made an entrance, it was one of the only times Abby had seen her walk into a room and not cause even the tiniest stir. Every eye was upon Ned Corcoran. His color was still heightened and there was a tight look around his jaw, but he held the inspector's gaze steadily.

"You wanted to see me, sir?"

"But who is this? And why is that young man holding those flowers?" Coco Chanel wanted to know. One way or another, it seemed, she was going to get the attention she obviously felt she deserved. Before anyone else could explain what was going on, the inspector introduced himself. "And you need no introduction," he added smoothly. "Miss Chanel, it is an honor to meet you."

Coco Chanel was never immune to attention from an attractive man and she looked at the inspector from under her lashes. "Are you the person I need to speak to then?" she asked. "Now that I understand this wedding has been postponed, there can be no need for the wedding dress designer to remain on site. As I'm sure you can understand, Inspector, I have many commissions and many clients. If I am no longer needed here, then I must leave."

Inspector Grenville was quite deferential but firm. "I'm very sorry, Miss Chanel, but I cannot allow anyone to leave this house until we have a much fuller picture of how Mr. Platt died."

She was outraged. Her eyes snapped fire and two spots of color burned like rouge on her cheekbones. "Are you accusing me, Coco Chanel, of being involved in this man's demise? A man I did not even know?"

"I understand this is very inconvenient," he said, "but I must ask you to remain until further notice."

Coco Chanel sniffed. "It is most inconvenient. I'm tempted to tell dear Sir Winston about this outrage."

Inspector Grenville's voice held a hint of steel as he said, "You may tell anyone you like, madam. So long as you do not leave Darrington Manor."

Realizing that he'd had the last word, she retired in a huff to the nearest sofa. And then, before sitting down, she said, "Let me take those ridiculous flowers from that poor man. He looks most foolish standing there holding a posy."

In spite of the rude way it was done, it was clearly a relief to Ned Corcoran when Coco Chanel took the flowers from his grasp. She placed them on a table where they would no doubt wilt until one of the servants cleaned the room. Still, Ned was patently more at ease without a bouquet of flowers in his hands.

"Please, sit down," the inspector said in a tone that was more command than request.

Abby watched Ned as he glanced first at Lord Wimborne, who nodded briefly. She wondered if the estate manager had ever sat in this room before. If so, perhaps never as a guest. She felt keenly his position because it somewhat mirrored her own. She wasn't a relative of the bride or groom or an illustrious personage, she was a reporter doing a job. That was the only reason she was sitting in this chair. Ned, like her, was part of the estate in a working capacity. And yet he wasn't a servant, in the somewhat complex strata of British society she suspected that she and Ned Corcoran were fairly equal. Neither fish nor fowl.

Even thinking the word fish made her shudder as she was reminded of poor Oliver and the reason they were now gathered here with a Scotland Yard inspector in their midst.

When Ned Corcoran was sitting, if not at his ease then at least not looking quite so horribly uncomfortable as he had before, the inspector asked him in the most genial of tones, "Do you often take flowers up to Miss Wimborne's bedroom?"

Lord Wimborne spoke before Ned could open his lips, and his words were like a lash: "I will not have you casting aspersions on my daughter. Especially not in my home."

Inspector Grenville was completely unruffled. "My apologies, Your Lordship. It is not, however, your daughter's behavior that worries me so much as Mr. Corcoran's."

Ned looked as though he'd like to speak with the same brutality that Lord Wimborne had, but of course he had no right. Instead he said in clipped, firm tones, "I have never taken Miss Wimborne flowers before. It was an impulse of the moment, when I heard that she'd had such a terrible shock. And

I had no intention of entering her bedroom, I merely wished to find her maid who could take them to her."

"Surely you would have found her maid below stairs?"

"No. I tried there first." There was a slight pause, then he said, "All the servants are gathered below, but Cre— Miss Wimborne's maid has been tending to her mistress so was above stairs."

"Ah, of course, you have the run of this house, I understand." Inspector Grenville made it sound like that was a suspicious activity.

Ned looked slightly puzzled by the question. "Naturally I do. I'm the estate manager. There isn't a nook or cranny of this house or the estate that I don't know quite well." Then, obviously realizing what he'd said, he immediately added, "Though not the family's personal quarters, of course."

Lord Wimborne nodded. "Quite right. Unless expressly invited. Such as when I had a leak in the ceiling of my dressing room. Naturally, Ned was the first person I called."

"So, Mr. Corcoran, you would know which bed chamber belongs to Miss Wimborne?"

"I do not understand why you are asking me these questions," Ned said, his brows drawing together. "Let me make my relationship with Miss Wimborne perfectly clear. I grew up on this estate. I have known Miss Wimborne since we were children. I have a great regard for her. I am also perfectly well aware that she is engaged to be married to Reginald Mitchell. My gesture was one of friendship and concern."

Gone was the affable young man who had picked her up at the station. This Ned Corcoran was showing his mettle.

Inspector Grenville let the pause lengthen and Ned Corcoran wasn't provoked into jumping in to fill the dead space. He merely waited. Inspector Grenville then asked, "You were shooting rabbits earlier in the day, I understand."

"That's right. It's not a task any of us enjoys, but if you don't cull them they'll destroy every crop on the land."

"And whereabouts were you shooting rabbits?"

Ned kept his gaze steady on the inspector's. "In the barley fields."

"I am not as yet acquainted with the geography of this place. Are those within shooting distance of the river where some of Lord and Lady Wimborne's guests were fishing?"

"No. It's far from where they were fishing, and besides, the shooting ended long before the fishing began. It would be fool-hardy to be out shooting rabbits when the guests were enjoying a fishing expedition."

He nodded. "But you were shooting this morning?"

"I've said I was."

Lord Wimborne spoke again. "You're not seriously suggesting that Ned here had something to do with Oliver's death?"

"Not at all. I merely wish to know everyone's movements today and Mr. Corcoran brought himself to my attention."

"Well, I can tell you that Ned was with me during the fishing expedition." Lord Wimborne waved a hand in front of his helpless legs. "As you can see, Inspector, fishing is a more challenging activity for me, though I refuse to give up the activ-ity. I'm quite addicted to the sport. Ned helps me."

"And was he at your side throughout the entire afternoon?"

Lord Wimborne was about to snap out an answer and then paused to reflect. He said slowly, "As far as I can remember."

The inspector nodded. "Very well. That will be all for now."

Ned Corcoran had clearly been dismissed. He turned to Lord Wimborne and in a low voice said, "I would never do anything to upset Miss Wimborne."

Lord Wimborne nodded. "I know that full well. Off you go

now. I understand the lads are being kept downstairs until they can all be questioned. Keep an eye on things for me, will you?"

"I'm on my way there now." And then he got up and, with a nod to the room, walked out with his back straight and his head held high.

After the door closed behind him the inspector stared at it for a moment and then said slowly, "An interesting man, that one."

"And an excellent estate manager," Lord Wimborne said.

After Ned Corcoran left the library the inspector turned, about to address Abby, but Charles Mitchell spoke up. His brows had pulled together and he had a thunderous look on his face.

"I don't like it. I don't like that fellow creeping around with flowers for my son's fiancée."

Lord Wimborne was about to speak but Reggie interjected, "Pa, if anyone should object it's me. The man explained himself. Cressida is a beautiful girl with a kind heart. Sure, he might have a little crush on her." He gave a faint smile. "Who wouldn't?"

His father looked at him from under beetle brows and said, "Well, I suppose if my son sees nothing wrong with the friendship, I'll let it rest."

There was a palpable lessening of tension in the room as it had been fairly apparent that Lord Wimborne would have defended his estate manager and possibly caused more friction between the two fathers than was already there.

Now, at last, Abby was allowed to tell her tale unhindered. She gave as clear an account as she could, trying to remember every detail. Inspector Grenville particularly wanted to know where the other people fishing had been situated. She tried to picture every detail of the walk she and Cressida had taken.

"I'm sorry, Miss Dixon, this must be painful for you, but I must ask exactly what you saw when you arrived on the scene."

She told again how Cressida had pointed and screamed out Reggie's name, and only then had she seen the body lying in the water. She said, "I thought perhaps he might have fallen in and still be alive... But he wasn't alive." She found her throat caught a little on that line.

He gave her a moment and then said, "Did you, too, believe it was Reginald Mitchell?"

"I think because Cressida had screamed his name, I did. He was wearing Reggie's coat, you see." The man raised his eyebrows and then she had to explain about the coats being switched. "But when I got closer, even before I'd seen his face, I knew it wasn't Mr. Mitchell. Something about the hair and the shape of the head was wrong."

"You went into the water?"

"I did."

"And could you see that he'd been shot?"

She shook her head. "I wasn't looking at his back, and he was in the water and there were waves and, well, no. I didn't see blood. I didn't see... I didn't see anything other than a man face down. I was more worried about whether he could be saved."

"And then I understand Henri arrived on the scene."

She realized that someone, most likely Henri, had already filled him in on most if not all of these details. No doubt he was asking each of them for their story in order to either see where inconsistencies might lie or to fill in what Henri didn't know. She suspected that, like Henri Deschamps, Inspector Digby Grenville could be a dangerous enemy to have. Even though she was innocent of any crime, she felt the uncomfortable quickening of her pulse.

"Yes, that's right," she told him. "Inspector Deschamps arrived at that moment. Alerted, I believe, by Cressida's scream."

"And then what did you do?"

"I walked back to the house with Cressida," she said. She felt again that awful feeling, as though she'd abandoned Henri when he needed her help. But Cressida's need had obviously been greater. "She was understandably very upset."

"Even when she realized it wasn't her fiancé who'd been killed?"

"Honestly, I'm not sure she could really take it all in. It had been such a terrible shock for her." She glanced toward Lady Wimborne and said, "And then we arrived back in the house and Lady Wimborne took her upstairs, and she will have to tell you the rest."

He nodded. "And you, Miss Dixon. What did you then do?"

"I was soaked through and chilled. My maid drew me a bath." She felt horribly entitled and spoilt saying those words, but it was the truth. She wanted to explain that she didn't really have a lady's maid and she could easily have poured her own bath, but it was hardly relevant. If the inspector thought it was surprising that a young journalist on a reporter's salary should have a lady's maid he kept his opinions to himself, for which she was grateful. She didn't want to have to explain the charade, not in front of Lord and Lady Wimborne.

"Did you see anyone when you were walking back?"

Had she? She'd been so focused on Cressida she'd barely glanced around. But now she tried to bring that walk back into focus. "I saw a man walking down the path toward the river. I didn't pay much attention at the time, but I believe it was Mr. George Smith."

They were then asked, each person in turn, where they had been during the fishing expedition. And he wanted to know who had been the last person to see Oliver alive. That would be important of course for establishing when he had been killed.

Reggie explained about his concussion and that he'd been in

his room sleeping. "I had a dreadful headache. The doctor left something for me to take and it knocked me out for several hours."

"So you were in your room alone?" the inspector asked him.

"Yes. I'm afraid so. Badger looked in on me, but I gave orders I didn't want to be disturbed."

Henri had already stated that he had arrived on the scene at five minutes past three o'clock. It hadn't occurred to Abby to check the time, but naturally the French inspector had immediately acted like the policeman he was when he came running at the sound of Cressida's scream.

Now it was important to clock Oliver's movements as much as they could. Who had last seen him and when?

"I saw him at lunch," Abby said, recalling the young man so full of life, wearing his borrowed coat. "That was the last time I saw him alive."

"And those of you who went fishing, did you all go down to the river together?" he asked them.

"No," Lord Wimborne replied for the group. "There are several excellent lies where the larger trout can be found. I'm afraid I take advantage of my disability and set up at the one closest to Darrington Manor." His tone faltered slightly as he continued. "Ned Corcoran was to take me down but was a little delayed on estate business. Jerry, one of the footmen who helps when I have guests fishing, showed the others where to find the best spots." He obviously realized he'd just admitted that Ned hadn't been with him the entire time as he'd first suggested. The inspector didn't bring up the fact, merely nodded and said, "And each person was on their own?"

"Yes. Trout can see and hear you if you're not careful so it's best to find a quiet spot and fish alone."

The inspector turned to face the group, asking the next question more generally. "And how did you decide who should fish where?"

Coco Chanel frowned and ran her hands over her pearls as though she were counting a rosary. She glanced at Charles Mitchell. He said, "Jerry suggested the spots that would suit us best. We walked along the path and Jerry pointed out a nice bit of ground protruding into the river. There was a flat boulder I could sit on and plenty of room to spread out."

Coco nodded. "And then Oliver and I walked on. Jerry promised me good sport at an area where the river curved. Nicely shaded by trees. A dead tree had lodged on the bank and he said the trout would likely be behind it." She brightened suddenly. "And indeed he was correct. I caught a lovely fish. I don't yet know how big, but I'm certain it was at least nine pounds." Then, recalling why they were there, she added, "And poor Oliver continued on. That is the last time I saw him."

"He and the footman continued on alone?"

"Yes," Coco confirmed.

"And did you see Mr. Platt again?"

"No."

"Miss Chanel, did you hear Miss Wimborne scream?"

She seemed to consider the question, her fingers once again busy at her pearls. "I thought I heard something," she finally admitted. "But could not be certain it was a woman's scream."

The inspector nodded, then turned to Henri. "And you, my friend, it does not seem you were with this group who were fishing?"

If Henri felt he was being interrogated as a murder suspect he didn't show any alarm. Abby was mildly pleased to see him being treated with suspicion, however slight. He smiled slightly. "I prefer to find my own way. And I have fished with Lord Wimborne before. I was a little downstream of Monsieur Platt."

"Close enough to hear Miss Wimborne scream?"

"The scream was faint, but I thought it was a woman in distress, yes."

"Did you hear a shot while you were fishing?"

It was as though everyone in the room held their breath for a second. Then Henri shook his head. "Unfortunately, I did not."

The inspector reminded them all once again that they must stay in residence until permitted to leave, and once more Coco Chanel tutted her displeasure. Then he said he would be back with them the next day.

He said, "I will interview each of you in more detail. If you recall anything, no matter how seemingly insignificant, please tell me tomorrow." And then he left.

Abby followed him surreptitiously. When she emerged into the hall, he was nearly at the front door. "Inspector Grenville?" she called.

He turned and his expression was rather forbidding. "Miss Dixon."

Conscious of an urge to lick her lips, she squelched the gesture, knowing it would make her look as nervous as she felt. She imagined Nellie Bly urging her on and said, "I'm not sure if you're aware, but I am a journalist with the *Chicago International Post*."

"My congratulations," he said in a tone so dry if she could have touched them the words would have crumbled to dust.

She plunged on. "Obviously, this is a significant news story. I wonder if I might interview you quickly before you leave?" She had her handbag and was ready to grab her notepad.

Inspector Grenville rocked back on his heels ever so slightly, then, in that urbane, smooth tone said, "Miss Dixon. I am at the onset of a difficult investigation. You may not interview me and you may not reveal any of what has passed this evening. Is that understood?"

Yes, he was intimidating but she knew that if she let him push her around now, he'd do it throughout the investigation. So, she narrowed her gaze and gave him her best steely-eyed stare. "There is no law that prevents me from doing my job." She had no idea what the law was in England but doubted very much he could stop her reporting the facts without some kind of injunction.

He tapped his driving gloves against the palm of his hand, the only sign he showed of irritation. Then he said, "Would you jeopardize a murder investigation in order to further your career, Miss Dixon?"

She recalled Oliver laughing with Reggie in the drawing room over cocktails and putting on that fancy fishing coat even when he hadn't wanted to. He seemed suddenly so alive to her that she had to swallow a lump of emotion. "No," she said honestly. "I wouldn't do anything to hamper your efforts to find Mr. Platt's killer."

He nodded, and began to turn away, clearly thinking the conversation was over. "But I'm here to report on the wedding festivities of Reginald Mitchell and Miss Wimborne. I must be allowed to give the bare facts." Before he could speak she went on. "And if I do, I want your word that whenever you have a statement to make or are willing to be interviewed that I have first access."

"Are you bargaining with me, Miss Dixon?" He sounded coolly outraged.

"Yes," she said, "I am."

He took a step toward her and lowered his voice. "Very well. But let me give you a piece of advice. Somewhere on this estate is the person who killed Mr. Platt. I would be very careful if I were you not to inflame that person. In my experience, one who has killed once will do it again more easily."

She returned to the library and didn't think she'd even been missed. They were all clearly tired and dispirited after the dreadful day and within an hour everyone went to bed, or at least to their rooms early.

When she reached her room, Abby got out her typewriter

and began to bang out a story for the newspaper. To her consternation she now had two powerful men in her life who didn't want her writing hard news stories about Darrington Manor. Walter Strutt and Inspector Digby Grenville.

Surely now that a man had died and the wedding of Cressida Wimborne to Reginald Mitchell Esquire had been postponed, Walter Strutt would allow her to write the hot news story that was burning off her fingers.

NINETEEN

To stick to her bargain with the inspector, Abby would be careful what she wrote. He'd emphasized that she couldn't share the specifics of the evening, nor the facts of the tragedy.

After writing her story she crept downstairs and into Lord Wimborne's office where he kept a telephone on his desk. She knew phoning her story in to Paris would be expensive but was certain that the *Chicago International Post* would pay the expenses. The operator connected her and she read out her story to the night editor. He was a colorless man named Gerard. After taking down the article, he said, "Looks like you got yourself into another mess, Miss Dixon."

She sighed, knowing he was right. However, she reminded him, "I'm in the middle of a hot news story. Now that Scotland Yard is involved, you know other reporters will be buzzing around Darrington Manor like flies at a picnic. I hope you'll hold the front page."

"I'll talk to Walter Strutt," he said solemnly. "Stand by." Then he added, "Good luck."

She wasn't certain what Gerard had meant by good luck. Good luck getting the *Chicago International Post* to print a news story that she'd witnessed firsthand? Good luck getting the story on the front page? Good luck getting a byline?

Abby was too unsettled to sleep. The only book she'd brought with her was Dorothy Canfield's *The Home-Maker* and there was an intensity to the prose that felt oppressive in Abby's current frame of mind. She wanted something light. She thought of the library full of books just down the hall and, knowing everyone was asleep or had at least retired to their rooms, decided to see if there wasn't something more soothing in the library. Even a dry and boring book about the family history might at least put her to sleep.

It was not quite midnight, but the house was still when she reached the library. She could smell a faint odor of cigarettes and the last of the fire in the grate. She perused the books and chose *The Inimitable Jeeves* by P. G. Wodehouse. The comic adventures of a hapless aristocrat and his indispensable man's man would surely help divert her mind from the tragedy she'd been involved with earlier today.

She headed for the door, book in hand, and noticed that Ned's flowers were gone.

Someone must have been in to clean the room and disposed of them. But then when she glanced around she realized the fire hadn't been reset for the morning, and while the cups and glasses had been cleared away, the decanter of whiskey was out of place on a side table. Had a maid or footman cleared away the forgotten flowers but not the whiskey? Or had someone taken those flowers?

Who would do that? And why?

While Abby stood looking at the spot where the flowers that Ned had picked for Cressida had been, her mind began to wander. She often did this when she was writing an article for the newspaper. There was an obvious through line to a story, but often the most interesting aspects were the less obvious. It was sometimes in asking the odd, unlikely or seemingly random question that truth would emerge. Sometimes a kind of truth that the person being interviewed hadn't even realized.

In this world in which she found herself, one which was alien to Abby, she felt that she perhaps had an advantage. She saw Darrington Manor and its inhabitants with the clearer sight that not being involved with this family and not even being British helped with. Then she shook her head at her own arrogance. Who was she to think she could figure out what had happened to Oliver Platt when both an inspector from Scotland Yard and one from the Sûreté in Paris were on hand to investigate?

She took a step toward the library door, thinking it was time to go back up to bed when the door began to open.

She didn't jump or cry out, but her heart beat uncomfortably fast in her chest as a man walked softly into the room and then shut the door behind him.

She let out a breath almost at the same moment that Inspector Henri Deschamps said, "Abigail Dixon. I thought you'd gone to bed." His tone was one of resignation rather than pleasure at seeing her in the library after midnight.

She felt defensive, and then was annoyed at herself. She had every right to be in the library of a house to which she had been invited. She put up her chin and said, "I might say the same about you." Then when he merely raised his brows she said, "In truth, I couldn't sleep. I thought I might find a book."

He nodded. "It is a library after all. Were you successful?"

It was such an odd conversation she nearly giggled. She held up *The Inimitable Jeeves*. "I think something light and humorous might help me fall asleep."

He looked at the cover of the book and smiled. "If you don't sleep, at least you'll be entertained. I wonder if there's another volume for me." She was surprised that a Frenchman would know the Wodehouse novels and then once more realized that there was more to Henri Deschamps than she'd discovered in Paris. He had a home in London, no doubt he'd hobnobbed with P. G. Wodehouse. She could only hope the author would parody Henri in a future novel.

Then, feeling she was being toyed with, she said, "I don't think you came down here to look for a book, did you?"

"I did not." It seemed as though he wouldn't say more, and then he let his gaze wander around the room. He stood very still and she watched him, wondering what he was seeing. There were the shelves of books, the dark wood paneling, the fireplace with nothing but embers glowing a dull red and smoking slightly, the furniture oddly lonely-looking without the people who'd so recently been sitting in there. She could smell a whiff of cigar smoke and the faintest hint of Chanel No. 5. It was a scent that made her shudder as she always associated it with the stepmother who had caused her and her family so much grief. There was the whiskey decanter that was out of place and a cushion that had been moved. She didn't know which of these things he was taking in and what other senses or impressions he was picking up that she was missing. In the silence between them she could feel the echo of the distress and pain of earlier, the loss of Oliver so keenly felt among them all, and then that strange scene with Ned Corcoran and his awkward posy of flowers.

Henri said, "I wanted to come back to this room and contemplate the very startling things that happened today."

She said, "Do you do that too? Do you let your mind wander and see if it picks up something new?"

His gaze came to hers looking quite startled.

She said quickly, "I do that in my journalism work. There are the stories that people tell us that are so often carefully rehearsed or curated. Sometimes they're stories they've been telling themselves for a very long time so that they believe their own version of the truth. And then there will be a glance, a moment, a thrown-out phrase, and it takes you in a different direction."

He rubbed the bottom of his chin with two fingers and said, "Then your journalism work is remarkably like that of a detective. I do hope that you are here thinking about journalism and not detection."

She said, "I am in the middle of a scoop of a story. Yes, I'm definitely thinking about my journalism career. You must know that I am tirelessly working to get moved off the women's page and into hard news. This could be my big break."

He was still looking at her rather suspiciously and then she decided to turn the tables on him. "And how about you? I don't imagine you're writing a newspaper article about Oliver's murder. And, as you've so clearly stated, you have no jurisdiction here."

His eyes glittered in what could have been amusement and he nodded his chin ever so slightly, acknowledging her hit. "I can, however, be of assistance to my colleague if he wishes it. Like you, I have the advantage of being in the middle of this extraordinary crime. In my experience, normally it's very clear who is the most likely perpetrator. But this is a genuine mystery. I keep asking myself, why would someone want to kill Oliver Platt?"

She couldn't have agreed with him more that it was a most strange and peculiar death on so many levels. "That's if you believe that Oliver was the intended victim. The fact that he was wearing Reginald Mitchell's coat does suggest that perhaps Reggie was the target."

"But suggestion isn't fact. And then there was the strange behavior of Mr. Corcoran this evening."

She cringed again thinking about the poor man caught red-handed with his posy of wildflowers, and the way Charles

Mitchell had done his best to humiliate him. She said, "Do you think his explanation was true?"

His eyes narrowed slightly. "That he's known Cressida Wimborne for years and wanted to take her some flowers to ease her distress?" Even as he said it, the excuse sounded unbelievable.

"What do you think he was doing then?"

"I cannot see inside the mind of Ned Corcoran. I find it interesting though, that the posy of flowers is no longer on that table."

So, he had noticed as she had. She glanced to where they had so recently lain and asked the question that was in her own mind. "What do you think it means?"

"As the servants haven't been in to do the final tidy-up of this room, I expect it means that someone came back and fetched those flowers."

She nodded. She'd come to the same conclusion. It might be strange to find a journalist and an inspector discussing what had happened to a handpicked posy of wildflowers, but she was glad that he felt, as she did, that there was something oddly significant about the missing posy.

"Either one of the servants picked it up while they were putting away the tea things or someone returned for those flowers," he mused.

"It could have been Ned Corcoran," she suggested, "wanting to remove them from sight and hopefully from all of our memories."

"It could."

"They could also have been fetched by Cressida's maid."

He nodded. "And, lastly, I suppose it could have been Cressida herself."

"Are you thinking what I'm thinking?" she asked curiously.

She saw a glint of amusement in his eyes. "That's a question guaranteed to get a man into trouble. What I am thinking is that when a boy and girl grow up in close proximity and she develops into a remarkably pretty young woman and he into a sturdy and fine young man, deep friendship is entirely possible. So is something warmer."

She nodded. Not wanting to beat around the bush she said, "You think he's in love with her?"

"I do not discount the possibility."

"And Reggie Mitchell is very much in the way of Cressie and Ned being together."

"There is much more than Reggie Mitchell standing between that happy couple. We must be careful not to make any hasty judgments."

That was so unfair. "I'm not making hasty judgments, I'm throwing out possibilities," she responded defensively.

"There's another possibility. Did you know that Oliver and Reggie were rather making nuisances of themselves at the local pub?"

Darn it, he was good. She'd thought she was getting privileged information from Vivian. How had he discovered what was going on at the local pub? Perhaps Inspector Deschamps liked to spend time there himself.

"Speaking of the locals," she said. "You haven't mentioned George Smith. I heard he and Reggie had an altercation in the pub."

"Mainly because Mr. Smith wasn't in the library tonight."

"No. But that is a very angry man and he has no love for Americans in general, or the Mitchells with their flashy automobiles and their flashy dollar bills coming over and lording it over the locals who are struggling to continue their way of life."

"It sounds as though you've already been working on your article in your head."

She couldn't help but smile at that. "I'd been thinking about writing about the impact of American prosperity on the old ways of life in Europe, that's true. But I had no idea that a murder would result."

"Again, we must be careful not to jump to any conclusions." He frowned. "I feel certain there is more that we do not know about Mr. Oliver Platt and his tragic demise."

"I've also been wondering about Gladys Trotter's death."

"You've been busy."

"There couldn't be a connection, could there?"

Those eyes that seemed to see everything held hers. "Why do you ask that question?"

"I don't know. Two murders close together, involving Darrington. It's such a coincidence."

"But coincidences do happen."

At that moment the door opened again and a footman came in with a basket of wood. He jumped when he saw them. "Shall I come back?"

"No," Abby said hastily. She felt suddenly awkward that she'd been caught late at night alone in the library with the inspector. Perhaps that's what made her blurt out, "I was only down here to find a book to read." And then she held it up. "And I found one."

She glanced quickly to Henri's face to find him grinning broadly now. He must know exactly how she was feeling and that simply annoyed her. In the coldest tone that she could manage she said, "I'll bid you goodnight, Inspector Deschamps."

"And I you, Miss Dixon."

And then with her head held high she walked out of the library and made her stately way up the stairs to bed.

TWENTY

When Abby woke up the next morning she felt as tired as she had been when she went to bed the night before. Her sleep had been broken by bad dreams and spells of troubled wakefulness where she had relived again seeing Oliver Platt face down in the river. It had been bad enough when she'd believed he'd somehow slipped and drowned by accident. But to be shot in the back? It seemed so cowardly to kill a man that way. Unless it had been an accidental shot... but then whoever had pulled the trigger ought to have stayed at the scene and tried to help the injured man. At least have called for help. Since they hadn't, she had to assume a cowardly employee of Darrington who hoped never to be discovered was the culprit.

Or, worst of all, a deliberate act of murder.

She didn't think that anyone deserved to end up that way, but certainly not a man who had arrived at Darrington Manor to be the best man at his closest friend's wedding.

As she rose and padded to the window, she gazed out on a promising morning. The gray skies had given way to sunshine which filled her with new energy. Abby wasn't a woman to wallow in the doldrums for long. She liked to be active.

Henri had reminded her she was not an investigator in this case. However, as an investigative journalist, or as someone who would like very much to be an investigative journalist, Abby had a vested interest in finding more about what had happened to Oliver. She was also well aware that the police were unlikely to share any of their findings with a reporter, so it was up to her to find out what she could if she wanted to not only discover the truth about what had happened to Oliver, but also accumulate enough facts to write compelling copy for the newspaper.

She wondered whether they'd held the front page of the *Chicago International Post* and if her byline would be the first thing readers would see when they perused today's paper.

When Vivian arrived to help her dress for the day, her temporary lady's maid looked quite heavy-eyed. Abby glanced at her sharply. "Were you out late again last night?" Not that it was any of her business what Vivian did with her spare time, but she was her friend and she cared about her.

Vivian nodded. "I couldn't leave Jerry when he was so upset, so I accompanied him to the Darrington Arms." She threw up her arms. "Don't worry. We were never alone. You see, Jerry had been acting as valet for Mr. Oliver, so he was understandably devastated. I think he was hoping that Oliver might take him on permanently and then he could move to New York."

Abby was quite surprised. "After only a week working for him?"

Vivian jumped to the defense of her new friend. "I told you, he's ambitious. And he's very efficient. And you know how much New Yorkers prize British servants. It's the height of fashion."

She wondered how Vivian would know any such thing. Perhaps she had discovered this from reading *Vogue* magazine.

And then Vivian went on. "Plus, it's customary for a gentleman to tip his valet at the end of a stay in a country house like this. Poor Jerry feels that he's been robbed of his tip. Not that he isn't also extremely sad to have lost Oliver. As we all are."

Abby supposed you couldn't blame the man for missing his tip, even though it did seem rather calculating and hard-hearted in light of the fact that the man he'd been working for had been murdered.

"And he's terrified that you'll turn him in to the police. Honestly, Vivian, he couldn't have killed Gladys. I can tell he liked her as a friend. He'd never hurt her. He said you told him to go to the police and tell them everything he knows, but if the Wimbornes find out he lied about visiting his mother and went for a job interview instead, he'll lose his position here."

"If the police find out he lied, bought the silk stockings that Gladys was strangled with and was in London at the time of her murder, he'll be in a lot more trouble than that. You must encourage him to tell the police everything."

"What if they pin it on him so they get an easy arrest?" Vivian argued.

Then she saw Abby's face and sighed. "Okay, I'll talk to him again."

Abby had a sudden thought. "Vivian, has Jerry been instructed to clean out Oliver's room?"

"No. He was ordered not to tidy it until the police have gone through everything."

"And have they?"

"I believe that Inspector Grenville is planning to search Oliver's things this morning. After that, Jerry's to pack everything up."

Abby felt suddenly very sad that Oliver had arrived with a week's worth of clothes suitable for balls and dances and dinners and social engagements of all sorts, that he would have packed the suit he would wear as best man, and now he lay dead. It was all so terribly unfair and so terribly wrong.

"Vivian, do you think Jerry could arrange for me to see Oliver's room? I probably can't tip him as well as Oliver Platt would have, but I'm sure the *Chicago International Post* would consider that a legitimate expense."

She used the word *tip* but the plain truth was she was willing to bribe a servant to access the dead man's things. However, since she was hoping to help the police discover who had killed Oliver Platt she convinced herself she wasn't doing anything too unethical.

No doubt Henri would strongly disagree with her plan, but she comforted herself with the thought that he would never know.

Vivian gasped. "Of course! I hadn't even thought that you were writing an article about Oliver's death. You are, aren't you?"

Abby didn't disagree. "I don't wish to profit from a young man's murder, but I believe I can help solve this crime, and at the same time as finding justice for Oliver I can write the kind of stories that I went to journalism school to tell." Then she opened the drawer of her dressing table and passed Vivian the typed article she'd sent to the *Post*. Vivian read the piece aloud and it helped Abby to hear her own words.

"*Tragedy Halts Wedding—Best Man found Dead*," Viv began. "*Joy turned to tragedy when Oliver Platt, best man to Reginald Mitchell, son of car king Charles A. Mitchell, died while trout fishing on Friday at Darrington Manor in Somerset, England.*

"Seeing it written down makes it so real," Vivian said. "And so sad. Imagine, going fishing, not realizing it's the last thing you'll ever do."

Vivian's voice grew thick as she read the second paragraph: "*Mr. Platt, twenty-five, was in England for his best friend's union with Miss Cressida Wimborne. After Mr. Platt's body was discovered by members of the wedding party, the Wimborne and*

*Mitchell families decided to postpone the wedding. 'Devastated,'
is how Reginald Mitchell described himself after hearing the
news of his friend's demise. 'Oliver was like a brother to me. I
can't imagine my life without him.'*

"Only twenty-five, Abby. The same age we are. It's so
terribly tragic. And poor Reginald. And the Wimbornes, having
put everything into this wedding, now having to postpone."
Then she glanced up at Abby. "Did Reggie really say all that?"

Abby's journalistic hackles rose. "Yes. He did. You don't
imagine I make up quotes for the newspaper, do you?"

Vivian immediately begged pardon.

"I wanted to get a quote from Inspector Grenville, too, but
he warned me against saying anything. I could see he'd have
vastly preferred it if there wasn't a reporter in the midst of his
investigation."

Vivian read one more paragraph: *"The circumstances are
considered suspicious and Scotland Yard has been called in to
investigate."*

"I should say they're suspicious. The poor man was shot in
the back." Then she glanced up, puzzled. "Is that further down
in your report."

Abby shook her head. "I promised him I wouldn't give
anything away until he's ready to release it. He said it could
hamper the investigation." Their gazes met in the mirror. "So I
made a deal with Inspector Grenville. I said I would do as he
asked so long as I was given first access whenever the press are
allowed to release the details."

"That's more than fair," Vivian said. She glanced at the rest
of the piece but Abby told her she didn't need to read it now. It
was merely background about Oliver Platt and a rehashing of
facts about the two families. Abby had barely mentioned Cressida. She might be a reporter but she hoped she was also a
woman with a heart and she couldn't say that the bride-to-be

had taken to her bed with the shock. At least, not without Cressida's permission.

Vivian buttoned the pearl buttons on Abby's fawn-colored day dress and then said, "Let me speak to Jerry and see what he says. But you know he could get into awful trouble if he was caught sneaking us in."

Abby considered he was already in a world of trouble. "Perhaps he could leave the door unlocked at a certain time? Letting you know beforehand which room belonged to Oliver."

Vivian approved of this plan. Then Abby said, "There's something else I want you to do. It's a bit of detective work."

As she had hoped, Vivian's eyes lit up at that. "Is it dangerous?"

She couldn't tell whether a hint of danger was a good or a bad thing. She shook her head. "It could be very important though; a vital clue, in fact."

And then she explained her plan. Vivian was both wide-eyed and thrilled to be an accomplice in sleuthing. Accordingly, by the time Abby went down to breakfast a plan was in place.

Similar to dinner the night before, it was a sober gathering at breakfast. The talk was desultory at best and Oliver's presence was larger than if he'd actually been sitting at the table. No one mentioned his name nor referred to his death. That was likely because Cressida was sitting among them, looking pale and fragile. She sipped at a cup of tea with hands that were shaking and her mother brought her over a plate with a slice of buttered toast on it.

She shook her head and tried to push it away, but her mother said, "You must eat something, my darling."

Cressida was wearing a sober gray dress with a black cardigan which made her look more like a young widow than a young bride. It was warm in the breakfast room and Cressie slipped off her cardigan, hanging it from the back of her chair.

Abby had her coffee and then got up to fetch herself food. As she walked by Cressida's chair she made sure to accidentally knock the cardigan onto the floor with her elbow. No one noticed. She fetched herself toast and scrambled eggs and, when she walked past Cressida's place again, she deftly kicked the sweater under the table.

She was sitting beside Charles A. Mitchell. He might be in mourning for the man he had said was like a son to him, but it hadn't impaired his appetite. He tucked into his bacon and eggs, sausage and kippers with relish and when he'd mopped the last of his egg off the plate with a crust of toast he said irritably, "When is that inspector coming back, may I ask?"

He stared at Henri as he said it, but it was Lord Wimborne who answered. "He said he'd be here after breakfast."

Charles Mitchell made an irritated sound. "What does that mean? Does the man breakfast early? Do you think he'll be here before noon? How am I to plan my day? I've things to see to. I must arrange for Oliver's funeral." There was a slight catch in his voice as he said the word funeral so Abby was certain that he was deeply affected, even if his appetite wasn't.

"I think we'll all be relieved when the investigation is behind us," Lord Wimborne said quietly as he looked at his daughter.

"It's the most confounded business!" Charles Mitchell almost shouted the words. "And where's the sense in it? A young man like that, in the prime of his life. Where's the sense in it?" he asked again.

No one answered him.

Reggie seemed very attentive to Cressida. He sat beside her and in a low voice asked, "What will you do today, my dear?"

She glanced up at him and her face was woebegone. "I don't know."

"Would you like to go for a drive?" he asked her.

Her shudder was violent. "No. I can't bear to be away from the house."

"Perhaps a walk, then," he suggested.

"Yes. Perhaps. Later."

"Is your head better now?" Lady Wimborne asked Reggie.

He still wore a sticking plaster on his brow but seemed in better health. He said, "A headache doesn't seem like much in comparison to..." He glanced at Cressida and trailed off. She had begun to weep.

"I'm sorry, darling," he said. "Thoughtless of me."

Charles Mitchell said, "I don't recommend you leave this property either, Reggie, until we know what's going on here. Don't forget you were driving that car and nearly killed. And, if the rest of you have forgotten, Oliver was wearing Reggie's coat when he was shot in the back. Doesn't that suggest that my son was the actual target?"

In fact, they'd been over this ground the day before. But she could see in Charles Mitchell's angry bluster a real fear for his son. And perhaps he had some residual guilt too. If the young man he'd called his adopted son had died by mistake in place of his actual son, how dreadful that would be for him. And to feel that his son's life was still in danger made her more charitable where the man's obnoxious behavior was concerned.

He motioned to the table and said, "If you've no objection, Lord Wimborne, I should like to use your telephone. I've sad arrangements to make."

"Certainly," Lord Wimborne said. "All my resources are at your disposal."

Reggie touched Cressie's hand and then rose.

Charles Mitchell called out, "Reggie, come with me. You can help me plan the funeral. You'll know more what he would have wanted."

Cressida dabbed at her eyes with a handkerchief, then said,

"I'm sorry to be such poor company but I'd like to return to my room." She and her mother left together and Lord Wimborne and Henri departed soon after, leaving Abby and Peter alone in the breakfast room. She had toyed with her coffee as long as she could and now she rose from her chair. Peter was looking down at his breakfast when she swiftly knelt down and retrieved Cressida's black cardigan, slipping it over her arm.

She left the room and then by preconceived design bumped into Vivian crossing the foyer with Abby's shoes that she'd been polishing in the servant's quarters.

Abby feigned surprise at seeing Vivian and said, "Oh, Vivian, I've done the silliest thing. I've walked away with Cressida's cardigan. Do you think you could find a way to return it to her?"

"Yes, miss," Vivian said, in a very un-Vivian-like way. She had never sounded so submissive.

Then Abby said, loud enough for anyone passing to hear, "Perhaps I'll come up with you and apologize to Cressida. I quite feel as though I've accidentally purloined her property."

"Yes, miss," her faithful servant replied, eyes firmly on the ground.

She followed Vivian up to the family's wing. She had dreaded bumping into Lady Wimborne, who would quite rightly take the sweater from her and tell her she would return it to Cressida herself. Fortunately, there was no one in the hallway. Vivian, through her own methods, had discovered which room was Cressida's and knocked softly on the door. There was no answer. She rapped softly again and the door opened to reveal Cressida's maid.

"I'm awfully sorry," she said, "but my mistress—"

Before she could finish her sentence, Abby swept past her right into Cressida's bedroom as though she had been invited. Cressida was sitting at her dressing table and turned in surprise at the sound of Abby's voice.

Abby said, "I'm so dreadfully sorry, I picked up your cardigan by accident and wanted to apologize and return it."

The woman was too polite to take offense at having her bedroom invaded like this. She rose and said automatically, "Not at all. Thank you so much for returning it. I'm sure the fault was mine. I imagine I simply left it behind."

The maid took it from Abby, who said, "It was a dreadful ordeal we went through yesterday. I'm sure, in time, the awful memory will fade."

Cressida looked almost desperate. "Will it? The most terrible day of my life, when all hope was lost." Her voice dissolved into tears.

"I'm so sorry this should happen so close to your wedding. If you ever want a friendly ear, I hope I can be your friend."

"That's very kind," she said mechanically. And then, "Thank you again."

If ever there was a polite exit line, that was it. She'd all but asked Abby to leave the room. With a final nod to the lady's maid, Abby stepped toward the door, which the maid opened for her. Then she stopped and pointed to a familiar-looking posy of wildflowers nestled in a vase on the table beside Cressida's bed.

In a bright tone Abby said, "Oh, good, I see you received your posy."

Cressida blushed and said, "Yes. Jane knew they were meant for me and very kindly brought them up. Mr. Corcoran is a very old friend. It was kind of him to think of me in my distress."

Her voice wobbled as she uttered the words "friend" and "distress."

"I'll leave you now," Abby said. But before she could there was a commotion outside. Cressida's room overlooked the front of Darrington Manor. She heard Charles Mitchell bellow: "Great Jupiter, what balderdash is this?"

She ran to the window and spied several men and a couple of photographers. They had their reporters' notebooks out and were calling out questions to Charles A. Mitchell. He rounded on them like a guard dog and pointed a stubby finger. "Now look, chaps. I know you've a job to do, but this is private property. What happened here is a terrible tragedy and that's all I have to say. You will stop bothering the family and get yourselves down to the road or I'll have the police on you."

Cressida had joined Abby at the window. "Who are those horrible men?" she asked.

"Reporters."

"Reporters! Why, they're like buzzards drawn to carrion, picking over the dead carcass. It's vile."

"I'm a journalist myself," she reminded Cressida. Then, as though compelled, she said, "I wrote a short, factual article for my newspaper. I barely mentioned you. I imagine it's been published in this morning's *Chicago International Post*."

"I see." She wasn't sure whether Cressida now lumped Abby with "those horrible men" or was simply shocked to discover that the death of her fiancé's best man was news.

With a final goodbye, she and Vivian retreated to Abby's bedroom.

When Abby and Vivian left Cressida's room, Abby had to squeeze Vivian's arm with a warning grip as she could just tell her friend and sometime dresser was bursting to talk about what they had seen. Fortunately, she must have got the message because she didn't say anything until they were back in Abby's room. Once the door had clicked shut behind them, her voice throbbing with suppressed excitement, Vivian said, "You were marvelous! And you were right."

Abby nodded. "It was just a hunch."

"You told me to look out for a small posy of wildflowers and there they were, in a vase sitting right beside Miss Wimborne's bed. Oh, Abby, what do you think it means?"

TWENTY-ONE

Abby was trying very hard not to jump to any conclusions. She said, "Honestly, I'm not sure. But it does seem strange that Cressida or her maid would creep back down and pick up those flowers. It's not like the flowers themselves were particularly special, it had to be the person who had chosen and picked each bloom."

Vivian put a hand to her chest and said, "Golly, do you think Cressida is in love with Ned Corcoran?"

"I think it's very likely that Ned Corcoran is in love with Cressida. But he must know it's hopeless. She's engaged to another man." Then Abby thought about it and said, "Or she was, until the groom's best friend was murdered."

"Nothing this exciting has ever happened to me," gasped Vivien. "To think, I'm on the scene of a famous murder. And you can write about it while all those other reporters have to kick their heels outside the estate gates."

Abby couldn't help but smile. "Well, I don't like to be causing any awkwardness for my hosts, but you're right, we're in the middle of a murder mystery. As a journalist, this is a gift. Walter Strutt will have to put my articles in the paper now."

Vivian sighed. "It's like one of those dime-store novels. The beautiful, titled debutante, marrying the dashing American whose father is one of the richest men in the United States, and then tragedy strikes. And now, it seems there's another love interest."

Abby had to laugh. Vivian was imbuing every line with throbbing eloquence as though she were Tallulah Bankhead emoting from center stage.

"It would be more exciting if it wasn't so sad. Oliver seemed like such a nice man. I still don't understand who would want to kill him."

Vivian glanced up at her. "Well, someone sure did," she said in a hushed whisper. "And those flowers were right beside her bed too. They'd be the last thing she saw when she went to bed and the first thing she saw when she woke up this morning Oh, Abby, do you think Ned Corcoran killed Oliver thinking it was Reggie?"

"I don't know," Abby said. "But I think I'm going to pay Mr. Ned Corcoran a call."

Vivian looked worried. "Abby, you do realize that he could be a killer. Remember when you warned me not to be alone with Jerry? I'm coming with you."

"No. It will look peculiar. I'll tell him you know where I am. But I can't think of a reason why he would kill me. Besides, I'll make sure I speak to him in company with his mother. Presumably she'll be in the cottage with him."

"Before you do that, Jerry said the police have finished with Oliver's things and he's to pack them up ready to be shipped back to America. He'll do that this afternoon. So, if we were to go to Mr. Oliver's room this morning, there'd be no one there," Vivian said with a pleased expression.

"Oh, Viv, you're brilliant! I'll make sure Jerry gets a good 'tip.'"

Vivian tossed her blond curls. "He doesn't need a tip. He

said he'd do anything for me. So please don't let the police send him to jail for a murder he didn't commit."

Deciding to postpone her visit to Ned's mother, she followed Vivian up a floor. They had no reason to be there, so she was extremely relieved when Viv opened a door leading off the deserted corridor and they found themselves in Oliver Platt's bedroom.

It was a comfortable room, though not as luxurious as the one Lady Wimborne had shown Abby to. A double bed, an armchair, a chest of drawers and a wardrobe. Unlike her room, this one had no en suite bathroom.

Abby stood very still for a moment and closed her eyes. She caught a slight scent of tobacco. Beside her, Viv whispered, "What are we looking for?"

"I don't know," Abby replied. "I don't know."

She walked to the wardrobe and opened it. Now she caught the scent of Oliver's cologne. His coats were hanging neatly, including, sadly, a black tuxedo with a black mask tied onto the same clothes hanger. It was his outfit for the masquerade ball that would never take place. His clothes were good but under-stated, as though he'd always been careful not to be too flashy. By nature as well as birth, he was the second in command. Serving Charles Mitchell, and being groomed to run Mitchell Motors, the able steward of a company that did not bear his name. She flipped through his coats, knowing the police would have searched all the pockets thoroughly. Then she stopped, coming upon the sporting jacket with the torn pocket. She removed it from the wardrobe. It was the last item of clothing he'd worn that day that was his own. She searched the pockets, knowing she was going over well-trodden ground. A box of matches with the name Edna written on it. She wondered who Edna was. A packet of pipe tobacco in another pocket and nothing else. Vivian looked over her shoulder. "My, that's some tear in the pocket." She reached out and touched it with her fingertip, making it flap. "He must have caught it on something sharp when he was out shooting."

A quick look through the chest of drawers showed nothing remarkable and Abby felt uncomfortable pawing through his undergarments even though the man was unlikely to protest. If he could see her, he must know she was only trying to help solve his murder.

On the bedside table was a slim volume entitled *Self Mastery Through Conscious Autosuggestion* by Émile Coué. In the flyleaf, Oliver had written, *Every day, in every way, I'm getting better and better*. To think of him earnestly working on self-improvement filled her with sorrow.

There was no fire in the grate and the fireplace hadn't been swept since Oliver had died. Presumably the police had sifted through the ashes, but still, Abby got to her hands and knees and, removing a hairpin, ran it through the ash.

"What are you looking for?"

"No idea."

She was about to give up when a hint of white paper emerged. She lifted it from the ashes with the tips of her fingers. Cheap paper, she noted. The paper had been burned but part of one letter remained. She showed Viv. "What do you think that is?"

Viv squinted. "You mean that smudge of pen? It looks like the beginning of a J. Or an L. Maybe a D? Or could it be a number. A one, perhaps."

There was nothing else in the room of interest. Vivian peeked out of the door and, seeing the corridor still empty, the two women made their way back to Abby's bedroom as quickly as they could.

"Did you learn anything new?" Viv asked when they had shut the door behind them.

"I learned that Oliver Platt was a tidy man who was interested in autosuggestion, and he burned something that could mean nothing. Or something," Abby said. "Maybe I'll learn more from Ned Corcoran."

Vivian said, "You're still going?"

She nodded.

"Be careful."

As Abby was leaving the house she bumped into Henri Deschamps. She would have greeted him and moved on but he fell into step with her along the path.

"I hope you found Cressida well?" he said.

She looked at him, startled. "What makes you think I would have any idea how Cressida is?"

He looked down at her in amusement. "I couldn't help but notice your little pantomime of knocking her cardigan off the back of her chair and neatly disposing of it under the table. Since I didn't imagine you were attempting to purloin that sweater for yourself, I'm assuming you were using it as an excuse to pay her a visit this morning."

Darn, that inspector was sharp-sighted. And sharp-witted, she ought to have remembered. There was no point pretending. "Fine," she sighed. "I did pay her a visit this morning. And you're right, I needed an excuse. Returning her clothing gave me the perfect opportunity." She only hoped he never found out she'd snooped in Oliver Platt's room. He wouldn't be amused by that, she was certain.

"Did you find her well?" he said in the smoothest of tones.

"As well as can be expected, under the circumstances."

He looked down at her, his eyes glinting. "Shall we stop fencing with each other? Were the flowers there? The oh-so touching bouquet that Mr. Ned Corcoran had picked with his own hands."

She nodded.

"Interesting."

Abby was curious as to what he was thinking. "Interesting as in what curious customs these English people have?"

"Interesting as in the gesture must have held value for Cressida. Or perhaps her handmaiden is more sentimental."

Abby felt suddenly as though she'd pulled Ned and Cressida into a mess that she hadn't meant to. She said, "I think it's entirely possible that what Lord Wimborne said was true. They've been friends for a long time."

"And I think it's entirely possible, as you do, that there's much more than friendship between those two."

She didn't answer. There was no point; it would only be speculating, and besides, she agreed with him.

Instead she asked him where he was off to. He said, "Inspector Grenville and his men are trying to find the gun that killed Oliver. I intend to lend my assistance."

She nodded and, even though he hadn't asked her, said, "I thought I'd take a walk. It's very unnerving in that house. There are so many complicated emotions swirling around."

"I would have thought you'd be in your element. A reporter, at the scene of a murder, and the only one here. It's an enviable position for a journalist. The English newspapermen are outside the gates waiting, and here you are in the middle of the story."

She heard his cynicism and felt justifiably annoyed. "I am not a monster. I'm extremely aware of how difficult this is for the Wimborne family, and the Mitchells too. I'm trying my very best to be sensitive while also doing my job. I received a telegram from my editor this morning asking me to interview Cressida. Can you imagine such a thing? Of course, I shan't do it. However, I do want to be the reporter who has the most thorough, accurate stories on the murder investigation."

"That is understandable," he said, almost on a sigh of resignation. "However, once more I must remind you that you are not a member of the police force. It's one thing to report the news, just make sure you don't insert yourself into the middle of it."

He didn't say "again," but it was implied. It was so unfair. It wasn't her fault that she'd been accused of murdering her own stepmother. If she'd inserted herself into that story, it was only because she'd been the unwilling victim. Naturally she didn't respond, she merely wished him a good day and strode on.

She'd been given the directions to Ned Corcoran's home by Vivian, who'd got them from Jerry. It was about a fifteen-minute walk until she came across the cottage. It was rustic but beautiful, made of the local stone, and at that moment bathed in sunshine looking as innocent as one of the lambs playing in the green fields that surrounded them. The garden was extremely well-tended and neat and she walked up the path hoping very much that she wasn't doing something very foolish. She decided that if Ned Corcoran was here on his own she would refuse any invitation to enter the cottage and remain outside. That should keep her safe.

She didn't want to think that Ned Corcoran was a killer. But, as she had already learned, almost anyone had it in them to kill, given sufficient provocation. Obsessive love could definitely be that kind of provocation. Everybody from the Ancient Greeks to Shakespeare to Eugene O'Neill had explored that theme.

She lifted the beautifully polished lion's head and rapped on the door. There was no answer. But it was such a beautiful sunny day she wondered if he might be working in this pretty garden. She followed one of the neat paths around to the back and discovered an older woman hanging washing. She was about to call out a greeting and then stopped, watching. The woman was pegging up a man's garments. Presumably Ned's. And it looked very much like the things he'd been wearing yesterday.

She called out, "Hello."

The woman had obviously been miles away and jumped slightly at the greeting. She turned her head and Abby could have told right away that she was Ned Corcoran's mother. They had similar features, the same open countenance and ready smile. Her hair was more gray than brown and tied back in a neat bun, and she wore an apron over a housedress.

"Good morning to you. Can I help you with something?" she asked kindly.

She had a pleasant voice with what Abby thought was a local Somerset accent. Ned's was more refined, closer to that of Peter's and Cressida's, but this woman sounded much more like the locals. She said, "Yes. I was looking for Ned."

"Oh bless you, he's never here at this time of day. He's always off working on the estate somewhere."

She wasn't sure why she'd expected to find him here, except that it was fairly obvious he would not be welcome anywhere near the house where Reggie and his father were staying. Somehow she'd imagined that, with a murder investigation going on, he'd be home. And yet, she supposed cows still needed milking and crops still needed tending and the estate still needed managing.

The lady said, "But I'm happy to make you a cup of tea and you could wait for him here if you like. He usually comes home for his lunch."

As much as she liked the idea of snooping inside Ned's house, she didn't have time to waste. Instead she said, "That's all right. Do you have any idea where he was going this morning?"

"As a matter of fact he mentioned something about tending to the Rolls-Royce. Oh, that young man and automobiles. He'd spend his whole life with his head under the bonnet of a car and poking around in the engine if you let him. His father was like that too, God rest his soul."

"Thank you very much. If I don't happen to find him, please tell him that Abigail Dixon was asking after him."

"Oh, he's mentioned you. He says you're a lady journalist."

"I am. I'm here in a professional capacity. I'm supposed to be writing articles about the wedding."

A shadow crossed Mrs. Corcoran's face. Abby couldn't tell whether it was sadness over the death of a young man she hadn't known or possibly over the blighted hopes of her son. Abby watched her for a moment and then the woman said, "What a terrible business. That poor young man, come to play best man at his closest friend's wedding."

She just shook her head and didn't say any more. She didn't need to, as they both knew how the poor man had ended.

"I'll let you get back to your washing," Abby said. "I see those are Ned's things. I imagine he keeps you busy."

"Morning, Mrs. C," a jovial voice called, and as Abby turned she saw George Smith. He hadn't seen her and his face shuttered so quickly she could have imagined the surly worker who'd been so rude to her. "I see you've got company. I'll come back later," he said, and turned away.

Mrs. Corcoran called back, "You come and have some supper with us, George."

Then she pointed to a section of stone wall around the garden that was freshly repaired. "He's a good man, that George Smith. Has a bit of a temper on him, I'll admit, but as good a nature as any man I know. Days he spent, helping fix that wall while keeping up with his other duties. He only got it finished the day you arrived."

"Really?" Abby went closer. "It looks like a very big job. How many days did it take him?"

"Well, let's see. He began on Saturday and by Wednesday morning he was done. I made him a nice big breakfast and then he was off back to the fields."

Which meant that George Smith could not have been in London murdering Gladys Trotter if he was building stone walls for Mrs. Corcoran. That made things look less good for Jerry. Had he gone to the police to tell them he'd bought those silk stockings and had been in London? She didn't want to be the one to give them that information, but if he didn't tell the truth today, she'd have to.

Mrs. Corcoran checked the washing to see if any of it was dry. "My Ned always has plenty of washing. For all he's supposed to be concerning himself with business, you'd be amazed how often he mucks in with the workers, helping bring in crops or birth an animal that's struggling. And the engine oil he gets all over him." She shook her head. "Yesterday it was blood."

Abby felt as though she'd suffered an electric shock. "Blood?"

"Aye, they were hunting rabbits all morning, weren't they? And a nice pair of plump ones he brought home for me to make a lovely rabbit stew."

"I'll let you get back to it then," Abby said, and wished the woman goodbye.

But as she walked away her heart felt heavy. Was it only rabbit's blood that Ned Corcoran had on his hands?

TWENTY-TWO

Abby walked toward the garage where the cars were kept, lost in thought. She passed a uniformed police officer who nodded to her and said, "Morning, miss," as she passed. Otherwise it was quiet. Peaceful. But an uncomfortable peace, if there was such a thing. She felt something was brewing. Something unpleasant. And because she didn't know what it was she was helpless to stop it. She quickened her pace, not that she even knew what she was headed for or why. As she grew closer to the garage she heard voices. Cressida was speaking and sounded in terrible distress.

"Please. Please just don't. Leave me alone. I wouldn't have come if I'd known you'd be here."

And then Ned's voice, passionate and urgent. "I had to see you. Cressie, whatever they're saying about me, you mustn't listen. You know me. You know who I am."

"Please. Please, you must let me go."

And then an anguished, "Cressie."

A moment later Cressida burst out of the garage, looking frantic, tears pouring down her face. If she even saw Abby she didn't acknowledge her, just ran toward the house.

Ned came out as though to follow her, and then seeing Abby the wind seemed to go out of his sails. He tried to put on a brave front, but she could see the desperation in his eyes.

"Miss Dixon. May I help you in some way? Did you need me to drive you somewhere?" He said, obviously pulling himself together with an effort.

She found herself in a quandary. She didn't know what to do or say. She did not think she'd ever walked in on anything so awkward or overheard anything so painful and personal. She hadn't meant to eavesdrop, but clearly she had and Ned must realize she'd heard at least some of what had passed between him and Cressida. She no longer in any way believed they were just friends.

"Oh, Ned."

He seemed for a moment as though he was going to keep up the façade, and then he seemed to crumble in front of her emotionally. "Miss Dixon, I don't know what you heard, but I can assure you—"

"I—"

She hadn't formulated what she was going to say, but in any case her speech was cut off by Inspector Digby Grenville, who walked around the side of the garage at that moment, holding a rifle in his hands. He looked almost jovial when he saw Ned Corcoran and her standing together.

"Mr. Corcoran," he began in a brusque tone, "I was on my way to find you."

Ned Corcoran gave him a curt nod. "Well you found me."

The inspector held up the rifle and said, "I believe this is yours."

Ned Corcoran nodded. "That's right. I keep it in the gun room."

"And yet I didn't find it in the gun room. No, indeed. Tucked in the trunk of a tree, not two hundred and fifty yards from where Mr. Oliver Platt was killed yesterday afternoon. Do you have any idea how it might have got there?"

She felt that he was toying with the man. The way a cat might toy with a moth caught between its paws. As much as the poor thing tries to flutter away, the cat pounces on it again.

Ned Corcoran said in a flat tone, "I do not. I do not leave weapons in tree trunks. I always lock them away in the gun room."

Inspector Grenville looked at the rifle and seemed to consider. Then he said, "Unless you're in a hurry, of course. Say, you'd just killed a man and needed to put distance between you and the victim as quickly as you could. Perhaps you intended to go back for it and relock it in the gun room and yet you didn't have a chance because you knew you were being watched."

"I can assure you, I locked up that gun yesterday afternoon."

Inspector Henri Deschamps came around the corner of the garage then and joined their little group. Several uniformed policemen stayed respectfully at a distance, ringing Ned Corcoran, presumably so he couldn't run. Abby's heart sank. Ned glanced behind her and obviously took in the fact that he was trapped.

The inspector said, "Why don't you just tell me what happened yesterday, in your own words."

"What happened yesterday? I believe I already told you that when you interviewed me. I went shooting rabbits in the morning, and then after lunch I helped Lord Wimborne with his fishing. I put the rifle in the gun room and meant to go back and clean it, but there wasn't time."

"But you weren't with Lord Wimborne the entire afternoon, were you?"

Ned looked quite annoyed now. "I most certainly was." And then he seemed to remember. "Except when I left to fetch him a rug for his knees. A breeze whipped up and he grew chilled."

"So you'd have had time to shoot Mr. Oliver Platt in the back, pop the rifle in the trunk of a tree, fetch Lord Wimborne his blanket, and who'd have been the wiser?"

"I didn't have a rifle with me to go fishing. Ask Lord Wimborne." Ned was furious.

"I hope I'm not a complete fool. You hid that gun in a convenient location, found an excuse to leave Lord Wimborne, made short work of Oliver Platt, returned the gun and, cool as you please, made your way back to Lord Wimborne."

"But why would I kill a man I've barely even met?" Ned pleaded angrily.

The inspector shook his head sadly. "You'll only make things worse for yourself, my friend. You killed for love."

She watched Ned Corcoran's face turn beet red. "I don't know what you're talking about," he retorted stiffly.

"I believe you do. When a man knows great love, there's nothing he won't do for the woman of his dreams. And Cressida Wimborne was that woman for you. Always unattainable, but so long as she remained single and in your orbit you could cope. You saw her every day, she was kind to you. Perhaps even friendly. Everything was fine until she became engaged to another man. And you were eaten by jealousy. Jealous in the utter impossibility of ever being able to have the woman you wanted so badly."

"This is absurd!" Ned spat.

"Absurd and tragic. Because, in trying to kill Miss Wimborne's fiancé, you made a mistake. He was wearing the jacket that Reginald Mitchell had been wearing that morning. A jacket you had certainly seen Reginald wearing as he came down that morning to check the car. He recalls engaging in conversation with you."

"Yes, he did engage in conversation with me. I couldn't have told you what the man was wearing though."

"Nevertheless, it was a fairly distinctive coat. You knew the wedding guests were fishing that afternoon and it's not a group activity. They were each tucked away in quiet spot where spotted trout might linger. It must have been much easier than shooting a rabbit. From behind, Oliver Platt and Reginald Mitchell would have looked very similar. Oliver Platt was wearing the coat you'd seen Reginald Mitchell wearing earlier. They were similar height, similar build. It was the work of a minute to end his life. However, you killed the wrong man. But you did it, and for that you will be punished."

"I am innocent," Ned cried, his hands curling into fists.

"That, my good man, is for a court of law to decide, unless you decide to end this farce and save poor Miss Wimborne and this family who have been so very good to you from the torment of a public trial. Admit your crime, it's the right thing to do."

"I assure you if I had committed such a crime I would admit to it, but I have done no such thing. I am an innocent man."

The inspector looked rather disappointed at this answer and wearily shook his head. He said, as though each word pained him, "Ned Corcoran, I am arresting you on suspicion of the murder of Oliver Platt. You do not have to say anything, however..."

He stood stiff and proud while Inspector Grenville read him his rights. Then one of the officers stepped forward and put him in handcuffs, after which he was led to a squat, black police car that was waiting in the drive. Before he got into the car he turned and his eyes sought out and found Abby.

"Tell Miss Wimborne, tell her... I'm sorry."

And then he could say no more for he was being pushed into the backseat of the car.

Inspector Grenville turned to Abby and said, "I will stand by our agreement. If you telephone my office later today, I will speak to you." With a nod to her and Henri he left and soon the rest of the police contingent followed suit.

"Well, that was a stunning conclusion to the next article you'll write," Henri said, turning to Abby.

But was it the correct conclusion? Abby's instincts told her this was far too neat. And yet, if Ned Corcoran hadn't killed Oliver, who had?

TWENTY-THREE

Henri had been watching Abby. She could feel his gaze on her. When she turned to him he said, "You don't seem entirely satisfied with this turn of events."

She couldn't explain the niggle of discomfort behind her breastbone, but he was right, she didn't feel entirely satisfied. With a helpless shrug, she said, "I can't explain it, it's just... something seems off."

His mustache tilted in a slight smile. "Not that I wish to malign my own profession, but the most obvious suspect is very often the correct one. Mr. Ned Corcoran is an amiable man, a good employee, liked by all. It's difficult to put such a man in handcuffs and send him to his just punishment. Much better when the criminal is a blackhearted villain, and ugly into the bargain. However, I can assure you, the prisons are filled with men just like Ned Corcoran. Often amiable men who have made a single bad decision or a series of bad choices."

Was that all it was? Was that why she felt so unsettled? "But Ned Corcoran isn't stupid. Why would he leave the gun he used to kill Oliver near the scene of the crime? He'd put it neatly back in the gun case, surely. Exactly as he said he did."

"You must make allowances for a man who is not by nature a criminal. Let us suppose he kills Oliver. Shooting a man in the back who is quietly fishing smacks of cowardice as well as villainy. He would have been too young for the Great War so it's likely all he's killed are rabbits and pheasants. To shoot a man and take his life is not like shooting a rabbit. It's entirely plausible that he panicked. He stashed the gun in the nearest hiding place. Besides, don't forget he had to get back to Lord Wimborne, who was his alibi. He may not have had time to retrieve his weapon, and then never found an opportunity to get it again without being spotted. Before he could go back and remove the gun, the police were here crawling all over the grounds and it was too dangerous."

"Ned looked genuinely innocent." And then she held up a hand. "Before you tell me that many an innocent-looking man is now behind bars, I will simply tell you that I have my doubts."

"I see."

She made a sound of frustration in the back of her throat. "You think I'm a hysterical female, like one of those women who write to convicts in prison."

He gazed at her for a moment with a curious expression in his eyes. "I think you are an extremely intelligent woman and a capable journalist."

She was so stunned by this that she felt her eyes widen. "But you're always telling me off for interfering."

His eyes lightened in amusement. "I also find you ruthlessly determined and only too willing to push forward when the wiser course might be to hold back."

Despite the insulting nature of his last words she was flattered by his more charitable observations, but she felt there was more he wasn't saying. She held his gaze. "You aren't completely convinced that Ned Corcoran killed Oliver Platt either, are you?"

"As I said, in my experience usually the person who seems

most likely to have committed the crime is the one who committed the crime. But, like you, I cannot help but find this resolution to be remarkably tidy. That does not mean however that it is the incorrect conclusion."

"Is Inspector Grenville leaving any other avenues of inquiry open?" she asked.

"I suspect the inspector fully believes he has the correct man in custody."

"Then what can we do?"

He let out a long sigh. "Abigail, have I not said, you must leave the investigating to the police?"

She'd heard this so many times before, and he'd said it so many times before, he must know she wasn't going to do that. "But you are the police."

She could see him bite back a smile. "Not in this country."

Not even bothering to respond to that most obvious observation, she said, "What else do we know? And, I suppose, more importantly, who else might have had a reason to want Mr. Oliver Platt dead?" And then she added, "Or, who might want Reginald Mitchell dead?"

He nodded. "Yes, that is what makes this a little more complicated. We are required to believe both that Ned Corcoran is the man who killed Oliver, and that the intended victim was Reginald Mitchell."

"If Reginald Mitchell was the intended victim, what about George Smith as the killer?" she suggested. He might have an alibi for Gladys Trotter's murder, but George Smith still seemed to her like a man with violence in him. "He was obviously angry, angry enough that he could have easily cut the brake line on the car that the Mitchells were parading all through the village in."

"And George Smith is exactly the kind of rude, unpleasant villainous type that you would much prefer to see as the criminal in this case, rather than a fine, handsome, young man like Ned Corcoran."

"Never mind that; the facts fit. Remember, I saw George Smith when Cressida and I walked back to the house after discovering Oliver's body. George Smith could easily have gained access to Ned's rifle."

"He was one of the men out culling rabbits in the morning, I'll grant you that."

She grew quite enthusiastic that he was at least open to the possibility that someone other than Ned had committed this terrible crime. However, before she could say another word he said, "However, you mustn't forget that Ned Corcoran also has a great deal of mechanical knowledge. By his own admission and from our own experience of him, he's a talented and enthusiastic mechanic."

This was true. However, she informed him that George Smith was also a mechanic who kept the farm equipment running.

"And then there was the obvious distress of Cressida over the murder," Henri countered. "Is she simply a kind-hearted girl who was devastated by the death of her fiancé's best man, and the postponement of her wedding, or was she suffering because she believed her secret lover killed the man he believed was her fiancé?"

She nodded. "The fact that she put his posy of flowers beside her bed does suggest there was an attachment between them, even if she was to marry another man."

"And her distress throughout this whole incident has been extreme," he concurred.

She turned to him. "Inspector, you seem to forget that a gently born and reared lady like Cressida Wimborne could hardly be expected to bounce back from discovering her fiancé's best man face down and dead in a stream on her property."

"You're right, of course. I shouldn't judge all women by you. You have a great deal more fortitude than most."

It seemed like a dubious compliment so she decided to ignore it. Besides, she didn't want to get sidetracked from her train of thought. "However, Ned Corcoran must have known that by murdering the man he believed was Reginald Mitchell, he was destroying any chance he would ever have with Cressida."

"The man never had any chance with her. That must be the motivation for his crime. A kind of madness seized him and he truly believed that nothing else mattered beyond destroying the man who stood between him and the woman he loved."

She'd never seen him so passionate. She began to see that there were hidden depths behind the inspector's cool façade.

There was a beat of silence and then she remembered the tiny piece of paper she'd retrieved from Oliver's fireplace. She'd tucked it into her handbag wrapped in a piece of typing paper.

If she was going to help Ned Corcoran, she'd have to trust Henri. Briefly, she told him that she'd gained access to Oliver Platt's room—after the police had finished with it, she emphasized—then she showed him her find.

He gazed at the scrap of paper. "And you say you found this after the men of Scotland Yard had completed their investigation?"

"Yes."

"You should be employed as a detective, Abigail."

"But does it mean anything?" she asked.

He rubbed the paper between his fingers. "Cheap writing paper. And a stroke of ink that could be a letter or a number. I should like to give it to Inspector Grenville. He's a competent detective, Abigail. He will be thorough in his investigation."

The back of her neck began to tingle as a thought occurred to her. A horrible thought.

The butler came toward them in his rather stately way.

When he grew close enough, he said, "Inspector Deschamps, I wonder if you'd be good enough to come and speak with His Lordship. He is quite agitated, if I may be so bold."

"I'll come at once." Henri told him.

The butler then turned to her. "He's asked for you too, miss."

"Me?" What on earth did Lord Wimborne want with her? She could quite understand that he wanted to speak to his old army friend, but what could she do?

Still, she was his guest, after all; the least she could do was go and speak to the man.

Abby and Henri followed the butler back into Darrington Manor. Coco Chanel's dresser walked by looking very self-important. She said to the butler, "Adams, Miss Chanel will be leaving in the morning. Please make sure there is someone to take her to the station for the ten forty train to London."

He bowed his head ever so slightly. "Naturally," he said in a condescending tone. In spite of the heaviness of the day, Abby's lips twitched. Lord Wimborne might be the lord of the manor abovestairs, but it was pretty clear that the butler played the same role downstairs and he clearly did not appreciate being dictated to by what he would have considered a lesser servant. No doubt in the world of Chanel her personal dresser was a person of enormous importance. Abby thought how important it was never to underestimate the power of an ego.

The butler knocked on Lord Wimborne's study door and opened it, and in the softest of tones, almost as though he were talking to a bereaved person, he said, "Miss Dixon and Inspector Deschamps, Your Lordship."

Then he opened the door and they were ushered in.

Lord Wimborne had already appeared older than his years, but looking at him now Abby saw a man who was utterly haggard. He seemed to have aged another decade in only a few hours. "One of the footmen witnessed the arrest. Is it true? Ned Corcoran killed Oliver Platt?"

"That is why he's been arrested," Henri said.

"But this is a terrible thing." He was speaking to Henri, so she remained quietly standing by the door.

"My old friend," Henri said soothingly, "you could not have known."

He made a fist and banged it down on the arm of his wheelchair. "I invited the Mitchells here as my guests, to celebrate my daughter's wedding to Reginald Mitchell. Now I find out that my trusted estate manager has killed a man, murdered him in cold blood, believing him to have been Reginald Mitchell."

He opened and closed his mouth a few times as though he couldn't find the words. Finally, in a rush, he said, "I've known Ned since he was a boy and I could see the intelligence and promise in him. I had him educated, all but groomed him for the role, and this is how he repays my kindness and that of my family?" He shook his fist, almost as though he were going to beat his own chest. "I feel almost as though it was Peter who had committed a terrible crime. To think he was obsessively in love with my daughter all this time, while I promoted him and gave him every advantage."

"*Mon ami*, he hid his secret passion well. And he was an excellent estate manager. How could you possibly have known?"

"I should have known. I've always considered myself an excellent judge of character." He turned his head to look out the window at the vast estate where the land as far as one could see belonged to Darrington Manor. "Perhaps I wouldn't have promoted him so far if we hadn't lost so many good men in the Great War. But he was keen and capable and, I would have said, utterly devoted to this family." He laughed in a very humorless way. "It turned out he was utterly devoted to one member of this family, to the detriment of us all."

Abby felt awkward witnessing this scene. Lord Wimborne had dropped his social mask. Seeing his raw anger and despair was like seeing him naked, something she'd really prefer not to do. She wondered if she could slip out the door again without either of the men noticing, but at that moment he brought his attention back to the room and looked straight at her.

"Miss Dixon, I understand that you are here in your professional capacity as a journalist. However, given the dreadful turn of events, I ask that as much as possible you confine your newspaper articles to the facts and try to—oh what's the use!" He banged his fist again on the arm of his wheelchair. "It's high tragedy and high farce all at the same time. The servant in love with the master's daughter, and then he kills the wrong man." He shook his head. "I wish my daughter had never met Reginald Mitchell."

"As much as I can, sir, I will report fairly and accurately and stay away from sensationalism," Abby promised.

He nodded. "I appreciate that, Miss Dixon. I'm only sorry you were ever dragged into the middle of this mess."

Then he said to Henri, "I suppose you can find me the best defense lawyer in England?"

"I imagine I could certainly get you that information. But I fear Ned Corcoran would not have the resources to pay for his own defense."

Lord Wimborne shook his head. "I shall foot the bill, of course. In spite of everything, he's been a fine and loyal manager until now. If it was obsessive love for my daughter that caused him to do this terrible thing, at least I can make certain he has an able defense, which I believe one needs these days in order to secure a fair trial."

She was impressed that, in spite of his harsh words of anger, Lord Wimborne was willing to pay for Ned Corcoran's defense. It emboldened her to ask, "Are you absolutely certain, sir, that Ned Corcoran committed this crime?"

He turned to her and his eyes were bleak. "Young lady, I would be delighted and relieved to my very soul to find that Ned Corcoran was not a murderer. But Chief Inspector Grenville seemed very certain he had his man."

Then to her horror he buried his face in his hands. She glanced at Henri for guidance and he quietly made a move to the door and opened it for her. She was deeply relieved to be able to slip out. When the door clicked softly behind her she felt the weight of sorrow and guilt that Lord Wimborne must be feeling. He'd been through so much, and now what should have been a joyous week had turned into a terrible tragedy.

But that sensation at the back of her neck grew stronger.

"Vivian," she said, when she next saw her maid, "I need you to do something else for me."

"Anything, Abby, especially if it gets me away from the servants. They're all too terribly upset about Ned being arrested. I never knew a man who was more liked."

"I've got a wild idea and it might be a crazy one. But here's what I want you to do..."

Viv's eyes widened as she listened, but, once she'd grasped exactly what Abby was asking of her, she headed off toward Darrington Village on foot.

Then Abby sat down and began to think.

Her next step was to speak to Henri and ensure that Inspector Grenville return that evening. She explained that she believed she had new evidence.

Henri Deschamps did not seem delighted by this news. "Then you should give the inspector this evidence."

"I will, when I see him. But I believe there is a certain person in this house who knows more than they are letting on. Please, Henri. I might make a total fool of myself, but I might also help serve justice."

He nodded slowly. "I suppose if we both make fools of ourselves, we will go back to Paris and hope the humiliation does not follow."

Not a ringing endorsement for her bold plan, but at least he said he'd try to get Inspector Grenville back that night.

That evening, for the last time, the assembled guests and family met in the library for drinks before dinner. This should have been the night of the masquerade ball and Abby imagined Paul Joubert's chagrin when he discovered she never got to wear the stunning black and silver gown he'd designed for her, or the jeweled mask.

She wore a gown of pale lilac with a sprinkle of iridescent beads at the bodice. She only chose it as it was the least flashy of the remaining outfits. When Paul Joubert had designed her clothing for the week, he hadn't envisioned tragedy causing the festive events to be canceled.

Coco Chanel had been the first to announce her intention to leave the next day, but was rapidly followed by Charles Mitchell announcing he and his family would also be leaving.

It was as though they were all searching for some kind of normality, or perhaps just something to do in the hour before dinner. Lord Wimborne had obviously pulled himself together since she had seen him so distraught in his study. But still, she could tell that Henri was keeping an eye on his old friend and was there to support him.

Lady Wimborne was also present, looking pale and brittle. Peter just seemed stunned.

The Mitchell family stayed together in one corner and Coco Chanel sat in solitary splendor smoking a cigarette with one hand and playing with her long string of pearls with the other. No one was relaxed.

Charles Mitchell looked at Abby from under beetle brows and said, "Well, girl, you've got yourself quite a scoop."

She flinched at the accusatory tone. It was he who had insisted she be here for this week. It seemed dreadfully unfair that he should suddenly treat her like one of those sneaky reporters who pretended to be someone else so they could gain access under cover to get a sensational story.

"I wish I was writing copy about the wedding of your son and Cressida, I truly do," she said. And to her own surprise she discovered that she did feel that way. Oh, she would do her job because she was a capable journalist and fate had handed her a fine news story, but she'd come to care for the Wimborne family and hated to see Lord and Lady Wimborne looking so broken. Ned Corcoran was no doubt sitting in a cell alone somewhere with his future and possibly his life essentially over. She thought for a moment of his mother at home in the cottage, desperately frightened and worried about her son. It was all so dreadful.

Henri came to Abby and quietly mentioned that Inspector Grenville had arrived and secreted himself in the butler's station of the dining room. Once they went into dinner, he would hear what was going on without being seen.

She thanked him, her voice dry with nerves.

Lady Constance bravely introduced the most banal topics of conversation and Mildred Mitchell and Lady Wimborne did their best to keep the conversational ball rolling. While they were discussing how shockingly difficult it was to find good servants, and what high wages they wanted, Abby moved to sit beside Reggie. She said, in a soft voice, "I hate to ask, but could you give me Oliver's home address? It's the kind of thing people like to read about in the newspaper."

"Of course," he said. He pulled out a pen and notebook from his pocket and in a very hand wrote out Oliver Platt's address for her. "He lived in Chicago, near Mitchell Motors."

She sipped a cocktail she didn't want and fervently wished the evening was already over.

There was no sign of Cressida, and in a subdued voice Lady Wimborne said, "My daughter sends her regrets. She's not well enough to join us for dinner tonight."

Charles Mitchell made a noise like "humph". Then he said, "Now that Chief Inspector Grenville's got his man, we'll head home tomorrow, but I shall return for the trial, of course."

Lady Wimborne nodded and Abby was certain she felt nothing but relief at the departure.

As though propelled by good manners, Mrs. Mitchell said, "But you've been wonderful hosts. I've quite fallen in love with Darrington Manor. It's only, well, such a terrible shame..." And then she petered out.

There was silence then. Until suddenly the door opened and Cressida walked in.

Everyone looked up, startled. Coco Chanel even dropped her pearls. It was so silent in the room that Abby could hear the clack as the beads banged into each other.

Cressida looked pale and her eyes were red from crying, which she hadn't even bothered to try and disguise with cosmetics.

Reggie stood up and took a step toward her. "Cressie—"

She shook her head and put out her hand as though she could ward off any further words. "I felt I had to come and tell you all..." And then she seemed to choke on a sob.

Her mother rose and put a hand on her shoulder. "My dear, I think perhaps you'd better retire to your room. You're not strong enough for this."

But her daughter shook her head firmly. "No. I've been silent and retiring too long. And look what's happened. It's all my fault."

She lifted an already damp handkerchief to her eyes and

wiped them. To Reggie she said, "Reggie, I'm so very, very sorry. I had no idea Ned would do something like this."

Charles Mitchell thundered, "So it's true then. You did encourage that fellow to fancy himself in love with you!"

She took a step back as though he'd physically attacked her. "We never meant for it to happen. Ned's always been so kind to me, and so jolly, and had such plans for the future. Naturally, we knew it was impossible, but I knew he cared. As I cared for him."

Her voice broke again. She swallowed and said, "Reggie, I truly believed that I could be a good wife to you. If I were in New York and miles away from here, I would have done my best to be a good wife to you. But that wasn't meant to be. And, well, I'm so sorry."

It seemed there was a lot that she wasn't saying in between her blurted divulgences, but it was as clear as the candles on a Christmas tree that she was as much in love with Ned Corcoran as he was with her. With shaking fingers she removed the very large engagement ring from her finger and held it out toward Reggie. She said again, "I'm so very sorry."

He held out his hand after a slight pause and the ring dropped into it. He said, "I'm sorry too, old girl."

It looked as though he would have said more, but Cressida turned and ran out of the room. Her mother looked toward Mrs. Mitchell, mother to mother, and said, "I had no idea," and then followed her daughter.

There was a long and extremely awkward pause and then Lady Constance Harroby said, "One cannot help but think she might have been better to keep her histrionics to herself."

Lord Wimborne, who looked as though this final blow might be the end of him, said, "I can only apologize to you, Reginald, and to you, Charles. If I'd had any idea..."

Reggie simply looked at the floor, but his father said, "If any of us had had any idea what we were letting ourselves in for, we'd have saved a lot of expense and bother, and I might still have a young man I cared about deeply."

"Father, I'm sure Cressida never meant to hurt me," said Reggie.

"Well she has. She's hurt all of us. And as for that Ned Corcoran, I'll do everything I can to make sure he gets the proper punishment. I'll come over here and testify against him myself. I'll see him hang."

Now it was Lord Wimborne's turn to shudder.

"And I'll arrange to have the car shipped back to North America," Charles Mitchell concluded his outburst.

Abby suspected that, after all the dreadful things that had happened in the past few days, having that flashy automobile removed from Darrington Manor would at least be one ray of sunshine for His Lordship.

There was so much hostility coming from Charles Mitchell that she almost expected he would take his family to the pub for dinner, but perhaps out of some sense of dignity, or maybe because he just didn't want to be accosted at the pub by reporters hungry for news of what had happened, the Mitchell family joined what was left of the Wimborne family and their guests for dinner.

Coco Chanel said, "I shall return to Paris, I think." Abby knew that once they'd all left there'd be no opportunity to sift through their recollections or work out what had happened. The sense of urgency was almost like panic in her breast.

While they ate smoked salmon, Charles Mitchell at his most officious said to Lord Wimborne, "Perhaps you could ensure that when my people come to take the sedan, they have access. And in the meantime, for God's sake, keep your garages locked. I don't want any more vandalism to my prize automobile."

The bluff, jovial Charles Mitchell was gone and in his place was a domineering man who no doubt terrified his workers and anyone he considered beneath him in the social strata. And at this moment she suspected the Wimbornes had been demoted to that level in his eyes. Mrs. Mitchell seemed to cower at the menace in his tone. Lord Wimborne, however, kept his dignity.

"I will make sure your automobile is well looked after." There was a cool undercurrent of sarcasm in his tone and she didn't blame him for it.

Oblivious, Charles Mitchell went on, "I'll leave you the name and telephone number of my agent in London in case there's any problem." He pulled out a notebook and then patted his pockets, looking increasingly annoyed. "I must have left my pen in my room. Reggie, give me yours."

"I haven't got mine on me either, Father," said Reggie. "I must have left it in my room."

"You had a pen in your jacket pocket just before dinner," Abby reminded him. "You wrote out Oliver Platt's address for me."

He shook his head at her. "You must be mistaken." And then patted his pockets as if to say, *There you go. Nothing there.*

His eyes darted to hers and away again. She could have let it go, but if there was one thing she'd learned in her journalism course—and it was one of the most unpleasant tasks of a journalist—it was to push when a subject clearly didn't want to be pushed.

"You wrote down Oliver Platt's address for me," she repeated. "In the library before dinner."

Charles Mitchell was glaring at his son as though promising retribution if he did something wrong. Reggie grew a little red around the neck and said, "That's right. Then I ran upstairs to get my cigarettes. I must have taken out my pen then. I can assure you, Miss Dixon, I do not have a pen. If I had one, I would give it to my father." He got to his feet. "But it's no trouble for me to run to my room and fetch it. If you'll excuse me."

"Wait," Abby said. And suddenly, in that moment, the final pieces fell into place. She felt as though the facts had been jumbled but staring her in the face, a bit like when she didn't know where to begin an article and went back to the journalist's standard: Who, What, When, Where, Why.

She'd been following the wrong Why.

But now, in a flash of insight, she saw the whole story laid out for her. If she'd had her typewriter in front of her she could have written the story straight through, but instead she had an audience of people staring at her and she knew how important it was to convey the terrible truth.

TWENTY-FOUR

"You do have a pen in your pocket at this very moment." Her heart was beating rapidly as she continued, believing she was correct but still feeling her way. "You have Oliver Platt's pen. That's why you don't want anyone to see it."

"Don't be ridiculous," he said, and took a step back as though ready to make a dramatic exit. But Inspector Henri Deschamps had maneuvered himself so that he was between Reggie and the door.

"What's all this about?" Charles Mitchell demanded.

And Abby, having trouble getting the words out because her throat was so dry, informed him, "I asked Reggie for Oliver's address before dinner and he wrote it down. Using a gold pen. I believe the pen he was using belonged to Oliver."

Charles Mitchell, who suddenly seemed bigger and more like a bully with every second, stormed up to his son and grabbed him by the lapels. Suddenly she saw the terrified boy that Reggie must have been growing up. He quailed before that furious face glaring into his. "Is this true? Answer me, boy."

"Father, please," he said desperately. But his father ignored him and shoved his hand beneath the lapels of his son's dinner jacket and began to feel around. He pulled out a pen and then dropped his son, gazing at the pen with a kind or horror. "She's right. This is the pen I bought for Oliver when he graduated from Yale. He carried it with him always."

Then he turned on his son. "What is the meaning of this?"

"No, Pa," Reggie protested. "That's my pen. I thought I'd left it in my room."

But his father was staring at the gold pen. Then he lifted it and examined it more closely. "The young lady's right. This is Oliver's pen. What in blazes are you doing with it?"

Reggie was full-on red in the face now. "All right," he said, "I wanted something to remember him by. He was my closest friend and the man who would have been best man at my wedding. When I went to say my goodbyes, I took the pen. Not for any malicious reason, but so I could remember him." And then his voice cracked. "It's all I have left of him."

Abby glanced at Henri and he picked up the narrative smoothly. "That's very fetching, except I personally made an inventory of everything on Mr. Oliver Platt's person when I brought him in from the river. He was never outside of my presence, and I can assure you that pen was not among his possessions. The only way you could have got that pen was before I fished his dead body from the river."

She felt that he had used those harsh words deliberately and saw the way Reggie flinched. His father was still staring at the pen. "Explain yourself, boy!"

"He's mistaken. He must be mistaken. I tell you I got it afterwards. He must have made a mistake in the inventory. Anyone could have." Reggie was talking too quickly, sweat beading on his forehead.

Henri didn't dignify that with a response. And in the heavy silence, Abby spoke up. "You killed Oliver Platt. It was jealousy, wasn't it? Jealousy that drove you. Your father spoke so glowingly of Oliver and clearly thought much more highly of his business skills than he did of yours, Reggie."

Charles Mitchell looked at her, quite puzzled. A tender expression entered his eyes. "That's true. Oliver had brains for business, while Reggie had the pedigree, the charm. I wanted them both to take over Mitchell Motors. There was more than enough for the two of them."

"But half wasn't good enough, was it, Reggie?" Abby turned from the son to the father. "I saw his face when you took Oliver into a business meeting with you and told him to go and socialize with his fiancée. He had a frozen smile which I think was the mask that he wore to hide the jealousy that's been seething inside him for a very long time."

"That's not true, I—"

"You didn't want to marry Cressida," she said, interrupting him. "I think you liked playing the field. But your father had chosen everything for you, hadn't he? Your school, your friends, even your bride. And you felt trapped.

"And then you came here. And met Gladys Trotter. A young, pretty girl who was only too happy to provide a distraction."

"What? That girl who was killed?" Charles Mitchell sounded like a wounded bull but she kept her gaze on Reggie's face. She needed to keep up the momentum, keep pushing. She felt he was teetering on the edge and she had to push.

"But Gladys didn't give anything away without getting something in return. First it was a red dress."

"How could you—that's ridiculous," Reggie protested. He was perspiring and wiped his forehead impatiently.

"You ordered your fiancée a coat from Coco Chanel at about the same time. But you got their measurements mixed up, didn't you? Gladys Trotter was a larger girl and her dress ended up too tight while the measurements for the coat you ordered were too large." She turned to Coco Chanel, who'd been listening fascinated.

"This is true. The measurements he sent me were entirely wrong. I assumed this was for his mother not Cressida. The coat had to be remade. But what is this red dress?" She looked quite confused. "I made no red dress for this man."

"Another dressmaker will have made that dress. Soon I'm certain the police will find the dressmaker who will be able to tell us that Reggie ordered it."

"This is nonsense. Anyone can get dress sizes wrong. This is absurd. Pa, please."

Abby now withdrew a letter from her bag and placed it in the middle of the dining table. "But then Gladys got greedy, didn't she? And she planned to tell Cressida what you'd been up to."

"What letter?" Charles Mitchell shouted. "What's all this about some servant girl?"

"Her mother found a copy of the letter you thought you'd destroyed. You burned it in Oliver's fire, either before or after you killed him."

"No. I didn't."

"What does this letter say?" Henri Deschamps asked the question quietly.

Abby retrieved the letter, in its schoolgirl handwriting so brilliantly copied by Vivian, on the paper that Gladys had practiced on, she was certain the same paper that she'd given to Henri.

"Dear Miss Wimborne," she read aloud. "I regret to inform you that your fiancé is not to be trusted."

"Stop!" Reggie yelled. "Stop reading that rubbish." A line of spittle hung from his lip and dribbled to his chin.

Abby ignored the interruption and continued. "When she threatened to tell the family what you'd done, you had to get rid of her. So you lured her to London, promising her an interview with a theatrical agent. You lured her with her dream of becoming an actress. And then you killed her, ruthlessly, in cold blood."

"No. It's not true."

"You were in London, and Oliver was seen in the area where Gladys was killed, driving the Mitchell 925. But he was alone. I think he was waiting for you. Did he know what you were planning to do when you went to meet Gladys Trotter?"

"No. Of course not. Oliver was too good to be true." The words came out in a sneer.

"Was it before or after you killed Gladys and seemed to get away with it that you saw Cressida and Ned Corcoran together? Because you did see them. And you came up with the perfect plan, how you could get rid of both the bride you didn't want, and the business partner you certainly didn't want, and blame it neatly on an innocent man."

"This is balderdash, utter rubbish," Reggie said. "You've no proof whatsoever. I never killed that girl and you can't prove I did. And it's disgusting to accuse me of murdering my dearest friend." Abby was fairly certain that no one in the dining room believed Reginald Mitchell, but she also didn't think there was enough evidence to convict him.

She cast a glance at Henri and he nodded, once. He was telling her to keep going. She pressed harder. "How did you get Oliver's pen?"

Reggie shot Charles a scornful look. "Father, are you going to stand for this? These people casting aspersions on your son's integrity?"

But his father was looking at him in dawning horror. "Is it true, boy?"

Now Mrs. Mitchell broke out in an almost hysterical tone. "For pity's sake, Charles, of course Reginald would never do such a dreadful thing."

Charles Mitchell was not to be moved. "How did you get the pen then, boy?"

"I tell you, I took it when I went to sit with him. Or maybe it was before. Yes, that's right. I remember now. I had a letter to write and got him to give me the pen before he went off fishing."

"But you went to your room with a headache," Abby reminded him. "You said you took a sleeping tablet and went to bed."

"Well, I wrote a letter first."

"To whom did you write this letter?" Henri Deschamps asked smoothly.

"That is none of your business."

"Did you give it to the butler to post?" Abby asked. It would be easy enough to check. Adams seemed like the kind of butler who recalled everything.

He turned to her and snarled, "I can't remember now. My best friend's dead. Everything's all mixed up in my head. Father, you're not going to let some two-bit newspaper hack speak to me that way, are you?"

"I will if my son is a murderer," his father said as he stared dully down at the pen he was holding, glinting gold in the candlelight.

"It's like the story of Cain and Abel," Constance Harroby said. "The son was so jealous of his brother he killed him."

"I tell you, I didn't!" Reggie looked very red in the face and his hands were opening and closing.

Inspector Deschamps asked, "May I see the clothes you were wearing the day Mr. Platt died?"

"No you may not go through my wardrobe. How dare you even ask!"

As the other houseguests looked on spellbound, the inspector said, "I've asked the servants, most especially the woman who does the laundry, to keep an eye open for any garments that are wet or water-damaged. Peter Wimborne sent down trousers that were both muddy and very wet. But no one else seems to have got their feet wet. And yet the person who murdered Oliver Platt would have become quite wet. The simplest way to prove your innocence, Mr. Mitchell, is to allow me to search your room."

"Well, I won't do it. This is outrageous." But his voice was shaking as he said it.

"Then, naturally, I shall request that my very good friend Inspector Grenville return with a warrant."

Charles Mitchell was staring at Reggie with a horrified expression. "Oliver was like a son to me. And a brother to you."

Reggie suddenly exploded. "He wasn't my brother." He shouted the words and she saw flecks of spittle fly from his lips. "He was no blood relation whatsoever. Just some poor kid that you took a fancy to. Oh, Oliver could do no wrong. 'Yes, Mr. Mitchell. No, Mr. Mitchell', until it made me sick."

His mother cried out, "Reginald, be careful what you say. Think of me, my darling boy."

But Reggie wasn't listening. It was as though the anger and fury and jealousy that had been boiling in his breast for years and years was suddenly pouring out like a volcanic eruption. "Every birthday, every Christmas I had to share with him. Oh the praise he'd get for being so clever. All the times you told him how far he was going to go in life. And wasn't I lucky that I had the name. I hated it, almost as much as I hated him." He took a deep, shuddering breath and then looked wildly around the room. She thought he was thinking of making a run for it, but Henri Deschamps was a very large presence standing between him and the door.

"But Gladys," Lady Wimborne cried out. "Poor Gladys, she was only a child."

"She was a harlot and a blackmailer," Reggie snarled. "You should be more careful of the servants you hire. A hundred men probably wanted to kill her. You can't blame that on me."

"Oh, I believe the red dress is even now being traced, and now the police have a person in their sights they will focus on your movements in London, Mr. Mitchell. It will only be a question of time until the truth emerges."

Lord Wimborne piped up: "I think perhaps someone ought to telephone for Inspector Digby Grenville."

"That won't be necessary," said the inspector, emerging from the butler's station.

Charles Mitchell looked up and said, "Lord Wimborne, I believe I may owe you an apology."

She could see how much those words cost him; he seemed to fade in front of her eyes.

"I didn't mean to do it. It was an accident," Reggie sobbed as he broke down, falling to the floor.

His father looked down at him. "I suggest you stop talking now. Don't worry, son, I'll buy you the best defense money can buy." Then with a bitter smile he added, "I've always bought you the best money could buy. Much good it's done either of us."

TWENTY-FIVE

Two policemen came through the dining room door and escorted Reginald Mitchell out. His parents followed, his father repeating his promise that he'd hire the best legal team money could buy.

Inspector Grenville came toward Abby and took the letter that she'd laid on the table in front of her, in the childlike writing that mimicked Gladys Trotter's. "Well, Miss Dixon. That was a fine performance. I imagine this letter isn't, in fact, evidence."

"No, Inspector. I admit, it's not."

"The police are not allowed to entrap a suspect into confessing a crime," he said in a conversational tone.

"But I'm a reporter. Surely, now he's confessed—"

"I believe we'll be able to build our case, certainly." He returned the letter to the table. "But when did you realize that Mr. Mitchell had killed Gladys Trotter?"

"It was a combination of small things. The too-tight dress, the meeting with a theatrical agent. She had to believe that the person could conceivably have set up such a meeting, which most of the men she associated with couldn't do. And then there was something you said, Inspector. That when a man has killed once, it's much easier to kill the second time. Once he'd murdered Gladys Trotter and seemed to get away with it, he turned his sights on Oliver Platt. He could neatly end the engagement he didn't want and get rid of the man he'd been jealous of most of his life."

When Ned Corcoran was returned to Darrington Manor in the back of a police car very similar to the one that had taken him away, the entire family was gathered to greet him. Abby was on hand to report on the thrilling conclusion of this drama, or at least the thrilling conclusion of the Darrington Manor part of the drama.

Reginald Mitchell had been arrested the night before. Inspector Grenville and several constables then carried out a methodical search of Reginald's room. As Henri Deschamps had suspected, they found trousers and a jacket, still damp, rolled in a bundle and stuffed under his bed. Presumably he'd planned to dispose of them as soon as he was away from Darrington Manor. In the meantime, he'd needed to ensure that Badger didn't discover the incriminating clothing.

When she told Viv all that had happened at dinner, and how Gladys had blackmailed Reggie, Vivian said, "That's why you should be careful when you employ servants, Abby. They find out all your secrets."

Indeed, once Reginald Mitchell had been arrested and taken away, Badger proved most willing to cooperate with the police investigation. He had been the recipient of many rants that his young master had voiced against Oliver Platt and he had been the one who procured the red dress given to Gladys Trotter. "But I never thought he'd go so far as to commit murder," he assured the police.

Abby had managed to catch Jerry alone and tip him ten

pounds. She hoped he would spend at least some of it on Viv, who seemed quite taken with the ambitious footman. She was delighted to see that Viv wasn't tearful about their impending departure and her separation from Jerry. In fact, she said she said she couldn't wait to get back to Paris and start searching for suitable openings for her new beau.

Abby was happy she hadn't been a witness to the departure of Charles and Mildred Mitchell. They'd left early that morning, catching the first train to London.

Coco Chanel had not been required to take the train after all. Her very good friend Lord Westminster had arrived with a car to take her away. Abby was witness to the aplomb with which Lady Wimborne handled the situation. She acted as though Bendor were a dear family friend of Miss Chanel, who happened to be passing through Somerset and only too happy to transport her to London. If they continued on to Scotland together, Lady Wimborne would remain blithely unaware. At least in public.

And now Ned Corcoran was free.

Abby watched as he got out of the car and then stood uncertainly on the gravel drive in front of Darrington Manor. Cressida was wringing her hands and weeping. Peter stood beside her patting her shoulder awkwardly. Lady Wimborne was standing beside her husband's wheelchair and Lord Wimborne himself was looking as aristocratic as she'd ever seen him.

Ned took two steps toward him and then stopped. In front of the gathered company he said, in a firm, clear voice, "Lord Wimborne, I've caused you a great deal of bother. Please accept my sincerest apologies."

Lord Wimborne's smile was wintry. "You have indeed, young man. But you've caused even more bother for yourself. What did you mean by making up to my daughter?"

Ned glanced over at Cressida, and Abby could see the devotion in his eyes. "I never meant for this to happen, sir. I've loved Cressida for years, but never would I have presumed."

"And yet it seems you have," Lord Wimborne said implacably.

"It wasn't until I realized that Cressie, I mean Miss Wimborne, shared my sentiments—"

"You still presumed upon your position of trust here in the family. I find that hard to overlook."

Then Cressida ran to her father and kneeled before him. "Please, Papa. I tried, I truly did. I would have done everything in my power to be a good wife to Reggie, but I never would have loved him. I love Ned Corcoran. I know we have no money and times are difficult, but Ned has ideas for the manor. I truly believe he's a man of the future." In a desperate tone, she went on, "You'd have married me to a murderer. Ned might have no money, but he's a good man and he loves me."

Lord Wimborne did not look particularly impressed by these fine words. He looked at Ned and asked in a rather dry tone, "And what are these fine ideas you have, young man?"

Ned visibly swallowed. But after sending a glance to Cressida, and receiving a look in response which seemed to fortify him, he drew in a breath, pulled back his shoulders and said with the air of a man giving his last words in front of a firing squad, "I believe there's much yet to be done with the automobile."

Lord Wimborne's face crinkled in distaste, but that was likely because of the fiasco of the Mitchell's royal blue show-off car which was still hulking in an outbuilding on Darrington Manor waiting for one of Charles Mitchell's men to collect it. Abby suspected the Wimborne family would heave a huge collective sigh of relief when the royal blue monstrosity rolled away for good.

Still, he didn't interrupt and Ned went on.

"For instance, when there's a collision and the windscreen

breaks, there must be a way to prevent the glass from cutting so sharply. I'm working on an idea for unbreakable glass."

"Unbreakable glass?" Lord Wimborne sounded anything but impressed. He gazed at Ned as though he wasn't quite right in his mind.

Undeterred, Ned continued. "I'm also very interested in improving comfort within the passenger compartment. I'm looking at ways to bring music inside."

"Music?" Lord Wimborne said, as though he couldn't believe his ears. "What, you're going to have an orchestra sit in on every journey?"

Ned Corcoran gave a slight smile, acknowledging the sarcastic humor, and said, "More like having a wireless inside the automobile." He turned to Cressida and his excitement shone. "Imagine, being able to turn a dial or push a button and have dance music playing while you were driving."

Her face lit up in response to his. "That would be divine."

Lord Wimborne drummed his fingers on the arms of his chair. Ned tried again. "As you know, two English ladies came up with a device to wipe rain and debris from the windshield. I'm searching for a way to automate this process."

"So, it sounds like you have little interest in running my estate then."

Ned looked stunned. "Lord Wimborne, I beg you to believe that Darrington Manor is my life. I was born here, I very much hope to die here, and in between you have my utter devotion." He raised his gaze and looked beyond the group of people to where Darrington Manor stood golden in the afternoon light with the fields stretching out behind it. Then with resolution he said, "However, you know as well as I do, sir, that the world isn't what it was before the Great War. Crop prices are lower than ever, so many of the men who used to tend our fields and crops are moving into the big cities for factory jobs. We've got to find new income."

Lord Wimborne might be very much rooted in the old ways, but he was no fool and that last speech had definitely got his attention. "And do you think these inventions of yours will help Darrington Manor?" he asked.

Ned was all enthusiasm now. "Undoubtedly. We've plenty of land where we could build our own facility to further my inventions. I've already applied for some patents. I'm convinced it's only a matter of time until I make my fortune." And then he gulped at his own temerity and added, "Sir."

There was silence. Everyone was looking at Lord Wimborne, knowing that Ned and Cressida's fate rested in his slender hands. He glanced at Henri Deschamps and asked, "What do you think, my old friend?"

Abby was a little worried. Henri tended to be very cold and rational, would he come out on the side of romance?

He turned his gaze on the hopeful lovers and then back to Lord Wimborne. He said, in his cool, faintly arrogant tone, "Well, the last man Cressida was engaged to turned out to be willing to murder his oldest friend through his terrible, deep-seated jealousy. One cannot help but think Ned Corcoran might be a better choice."

Cressida's eyes filled with tears and she said, "Truly, Papa. I never wanted to leave you or dear old Darrington. And you know you and Mummy didn't want me to go to New York, not really."

Her father shook his head sadly. "No, but I did and do want to see my daughter settled creditably. Peter will have his work cut out trying to hold the estate together when I'm gone. Who knows if he'll even manage it?"

"I'll do my best, Papa, you know I will," Peter said.

Cressida looked to Ned. "And we can help, Papa. You know Ned is as devoted to this estate as I am, and Peter and you and mama. Between us all, we can do remarkable things."

Lord Wimborne smiled at his daughter. "When you put it like that, my dear, you almost give me hope."

Then to everyone's surprise he held out his right hand toward Ned Corcoran. "I don't pretend you were my first choice for my daughter's hand, but it seems you are to be part of the family."

Ned almost ran forward and grasped the outstretched hand. "You won't regret it, sir. I promise to do everything in my power to be worthy of the trust you've put in me." And then he turned to Cressida and his face was glowing. "And I will do everything I can to make Cressie happy."

Lord Wimborne nodded curtly. "Very well. I think that's quite enough high drama for one day." He turned to his wife. "My dear, shall we go in to lunch?"

It was a happy and relieved group that sat around the table for lunch. Ned was bashful at first to be included in the family meal, but soon gathered enough courage to take part in the conversation.

Now that she knew the man she loved wasn't a murderer, Cressida was like a new woman, happy and radiant. She said, "It must have been awful for you stuck in prison, knowing you were innocent."

"The worst part was knowing I hadn't killed Oliver Platt, which meant the real killer was still out there. I had wild ideas of somehow escaping so I could warn you all," he said, then shook his head.

"But I don't understand," Lady Wimborne said. "If George Smith cut the brake cable and caused Reginald Mitchell's accident, are the police not going to prosecute him? I must confess I don't feel entirely safe knowing there's a vandal among us. He's probably one of those anarchists too. One of those who wishes to see all of our kind done away with."

"My dear Lady Wimborne," Henri assured her, "George

Smith may be all those things but it was not he who cut the brake cable on the automobile. That was Reginald Mitchell."

Lady Wimborne gasped in surprise. "Are you suggesting the young man nearly caused his own death? He must be more disturbed than we'd realized."

Henri shook his head. "He was so determined to get rid of Oliver that he was willing to cause himself a bit of hurt. He was an excellent driver and had the advantage of knowing the Mitchell 925 had no brakes when he set off. He'd likely already chosen the perfect spot for his accident. Yes, he knew he'd likely bang his head, maybe suffer a few cuts and bruises, but he was never in danger of serious injury. However, the vandalized automobile began the narrative that someone was out to get him. It was simple but diabolically clever. Who would suspect Reginald Mitchell of sabotaging his own vehicle or causing an accident where he was the person hurt?"

"But he invited Cressida to go with him that day. Surely he wouldn't have injured her?" Lady Wimborne wanted to know.

Again Henri shook his head. "You will recall that Cressida had arranged a dress fitting with Coco Chanel. He knew perfectly well when he asked that Cressida wouldn't be able to drive out with him.

"He systematically acted in ways that threw suspicion away from himself and onto Ned Corcoran," Henri went on. "After the vandalism was discovered and he'd planted the idea that his life was in danger, it was much easier for us to believe when Oliver died wearing his jacket that in fact the death of Oliver was meant to be the death of Reginald."

Lady Wimborne still looked quite confused. "But all along I thought George Smith had vandalized that automobile."

"Yes, that must have been annoying for Reginald, to find that there was a suspect other than Ned Corcoran. But once he'd used Ned's rifle to kill Oliver and then planted the murder weapon where it would easily be found, Ned seemed like the only possible suspect. He was the man who'd been seen tinkering with the Mitchell 925. He played right into Reginald Mitchell's hands. He could easily have cut the brake cable, knowing Reginald was going to drive the car."

"But Ned would never do such a thing!" Cressida cried out.

"No. But because Reginald Mitchell understood the power of jealousy so well, he set the stage for Ned to be perceived as the jealous lover who would kill his love's fiancé rather than see her married to another man. And he very nearly got away with it."

"But how did he know to blame Ned?" Lady Wimborne continued, perplexed.

"I can answer that," Abby chimed in. "Ned and Cressida met clandestinely, and I'm certain Reginald saw them."

Cressida nodded. "I was saying my final goodbyes to Ned." She glanced up at her mother. "I know it was wrong of me, Mummy, but I couldn't go off to America without a parting word to him." She dropped her gaze to her pale hands. "Are you suggesting that my behavior caused Reginald to do the terrible things he did?"

It was Henri who answered her: "It's my belief he knew long before he saw you that your affections were engaged elsewhere." And then he looked at her with some amusement in his face. "Knowing your character as I do, I suspect you may have confessed to the man you planned to marry. It's the kind of honorable thing you would do, and that Reginald Mitchell could never understand."

She raised her face to his and nodded slowly. "I never said who it was. Only that I had broken it off with a suitor because our future was so hopeless. I did not want to start my married life with even the suggestion of duplicity between us."

Ned turned to her, an adoring look on his face, and said, "And I honor you for that. And I very much hope that Reginald's behavior won't put you off having complete trust in our marriage."

Lady Wimborne was still following her own train of thought. "So, Reginald caused his own accident, and then swapped coats with Oliver on that fateful day. But how could he know that Oliver would need a new coat?"

"Because he had vandalized Oliver's coat," said Abby. "Just as he'd vandalized that beautiful automobile. I watched him walk toward the house beside Oliver. He must have had a pocket knife on him and managed to distract his friend long enough to damage his coat. It would have been the work of a moment. He couldn't point out the damage himself, so he had to trust that Oliver himself would notice or, as it happened, and even better, his father, who then insisted Oliver change into a more respectable coat."

Lady Wimborne still looked very confused. "You are suggesting then that Reginald Mitchell never had any intention of going fishing that day?"

Abby nodded. "That's right. He wanted you all to think that he was bravely attempting an outing he was too weak for, when in reality he was setting his friend up. Then he maintained he was going to lie down and rest in his room and he wasn't to be disturbed, which gave him a perfect opportunity to sneak out. He waited until Ned Corcoran had returned his gun to the gun room. Then he must have put on some gloves to throw off any fingerprint experts and helped himself to the weapon, knowing that so long as he remained unseen he was at liberty to shoot his good friend in the back." She tried to picture Reggie going through with his deadly plan. "The most difficult thing must have been plunging into the river so that he could retrieve the pen he wanted so badly."

"I rather think he went in after Oliver Platt to make certain the man died," Henri said. "The autopsy will tell us more, but a .22 caliber rifle would probably not kill a man unless it was a very skillful shot. I expect he waded into the water and held Oliver Platt's head under until he drowned. Then he made sure to take the pen."

Abby shuddered, she hadn't thought that Reginald could be quite so cold-blooded, but she had no doubt the inspector was correct. "I suppose if anyone had seen him, he'd have claimed he had seen his friend floating in the river and was trying to save him."

There was a moment of heavy silence as they all contemplated Oliver Platt's end. But then, with the resilience of youth, Cressida and Ned were soon talking about their future.

"I want to be married as soon as possible," Cressida said. "And I want our local dressmaker to create my gown."

"I like this new economizing streak," her father said with a smile.

"I can indeed be economical," she insisted. "Our wedding will be very small. I don't want fuss and show, only the people I truly love around me."

Abby thought this was the nicest meal she'd shared with the Wimbornes. There was relief, and laughter, and a shimmer of possibilities. In securing a spectacular marriage for Cressida in the United States, Lord and Lady Wimborne had essentially been accepting the defeat of Darrington Manor. But somehow, with Ned's fresh eyes and enthusiasm and Peter's love of the land and Lord Wimborne's steady hand guiding them all, Abby had a feeling that Darrington Manor might have a reasonably bright future. She'd come to like all these people so much that she sincerely hoped so.

When luncheon was over, she said, "If you'll excuse me, I've an article to write."

Lord Wimborne's eyes twinkled as he replied, "For you at least, Miss Dixon, this week has been very profitable."

"I'm doing my very best to keep my coverage factual and tasteful and not take advantage of the fact that I've been privileged enough to be in your home," she assured him. But she couldn't help a slight smile as she added, "However, I can't deny it's been quite beneficial to be the only journalist on the scene when Reggie all but confessed to the murder of his best friend."

"I foresee great things for you, my dear," Lord Wimborne said. "I believe we've another Nellie Bly in our midst."

Since he'd referred to her absolute idol, Abby was buoyed up by the notion that she might one day become as famous as the woman who had encouraged her to enter journalism school in the first place. However, her good mood soon dimmed as she recalled the telegram currently sitting on her dressing table.

Abigail. Congratulations on the scoop. Need you back in Paris office soonest. I've secured you an interview with Mrs. Penelope Greenwood, the hostess du jour about the current trend in literary salons.

Her editor Walter Strutt was letting her know in no uncertain terms that she was still very much a reporter for the women's page.

However, Abby was an optimist at heart. She was convinced that if she worked long enough and tried hard enough she'd find her place on the hard news team.

Ned Corcoran offered, "Whenever you're ready, Miss Dixon, I'll be happy to drive you to the train station."

But to her surprise, Henri said, "It would be my pleasure to drive Miss Dixon and her maid to London."

"Why thank you," she said.

"Family business will keep me in London for a few days, but no doubt I will see you in Paris." Then, with a kind of resigned amusement, he added, "In a social capacity, I hope."

A LETTER FROM THE AUTHOR

Dear Reader,

Thanks for reading *Death at Darrington Manor*. I had a blast writing about Abigail's latest exploits leaving the glitz and glamor of Paris for a genteel Somerset manor house. I so enjoy researching the 1920s period—the fashion, the food and in this particular story, the cars! I can't wait to take readers on Abigail's next adventure to the French Riviera where a new mystery awaits her.

If you'd like to join other readers in keeping in touch, here are two options. Stay in the loop with my new releases by clicking on the link below. Or sign up to my personal email newsletter on the link at the bottom of this note. I'd be delighted if you choose to sign up to either—or both!

www.stormpublishing.co/nancy-warren

If you enjoyed reading *Death at Darrington Manor* and could spare a few moments to leave a review, that would be hugely appreciated. Even a short review can make all the difference in encouraging a reader to discover my books for the first time. Thank you so much!

Join other readers in hearing about my writing (and life) experiences, and other bonus content.

www.nancywarren.com/newsletter

You can also connect with me via my private Facebook Group. It's a lot of fun.

www.facebook.com/groups/NancyWarrenKnitwits

Until next time, Happy Reading,
Nancy

www.nancywarrenauthor.com

 facebook.com/AuthorNancyWarren

 x.com/nancywarren1

instagram.com/nancywarrenauthor

Made in the USA
Middletown, DE
27 June 2024

56478372R00165